SUNNY COLLINS

The Pursuit of Love and Fame

Jennifer,
Love, Your Cousin! All the
Best, Your Louisiana
trouble maker :)

JACOB DIAMOND

Sunny Collins
Copyright © 2015 by Jacob Diamond
All rights reserved.
First Edition.

This book is a work of fiction and does not represent any individual, living or dead. Names, characters, places and incidents either are products of the author's imagination or are used fictitiously.

Interior Formatting by: Cassy roop of Pink Ink Designs

Acknowledgements

First and foremost my amazing mother,

Sylvia Diamond:

Thank you for teaching me the ways of the world, for always leading me in the right direction, and for showing me the human experience, both good and bad. I learned through you that people can touch us in the most incredible ways and also be cruel and disappointing. You've always encouraged me to dream big with unlimited possibilities. For that I am forever grateful. I love you Mom, more than anyone else in the world. Nothing will ever separate us, not space or time. I am a part of you, and you are a part of me. Your courage to battle the ups and downs of life is nothing short of greatness.

My larger than life grandmother,

Faye Diamond:

Your fire, leadership, warmth, humor, laughter, and presence when you walked into a room, there hasn't been anyone quite like you. You dined with presidents, senators, and governors. You shaped Cleburne into a booming little Texas town. Most importantly, you created the best family I could ask to be a part of. You always rose above adversity with style, grace, and class and taught me to strive to do the same. I hope I make you proud and continue the Diamond legacy.

Mrs. Peggy Rawland:

My time with you was so meaningful. Your elegance and sophistication have been a great influence in my life. The most important advice you ever gave me was "Don't be a star for everyone else; be a star for yourself." I will always cherish these words. I know you would have been tickled by this book.

Gaye Beasley Roden (Gaye Gaye):

My big sister, my soulmate, my heart. I can't imagine who I would be without you in my life cheering me on all these years. From boybands, to movie roles, to reality shows, and now to books, you've never given up on me no matter how big the failure. I'm forever grateful. You truly hold the magic of life. We share a bond that no one will ever understand because we see life in such a strange and different way. You've taught me kindness, discipline, loyalty, courage, honor, strength, and how to be a pretty damn good cook. Some of the best nights of my life have been in your kitchen roasting ducks and Brussels sprouts with warmth, love, and laughter. My sense of what family is supposed to be like comes from you.

Staci Dang:

Where do I begin? One of the most amazing women I know? One of my greatest teachers in life? How about THE queen of Cleburne, Texas? There are so many things I love and admire about you, and I am truly blessed to have you in my life. I've had many guides and teachers, but you have worked very hard trying to teach me two of the most important lessons in life: 1) No matter where you come from, stay humble. Be a Cleburne boy at heart. No matter how many people attack you, say negative things about you, or try and take you down, rise above it. The higher you rise, the more they want to see you fall. Don't let them, and don't respond. I try hard to remember this every day. 2) IT IS WHAT IT IS!!.......That says it all.

Pamela Massey:

You took a young boy from Cleburne, Texas under your wing and gave him a crash course on how to be cool. The right clothes, the right hair, and the perfect tan. You were hard on me at C.H.S. and over the years, but it's because you cared about me and expected only the best. I learned from you how to be strong, how to stand up for myself, and how to deal with people who try to take me down. For your guidance on my journey, I will be forever grateful.

Georgeann Meek:

My crazy Gemini sister. I am so happy we've gotten closer over the years, and I love some of the wild nights we've had out. You are the least boring person I know. You've been through so much over the years, yet you always persevere. You are an inspiration, and I love you.

Steven Meek:

The eldest and the grooviest in the family. Thank you for always sticking up for me, and thank you for listening to me when I need you. Your talent is incredible, and your outlook on life always gets me thinking.

Sam Moore:

You define shifty, and it's my favorite thing about you. You were there in Orlando in the beginning, teaching me, molding me, and guiding me through the strange and mysterious adventure called our twenties. You pushed me out of the nest in Louisiana and watched me fly in L.A. As cynical as you can be at times, one thing always rings true: you never question my drive to succeed; you always told me it's a matter of *when*. No matter how bad I crash and burn, you are one of my best friends, and for teaching me how to play "the game," I will be forever grateful.

Brittany Musso:

My partner in crime, my confidant, and my strength though the darkest most difficult period of my life. I look back, and I'm not sure how I would have survived it without you there holding me every time I fell. We shared a special bond during those trying times, and I will be forever grateful for your patience and understanding and for being on my side when no one else was.

Lisa Beaumann:

Momma Beaumann. Why you took me under your wing and showed me the ropes of life in the French Quarter, I will never understand, but I will never forget a second of it. What an adventure. Some of the most curious, fascinating encounters I've ever had were when I was with you. You have been one of the most fascinating people I've met in this life, and the things you taught me will always stay with me no matter how far away I am. There is something magical about you, and I can't wait to see how this all plays out. After all, "No one could play Lisa Beaumann, but Lisa Beaumann."

Luanne Bailey, Susan Yates, Wallis Ann Foster, Vicki Pullin, Freda Gray, and Ann Hunter:

We all have teachers in life, but God blessed me with these special women. From each of these southern ladies, I learned so much. Some teachers just teach, just do their jobs, but not these women. They stand out because they guided me, and they took extra special time with me because they knew I was different in more ways than one. It takes a special woman to take a student aside to deal with the problems he causes, to get to the root of the problems, and then try to find solutions and show him how to grow up and be a respectable young man. After jumping from school to school, dozens of other teachers came in and out of my life. Many of them wrote me off as a troublemaker, as a bad seed, as the kid they didn't want in their classes. To these spectacular women, you will always be in my heart. Thank you for taking the extra time with me; that will stay with me for a lifetime.

Andrea Sciarallio and Claudine Smack:

My girls at the end of the rainbow from Louisiana to Houston. Life has a funny way of bringing people back to you. I know this because this book wouldn't be finished without your constant encouragement. Thank you for all you have done and for letting me blow off steam when others frustrated me. We made it!!

Author Rhonda Dennis and my editor Donette Freeman:

My guardian angels. I would be lost in the literary world without your constant guidance. I could never ask for better mentors, not to mention such sweet southern women. You both add to my love affair and fascination with the great state of Louisiana.

And last but not least:

Lance,

I dedicate this book to you.

CHAPTER ONE
The Greyhound Bus

I MAKE MY WAY inside the Greyhound bus station and purchase a one-way ticket to Los Angeles, California. When the ticket agent hands the piece of paper to me, I can't help but stare at it for a minute. Dallas to Los Angeles, departing at 7:10. Am I really going to just get on a bus and go to a city I've never been and where I know no one? I must be out of my mind. I step out of the Greyhound station into the cool Texas night air. The smell of exhaust fumes coming from the running buses and the lights of downtown Dallas twinkling in the distance send chills down my spine. There are fourteen buses lined up in the terminal, so I ask one of the attendants which bus is headed to L.A.

"Bus number three," an old man grumpily says to me.

A sense of fear and a tinge of excitement come over me at the same time. I give the driver my suitcase, and he loads it into the luggage compartment.

I step up to the running bus and feel the heat from underneath it run past my legs. Anxiety shoots through me and presses down on my chest. I freeze in place and can't climb onto the bus. There's only one way I can do this; I pull out my iPod, put in my earphones, and hit *play*. Leann Rimes' "One Way Ticket" begins to play. ...*buy a one way ticket on a west bound train, see how far I can go, gonna go out dancin' in the pouring rain, talk to someone I don't know*... I take a deep breath and step up onto the bus. I find a seat three rows back and plant myself there. I pray no one scary sits next to me.

I think about Madonna and how she loaded up her suitcase and went to New York City. Look how that turned out. Ok, I can do this. There's no turning back now, nothing left for me in that country town except a dead end. I'm going to Hollywood, I'm gonna make it big, and I'll show every last one of them who laughed at me who Sunny Collins really is. I take a deep breath as the bus begins to pull out of the station. When you've got nothing, you've got nothing to lose.

THIS STORY BEGINS in a small country town called Cleburne, sixty miles outside of Dallas, Texas. Things never change there. It looks exactly the same as it has over the last hundred years. It's the kind of town you see in the movies. There's a court house and clock tower right in the middle of the town square that was built in 1912. It has one little movie theater called the Esquire, The Redwood, which is the town cafe, and like any small town in the south, it's divided by wealth and poverty.

She was born Sunny Faye Collins to her mother Daisy Collins and daddy Dusty Collins. Daisy was very young when she had Sunny, eighteen to be exact, but before that she grew up the pride of Cleburne. It was said that she was the most beautiful girl in all of Johnson County. She was a straight A student, homecoming queen, a cheerleader, a dancer, and was one of the most popular girls at Cleburne High School in the early 1980s.

During Daisy's senior year, she started dating and fell in love with the captain of the football team. At the end of the school year she found out she was pregnant with a baby girl. Daisy never dreamed of having a baby so young. She had planned on going to school to become a college professor or maybe a lawyer, but as fate would have it, these dreams would have to be put on hold. She truly believed her love for Dusty would get them through what she knew was going to be a rough patch: having a baby and starting a family so young. Soon afterwards, Daisy and Dusty were married, and their parents helped them get a small farm house that sat on five acres of land.

On August 17th, Sunny Collins was born with big blue eyes, a head of golden hair, and left-handed just like her mother. From the moment Sunny was born, Daisy knew there was something special about her. She named her Sunny because every time the baby smiled, the whole room lit up with sunshine. The first couple of years of Daisy and Dusty's marriage were happy and blissful: church every Sunday, small vacations to Galveston on the Texas coast, and wonderful and magical Christmases. Daisy stayed home, took care of Sunny, kept up with the washing and cleaning, and had a nice hot supper on the table when her husband would come from work. Dusty had gotten a good job working as a foreman on the railroad in Cleburne, so they bought some dairy cows, a couple of horses and some chickens. Life was good. But as time went on, things took a turn for the worse. Both Daisy's and Dusty's parents passed away, and worst of all, the Cleburne railroad shut down, leaving hundreds of people out of work. Steam engines were out and diesel engines were in, which meant they could travel further and faster than ever before. Unfortunately there was no longer a need for a stop in this once booming little Texas town. That also meant a decrease in livestock and agriculture, and the whole town really suffered for it. Dusty had always had a beer or two after work, but that led to bottles of Jack Daniels now that he was stuck at home and not able to find work. He became extremely abusive and began to knock around Daisy with his fists during his drunken rages. His mental and physical abuse became worse and worse over time.

Finding a job in town was almost impossible, so Daisy traveled to Dallas where she found a job as a cleaning lady at the Theater in the Round: a huge domed indoor theater with a round stage built in the middle and surrounded by three thousand red velvet seats. The Broadway musicals and plays that were on tour from New York City ran there for two weeks at a time. After the performances were over and the crowds of people poured out of the theater, Daisy spent several hours cleaning the mezzanine and sweeping the stage. After school every day, Daisy would pick up Sunny, and they would make the long drive to Dallas, clean the theater, and pray Dusty would be asleep by the time they got back to Cleburne. Every night at 7:00 p.m. Daisy would find Sunny an empty seat, the show would begin, and Sunny's imagination would soar. The theater was such a curious place for her, and it was also an escape from the mundane existence of Cleburne. Watching the dazzling performers come from all around the world was a magical experience. Big names like Carroll Burnett, Liza Minelli, Debbie Reynolds, Bob Hope, and Ruta Lee played the theater week after week.

Every night the lights would dim, and the stage came to life as actors and actresses performed with such passion and charisma. Her favorite shows were *Annie*, *The Wizard of Oz*, and *The Phantom of the Opera*, and Sunny knew every word by heart. They sang, and they danced and introduced Sunny to a world that she never knew existed. When the show was over and the crowds had emptied the theater, Sunny climbed up on the stage and sang her heart out, acting out whatever performance she had seen that night. Daisy would instruct her on her singing as she swept, making sure she hit the right notes. Back home in Cleburne, Sunny would open the windows to her bedroom and let the gentle breeze of the night air flow into her room. As she lay in bed, she dreamt of what it would be like to grow up, be a famous actress, go to Hollywood, and live in a beautiful home in the Hollywood Hills that over looked the ocean, just like the movie stars. Being famous meant being rich, and being rich meant having enough money to move her and momma into a safe place away from the turmoil and chaos Dusty created. Being famous meant escaping a terrible life and creating a new one. Achieving fame and fortune became her number one goal.

One Sunday morning Sunny woke up to a crash in the living room. Dusty had turned the television over, and it crashed onto the floor. Daisy had asked him if it was ok that she and Sunny watched the Oscars that night which was something they had done every year together as far back as she could remember. It was especially exciting because their favorite actress, Julia Roberts, was nominated for best actress for her role in *Pretty Woman*. Sunny and Daisy rented that movie at least a hundred times since it had come out on video at Blockbuster. Just to be mean and hateful, Dusty destroyed the only TV in the house… not the smartest thing to do considering that all he had done for the past couple of years was get drunk, sit on the couch, and watch TV. He became enraged, yelling and screaming, and called Daisy a stupid, worthless, bitch.

Sunny watched in horror as her daddy slammed his fists into her momma's face, bloodying her nose as she begged him to stop. Sunny turned and ran as fast as she could through the back door and out to the barn, the whole time blood-curdling screams from Daisy echoing behind her. She knew had she stayed, she would have been next in line for a beating. Sunny called the police at least a dozen times before, and every time they showed up, they sat outside and did nothing. They told Sunny this was a domestic dispute and they weren't getting involved. Several of the officers were on the C.H.S. football team with Dusty and did the same thing to their wives. Unfortunately, this happens a lot in small Texas towns. Sunny saddled up her horse Shorty and called her dog Little Red. She loved that horse and dog more than anything. Shorty was a beautiful Arabian mare, and Little Red was her German Shepard she had raised from a puppy. The two of them kept her company deep in the woods when escaping from her daddy's drunken tirades. Little Red was a loyal companion and slept in bed with Sunny every night. She would hold him close when Dusty would come home from Second Chances, the town bar, and pull Daisy out of bed and beat the shit out her for no reason. That night Sunny stayed out until around 9 p.m. She rode down through Buffalo Creek all the way to the Redwood for a Coke. Sunny tied up her horse and dog to the hitching post out back. Soon after she got there, two patrol cars pulled up, and the officers came into the cafe. Dusty called in Sunny as a runaway, and the police escorted her, her dog, and her horse back to the house. When the police left, Sunny found her mom black and blue on the floor of her bathroom, too weak to walk.

As she lay on the floor next to Daisy with tears running down her face, she heard Little Red begin to yelp. Sunny raced to the front door to see her daddy tying Little Red to the clothes line pole next to Shorty. Just then it began to sprinkle. A thunder storm was moving in fast from the west, and a feeling of terror came over Sunny. Why was Dusty tying the animals to the clothes line? Her father appeared from around the side of the house unexpectedly with a long chain in his hand. Sunny began to run, but to no avail. He was able to catch her before she could get over the fence. She turned and saw his hatred for her for burning in his eyes, and the smell of whiskey on his breath was suffocating. Dusty drug her through the wet grass and over to her old rusted swing set. He wrapped the chain around Sunny chaining her to the swing set, so that there was no way for her to escape. Then it began to pour. The rain pounded the fields around the house, and the lightning lit up the Texas sky. As the thunder cracked, Shorty started to buck in fear. Dusty went into the house, and came back out with his shotgun. It dawned on Sunny what was about to happen. He slowly closed the screen door, and sat down on the front porch with his gun and a bottle of Jack. Sunny could barely make out the evil grin on her father's face through the rain. She refused to scream or beg him to stop because she knew how much pleasure it would give him. She simply sat there horrified as he began to shoot, not bullets, but pellets at Shorty and Little Red. This way they would be wounded and die a slow and agonizing death instead of it being over with quickly. Little Red howled in pain for hours before he finally died, and Shorty continued to try to stand up while she whinnied for a while before she finally died as well. The worst part was that Sunny couldn't even be by their sides to console them as their lives slowly and painfully ended. She had to sit in the rain and lightning storm watching the only two friends she ever had die agonizing deaths. Sunny woke up the next morning, and for a minute thought it was all a nightmare, but the nightmare was real. Still drenched from the rain and still chained to the swing set, she looked over to see the dead bodies of her beloved horse and dog lying on the ground still tied to the clothes line.

A COMMOTION IN the back of the bus startles me, and I snap back to reality. I turn to see several passengers scattered about, but mostly I see empty seats. At the very back of the bus I see a group of guys play-fighting. Three of them are sitting, but one is hovering over the others. The guy standing is probably six foot three, spiky jet black hair, scruff, thick eyebrows, dark brown eyes, very long eyelashes, and dark complected. He is dangerously good looking. He's wearing faded gray jeans tucked into motorcycle boots, a black wife beater, and a black leather bomber jacket. I can't take my eyes off of him. He's dark and fascinating. I watch him twisting one of the guys' arms and demanding he say please before he stops. I watch as the tall one glances in my direction, and he immediately drops the other guy's arm midsentence. His face changes from playful to domineering.

"Can I help you?" he shouts in my direction as I turn around quickly and face the seat in front of me. Shit! I'm sure I look like a total creeper. I grab my purse and pretend to dig through it. After a minute or so, I glance back hoping they've resumed arguing. Unfortunately, I'm staring right into the face of the tall sexy guy. He is sitting in the seat behind me, his arms perched on the back of my seat, and his chin covered in black scruffy facial hair is resting on his hands.

"Hello," he says as his mouth curls into a devilish grin. Wow! Up close he is even more handsome, but in a sinister way.

"Hey." My voice sounds small as I go back to digging in my purse. I've always been pretty fearless ever since I was a little girl, but in the presence of a guy who is this hot, I lose all sense of composure.

"I'm Eric...who are you?" he asks, as his dark brown eyes study me intently. I try not look at him.

"Hi, I'm Sunny," I say politely.

"Ohhh...southern girl, huh? That little accent's pretty cute." He grins at me, and he's so close that I can smell the mix of liquor and stale cigarettes on his breath. This doesn't surprise me.

"Well I'm not sure if you've noticed, but we're in the south," I say sarcastically.

"Are we?" He laughs mockingly at me. "I hadn't noticed. I don't have a fucking clue where I am these days!! What city did you say this is Sunny?"

"Dallas, Texas," I say sarcastically. He knows damn well where he is, but I'll go ahead and play his stupid game.

"Guys!!" he shouts to the back of the bus, "Did you know we're in Dallas, Texas?? How fucking insane is that!!"

"Yes Eric, we are all aware of what city this is," one of the guys, who is very pretty for a guy I might add, calls out to him as he sits reading a magazine without looking up. "Stop being a fucktard and leave that poor girl alone."

"So Sunny, what's a cute little blue-eyed southern girl like you doing traveling all alone tonight?" Eric leans back, props up his boots on the back of my seat, and puts his hands behind his head like he's about to give me a full interrogation. I know better. He might be good looking, but he could also be a serial killer. Momma would kill me if she knew I was talking to a shifty guy like this. I can't help but be entranced though; I've never seen a boy like this before.

"Listen, I'm really tired, and we have a long ride to L.A., so if you don't mind, I'm gonna close my eyes for a little bit." The look on his face turns from inquisitive to disgust.

"Not gonna talk to me huh? Alright, fine." He gives me an icy glare and then jumps up and struts towards the back of the bus. I get the feeling not too many girls have ever told him they would rather sleep than talk to him. He turns around and looks back at me. "Hey Blondie, just so you know, this bus is headed to Miami, not L.A...Looks like you're in for an adventure." His lips curve into a sinister smile. "Do they not teach y'all how to read in Texas??" I give him a go-to-hell look, but he just keeps grinning from ear to ear. An elderly black lady in the seat across the aisle from me is shaking her head.

"Girl, you on the wrong bus. The one going to L.A. was next to us at the terminal."

I get up frantically and ask the driver what to do. How could this happen?

"We're not stopping again till Mississippi darlin', and you won't be able to buy another ticket till morning anyway."

I begin to panic. I don't have enough money to buy another ticket! My plan is completely screwed. What a disaster. I grab my stuff and start to slowly shuffle towards the back of the bus. My ponytail swings from side to side as I walk between the seats embarrassed. I sit down in the seat across the aisle from Eric as he chats away to the pretty boy. His other two friends are sitting in the seats behind him looking at me inquisitively. Eric stops talking to his friend and turns to look at me.

"Changed your mind, I see." he says smugly as he cocks his head sideways.

"Listen if you're gonna be a dick about it, I can go back to my seat," I say not in the mood for his smugness.

"Wow, look at that guys, we've got a feisty one here." His eyes gleam with excitement. I roll my eyes at him. In the back of my mind a sign is flashing danger ahead, but I completely ignore it. I'm freaking out, and I'm desperate. "Sunny, this is Zack and Kevin." Both guys are handsome, seem kind, and have an innocence about them. Obviously Eric is their leader. They probably do whatever he tells them, I think to myself. Momma always said I have a talent for instantly sizing up people. "And this is Sam," Eric says, pointing to the guy next to him. Sam is short, has striking blue eyes, cropped jet black hair that is swept back, and is clean-shaven. His face is very pretty, and he reminds me of a Ralph Lauren model. Very clean cut.

"Charmed, I'm sure," Sam says dryly without looking up from his *US Weekly*.

"He's a little bitch, but we don't hold it against him," Eric says grinning.

"Fuck off, E.J," Sam blurts out, as he lights up a Marlboro Light cigarette.

"Nice to meet you, Sam. I'm Sunny." I twist my finger through my ponytail nervously, not sure if this guy wants me around. Maybe I should have just stayed in my seat.

"Aww… your accent is cute, isn't it?" Sam gives me a fake smile. He rolls his eyes as he takes a puff of his cigarette. "PUT THAT CIGARETTE OUT, BOY!! I told you last time you was on my bus I wasn't gonna put up with your shit anymore!!" the driver screams from the front of the bus.

"Blow me bitch!!!" Sam yells towards the front, as he smashes out the cigarette on the seat in front of him and then pitches it out the window.

"So why are you heading to Miami?" Eric smiles at me and winks. I'm grateful he's not telling the guys what a complete idiot I am for getting on the wrong bus.

"Um, well, I just got a job down there." I lie to him purely for the sake of the other guys listening. I glance at downtown Dallas glittering in the night sky. I can see the lit-up ball at the top of Reunion Tower and Reunion Arena next to it. I wonder how long it will be before I see Texas again. "Why are you guys going to Miami?" I ask.

"I'm a DJ, and we have a gig there tomorrow night. Sam books jobs for me at different clubs all over the country. A lot of them are the top gay clubs. He handles the money and business side of things. He's good at that. I eventually want to be a resident DJ at one of the big clubs in Los Angeles or New York, but Sam says I have to play the circuit and get some recognition first. The gay scene's the best way to do it."

"Oh, so you're a DJ… that's cool. Are you gay?" I say, secretly hoping he's not. Momma always says the really cute guys usually are.

"Haha, no, I'm not. Sam is though, which is great because he's slept with all the club managers and owners. He has no problem persuading them to give me a chance," Eric says happily.

"Oh, I see. So how do you guys all know each other?" I ask inquisitively.

"I met Sam about a year ago at an after party. I DJ'ed at a club in Boystown one night, that's the gayborhood in Chicago. Afterwards I got invited to an after party, drank way too much and passed out. Some guys at the party tried to take advantage of me, but Sam found a baseball bat and threatened to bash in their skulls if they touched me!!" he explains animatedly. Sam yawns with boredom, and I get the impression he has heard this story a thousand times. "Anyway, we've been friends ever since. Kevin and Zack carry equipment and set it up for me; we don't pay them much, but they're mostly in it for the adventure anyway. Kevin here just got discharged from the army and was living in a veterans' facility in Santa Monica. We met him on a bus ride to a gig in North Carolina about three months ago, and he's been tagging along with us ever since."

"You lived in California?" I ask him excitedly. Kevin is very good looking and is somewhat sunburned. He's wearing a backwards hat and is dressed like a skater but still has a wholesomeness to him. Not like Sam or Eric who both exude shiftiness. They remind me of puppet masters, who find groupies to cater to their every whim. Kevin beams at me.

"Yeah, it was great. I love it out there."

"I want to live in L.A. one day," I say to him longingly. This instantly reminds me that I'm supposed to be on my way there right now.

"Oh no, please tell me you're not another girl with the bright lights of Hollywood in her eyes, are you? Let me guess, you want to be an actress," Eric says to me in an annoyed voice. I give him a look that says, *keep it up and I'm going back to my seat*, and he quickly changes the subject. "Anyway, this is Zack; we found him at a club in Vegas, he had just gotten fired, and his girlfriend broke up with him, and he had nowhere to go." Zack gives me a little nod. He seems more shy than the other three, and reminds me of Teen Wolf. High, brown, spiky hair, and very scruffy.

"So you guys just go from city to city together? That must be pretty exciting to be in a new place every couple of days," I say to Eric.

"Yep, it's the good life, never gets old. If you screw up or get in trouble in one place, you just move on to the next!" I wonder if he's kidding, but I have a feeling he's not.

Eric and I sit up talking for the rest of the night. At 4 a.m. we make an hour-long stop at a gas station in Mobile, Alabama. The other boys have been sound asleep for hours, so we get off and walk to the Waffle House next door to the gas station. We split breakfast which Eric gobbles up, leaving me with very little. Even though I'm wary of Eric, I'm glad to have someone to talk to. It takes my mind off what I'm going to do when I get to Miami tomorrow.

CHAPTER TWO
Welcome to the Jungle

I WEARILY OPEN MY eyes and try to sit up straight. Sleeping in a bus seat is really uncomfortable. I look over at the boys who are still passed out, and Eric is snoring away in the seat next to me, drool running down the side of his mouth. The bright Florida sunshine is flooding through the windows as we speed down Interstate 4. I see a sign that says that downtown Miami is in seven miles, and ten minutes later we arrive at the Miami Greyhound bus station. I reach over and tap Eric to let him know we've arrived and make my way out of the bus to grab my suitcase. The driver hands us our bags as we sleepily climb off the bus. I stick out my hand to shake Eric's.

"Well, it was nice meeting you, and if I can get a ride tonight I'll come see you DJ. That is if you still want me to," I say looking around, distracted with thoughts of where to go from here.

"Why don't you just come to our hotel with us, and your friend can pick you up there." He winks at me, knowing damn well I have nowhere to go.

"No, it's cool. I've got to get to my friend's house, but it was nice to meet you guys. You made the bus ride way more fun." Why I just said that

I have no idea. I clearly have no other options but to go with them, but I'm a little afraid of Sam, who's silently standing by Eric. Suddenly Sam grabs me by the arm and pulls me away from the others. He jerks his Ray- Bans off his face, crosses his arms, and takes a deep breath.

"Now listen to me because I'm only going to say this once. I don't believe for one second you have a job here, nor do I think you have anywhere to stay now that you're here. My guess is you're running away from something in that shit hole of a state Texas, and you have no idea what your next move is," he says hatefully.

"Actually I was on my way to Los Angeles." He sticks his finger in front of my mouth hushing me.

"Pip pip pip. I don't buy that sweet little southern girl act for one second, so don't even try it. I see right through it, so let's just get down to business. We don't need any more people traveling with us, but Eric will hound me until he gets his way, so here's the deal. I'm running this show, not Eric, so when I say jump, you say how fucking high. Got it?" Even though it's 80 degrees in Miami, I feel frozen in place.

"Umm ok," I say shyly. Wow, he sure has a big bark for such a little guy.

"Now, let's go," he says, as he puts his nose in the air and marches off. I make my way back to Eric who is smoking a cigarette. He grins at me.

"So you coming with us?" he asks with a smirk. I take a deep breath.

"Apparently so," I say half-heartedly. "Is Sam always that mean?"

"Haha, he's a little bitch, huh!?? But I always get what I want, remember that!!" Eric says, sticking his tongue out at me.

We make our way from the bus station to a Holiday Inn, check in, and then taxi it to The Jungle. They tell me it's one of Miami's hottest new gay clubs located on the South Beach strip. I'm really excited because I've never been to a real club before, much less a gay club. I keep this to myself because I don't want them to know I'm only eighteen, not twenty one. As we drive down Ocean Avenue, I'm amazed at how beautiful it is. Each building is painted a different shade of pale pink, baby blue, and bright yellow. I'm mesmerized when we pass the Versace mansion. On the other side are the white sandy beach, shimmering blue ocean, and hundreds of palm trees, swaying in the breeze. When we pull up in front of The Jungle, I'm not too impressed. It's an enormous gray building with a front door covered by a canopy; however, when we walk through the front door, I am absolutely shocked. There are dozens of palm trees everywhere, and the landscape is plush with greenery and every kind of tropical flower imaginable. The oversized pink, purple, and yellow flowers are all lit with LED lights and glow inside the dark club. Thousands of spotlights flash around inside, and one whole wall is a massive waterfall surrounded by large boulders on both sides. The ceiling is purple and glows with thousands of tiny stars to resemble the night sky. I feel as if though I've been transported into a rainforest. A far cry from the cow fields of Texas! I watch as Zack and Kevin start unloading Eric's equipment into the elevator to take to the DJ booth on the second floor.

"I forgot to ask you last night how old you are," Eric turns and says to me.

"Oh… I'm… uh, twenty two," I say nervously.

"Are you sure about that?" He grins. "You have an ID, right?"

"No, I'm a…actually…I lost it yesterday. Yeah, on the bus. I was looking for it everywhere." Eric shakes his head at me.

"Jesus, I have to teach you how to be a better liar. You're gonna need an ID I'll be back in thirty minutes, don't wander off." He winks at me, slaps me on the butt, and makes his way out the front door.

Eric is gorgeous and charismatic, but there's also something dark about him. I can't put my finger on it, but it scares me a little. He's beautiful, seductive, manipulative, and obviously a hustler. I know Momma would tell me to run the other way and that a boy like him will only get me in trouble. I'll just hang out with these guys until I can figure out a way to get some money together and then I'll hit the road again. Besides, I really don't have any other option right now.

"Sunny!!" Sam startles me as I lose my train of thought. "Ok, so I talked to the club owner, and you're going to be go-go dancer in a cage tonight. He had a girl quit last night, so it's your lucky day. Here's fifty bucks, go to one of the shops on the strip and find an outfit to dance in, then get back over here. You can pay me back when you get the hundred for dancing tonight. You can dance, right?" he asks me skeptically.

"Yeah, I think I can handle it." I smile at him. I walk up and down the strip for an hour checking out all of the little shops. Finally, I find a cute baby blue tank top that matches my eyes perfectly and a pair of cute cut-off shorts. When I get back, all four boys are standing outside the front door smoking.

"Where the hell did you go??" Eric yells at me outraged, his eyes are burning with anger.

"I told you I sent her to get an outfit!" Sam yells at him.

"I told you not to wander off!!" he screams at me, ignoring Sam. I wonder why the hell he is so mad.

"Let's go everyone. We gotta eat dinner and get ready for the show tonight," Sam barks out as he flicks his cigarette and begins marching down Ocean Avenue.

"I'll see you guys later," Eric grumbles, then storms off in the opposite direction.

"Wow, talk about a mood swing!" Kevin laughs and looks at Zack who shrugs and starts to follow Sam. "C'mon, Sunny, don't worry about him. He has serious anger management issues!" Kevin lightly punches my shoulder and follows behind Zack.

We find a small cafe that serves fresh seafood, and Sam tells the three of us to order whatever we want because it's on the Jungle owner's tab. I get grilled Australian lobster tail, and it's amazing. I feel very fancy eating this meal after being on a bus for twenty three hours yesterday.

At 8 p.m., we get back to the club, and I see the giant steel cages where I'll be dancing lowered to the floor. Sam directs me to the dressing rooms, while he, Zack, and Kevin make sure all the equipment is working properly. There are six other girls in the dressing room when I walk in, buzzing around with exotic patterns painted on their faces. All of them are wearing extremely tight and revealing outfits, each of which has a different animal print. I am mortified realizing my new cute little outfit is not going to work.

"Hey girl, I'm Clark. You need help getting ready?" a very tall girl with big green eyes and long golden hair says to me.

"Oh my goodness, yes, I would really appreciate it," I say trying to hide the anxiety in my voice. "I had no idea y'all were wearing these kinds of outfits."

"I love your accent!! Where are you from?" she says to me curiously.

"I'm from a small town in Texas, right outside Dallas," I say smiling at her.

"Cool!! I've never met anyone from Texas. I'm from Pennsylvania. Here, Amanda quit last night. This was her outfit, and you look about the same size as her." She hands me a yellow snakeskin jumpsuit. "It'll look great with that blonde hair of yours." *Thank you God for Clark*, I think to myself, as none of the other girls have even bothered to look up and acknowledge I'm here.

At 10 p.m., Clark walks me to my cage as Ja Rule's "Livin' it up" blasts through the speakers. I see some of the other girls in costume, and two girls even have six feet long yellow and purple pythons wrapped around them. There are a dozen male dancers wearing the same animal print as the girls, but their outfits are tiny boy shorts. Holy shit! I've never seen anything like this. The lights are in full effect, and the music is pulsing. I get in my cage which has big pink and purple flowers and vines twisted through the bars. As the cage rises up to the second level of the club,

I realize I'm directly across from Eric who is in the DJ booth. He has earphones up to one ear and is typing on his laptop. He looks up at me and gives me a wink. I frown and look away remembering his outrage earlier in the day. That was so crazy; I don't even know what made him so angry. What a dumb thing to lose your temper over. My mind flashes back to daddy's rages...but I quickly shake off those memories and get busy doing what I'm being paid to do.

The night is insane. The drinks are flowing, the music is pumping, and hundreds of people below seem to be having a blast. Dancing in this cage isn't too bad either for a hundred bucks. Two a.m. finally arrives, and the house lights come on. I get changed, thank Clark, and go to meet up with Sam who is collecting money from the club manager.

"You boys did great as always, Mr. LeBlanc," the manager says to him.

"LeBlanc... that's an interesting last name," I say to Sam as he hands me fifty dollars. "What is your background?"

"It's French; I'm from Louisiana," he says, annoyed.

"Oh cool! What was it like growing up there?" I ask him, my curiosity piqued.

"Listen, as much as I'd love to sit and braid each other's hair and have a heart to heart right now, we have to get the equipment loaded up and get it back to the hotel. Why don't you run along, find Eric, and bother him," Sam says as he makes his way to the DJ booth. I sigh to myself. Ok, no small talk. I get it. He really doesn't like me. I don't know who's more high strung, Sam or Eric.

I GET OUT OF THE shower and look at the clock on my phone; it's 2:45 a.m. So much has happened in the past forty eight hours, I haven't even had a chance to stop and catch my breath. I'm in a strange new city with a bunch of guys I don't know and dancing in a club that looks like a jungle. This was not at all my plan, but at the same time it's thrilling. It might not be L.A., but right now anything's better than being stuck in Cleburne. I open the bathroom door, and the bedroom is empty. There are two beds and a roll up bed that Sam has sent up for Eric, so Sam and I can sleep in the hotel beds. I hear a card slide through the door and in walks Eric. His face is hard to read.

"Hey. I just wanted to apologize for earlier. I kinda lose my temper sometimes. You forgive me right?" he says in a childlike tone. Not much of an apology, but the apologetic look on his face is so cute, I have to forgive him.

"Yeah I forgive you...I'm still not really sure why you got so mad though, what did I..." He puts his finger up to my mouth.

"Let's talk about something else. How did you like the music tonight?" He looks at me inquisitively. I figure it's pointless to push the subject.

"It was great, and the crowd seemed to love it," I say smiling up at him. "You're a really good DJ."

"Thanks, I'm glad you liked it." He grabs my hands. "Listen, it's been a long night, do you wanna go down to the lagoon with me for a swim?" His face changes as he looks at me seductively, with one side of his mouth curling into a smile.

"Um, yeah, I don't have a swim suit, though." Holy shit! There's something so dark and mysterious about him behind those magnetic brown eyes.

"I bought you one earlier when I got your ID." He opens the closet and then hands me a small bag. I pull out an ID and check out the picture which looks very similar to me. It says I'm from Georgia, and my name is Sandra Bullockson. He flashes a grin at me. "I remembered last night you said Sandra Bullock was your favorite actress. This way if anyone asks your name, it won't be hard to remember. It's a real ID. You can scan it and everything… use it to fly… whatever…"

He pulls off all his clothes and walks over to his suitcase and rummages through it. I'm in shock. I can't believe he's standing in front of me buck naked. He's tall and lanky, but still has a hard, muscular body. His skin is beautiful and dark, and his chest and stomach are covered in black hair. The only thing he's wearing is a shiny black diamond encrusted dog tag. I look away embarrassed and can't help but think he's doing this on purpose. He pulls out some swimming trunks and slides them on. I quickly head to the bathroom and put on the Hawaiian print bikini he bought me. After a couple of minutes I hear him tap on the door.

"You ready?" he asks impatiently.

"Yeah, just let me put my hair in a ponytail," I say feeling rushed. I wonder if we are really going to swim, or if he has more in mind.

WE GET DOWN TO the hotel's lagoon themed pool, which is enchanting. It's in a very quiet secluded area, very dimly lit, with a small cave and a waterfall on one side of it. We are completely alone. I stick my foot in the water which is warm and feels amazing. It sends tingles up my body.

"You ready?" Eric asks excitedly, and then grabs my hand and pulls me in along with him. When we both come up for air, I feel him slide his hands around my waist as he pushes me up against the side of the pool.

"You're pretty fucking cute, Sunny," he says in a hushed tone, as his eyes narrow and stare into mine. "I told you not to wander off today, and you did it anyway. That drives me crazy." I look at him perplexed, not sure what to say. "Don't ever defy me again, understand?" Eric's voice lowers to a whisper, as he thrusts himself between my legs. I feel my heart begin to beat faster as he slowly wraps himself around me like a snake squeezes its prey. He tilts my head back and bites into my neck, then does the same thing on the other side. He presses his warm lips against my shoulders, bites deep into my skin, and then looks me in the eye to see if I'm enjoying the pain. It hurts, but I'm entranced. I don't want him to stop. He pulls me up higher and bites into my bikini top. I feel his hand untie the knot, and he slips it off. He moves his mouth around my neck, his tongue licking my wet skin. Even though the pool water is warm, I can feel the heat radiating off Eric's smooth dark skin. I put one hand on his bicep and the other I use to run my fingers through his glistening black hair. He looks me in the eyes, and I feel a slight amount of fear. He looks at me like a predator who's caught his prey. Eric is sexy and terrifying all at the same time. He pulls off his swim trunks and pitches them to the side of the pool, never taking his eyes off me. He then slides off my bikini bottoms, I wrap my legs around him, and he enters me in one swift thrust. I feel sharp pain at first, and I let out a whimper. He quickly cups his hand over my mouth.

"Shhhh," he whispers. "Just let me in. It'll only hurt for a minute." I wish he would go easy, but I'm afraid to ask him. It takes a while, but the pain stops and I wrap my arms around him as he thrusts himself into me deeper and faster, never taking his eyes off mine. Every time I whimper in pain, I see a flicker of delight in his eyes. He enjoys watching me suffer, so I do it even more to turn him on. His face lights up with excitement. *This is wild,* I think to myself as I lean back and try my best to submit to Eric Jordan.

THE BOYS DECIDE to stay in Miami for another week because their next gig in Atlanta is not for another four days. We spend most of the time just hanging out on the beautiful white sandy beaches. Eric and I relax under a huge umbrella while he sips his favorite drink, a giant blue frozen margarita. He can't keep his hands off me, which I don't mind at all. Every time he brushes against me, I get chills, and I'm thankful I haven't seen the frightening side of his personality again. I've never seen someone as beautiful as he is in real life. He reminds me of the male models in *Vogue* or *Vanity Fair*, and he's not afraid to remind me he's the best looking guy in the world. His narcissism is annoying, but I try to ignore it. We talk about how he learned how to DJ, what growing up in Washington was like, and some of the wild nights he and Sam have had together. He doesn't ask many questions about me, which I'm fine with because the less I tell him the better. Sam usually cruises up and down the beach in his speedo and signature Ray-Ban sunglasses. I can't help but notice that Sam has an incredible body as well, with a six pack to die for. He finds gay muscle guys to talk to, sometimes disappearing with them for hours to something called a bath house, but I figure it's best not to ask questions. Kevin and Zack usually rent bikes or skateboards and make their way up and down the boardwalk to find Cuban girls to hit on. On our last day in Miami, Eric, Kevin, Zack, and I wake up and go to the South Beach Yacht Club. Eric has arranged for us to have brunch on the biggest yacht I've ever seen. He met the owner of the yacht, a business man from Dubai, on the beach and used his dazzling charm on him. So here we are. Later in the day as are lying out on the deck of the boat drinking Veuve Clicquot, Sam rushes aboard excitedly.

"So tonight is the opening of VICE, the newest and hottest club in Miami, inside the Mondrian Hotel," Sam states to the group in his usual arrogant tone. Eric jumps up wide-eyed.

"Bro, that's sick. I heard they were building VICE, but I didn't know it was opening so soon!! Can we get in?" Sam holds up five red tickets with gold writing on them. He's grinning a triumphantly from ear to ear.

"Just had a meeting with the general manager. Not only did I get all of us in, I set up a meeting with the owner to discuss you spinning one night a month, and it comes with a huge paycheck." Eric scoots his chair out and rushes over to hug Sam, who tries his best to wiggle out of Eric's grasp. Sam is barely 5'8", so unfortunately he has no choice but to wait for Eric to let him go. Eric puts Sam in a headlock and rubs his knuckles into Sam's head.

"You sneaky little gay, you, I love how your foul little mind works!!" Kevin and Zack burst out laughing, and Sam is visibly pissed. He looks like an owl who has his feathers ruffled. Eric finally lets him go, and he starts trying to put his hair back in place. "C'mon, Sunny, let's go. We need outfits!!" Eric says to me excitedly. His face lights up like a little kid, as he grabs my hand and drags me off the yacht. We make our way past each of the luxury stores along the ocean front strip, Versace, Prada, and Gucci.

"Nope...nope...nope...," Eric says as he pulls me away from each window front. "Ah-ha!!" he shouts, as we pause in front of Dolce and Gabbana. "Find a dress you like while I talk to the store manager," he orders as he makes a bee-line for the sales counter. I have no idea what he's planning to do, I just hope he's not going to try to steal us something to wear. I make my way through the women's dresses and find a short sexy white dress with gold zippers and gold shoulder pieces that I'm in love with. I take it in the dressing room, and it looks even more gorgeous on me. I look at the price tag, and my heart drops. It's almost two thousand dollars. Well there goes that idea. I walk out of the dressing room, and Eric is standing with a small middle-aged Latin man with a huge smile on his face.

"*Hola,* Miss Sunny!! I'm Javier the store manager! Is that the dress you would like to wear to the event tonight?" I look at Eric, and he furrows his thick black eyebrows and shakes his head *yes.*

"Um... hi Javier, yes it is," I say politely.

"Very well, I'll put it in a dress bag for you!! Mr. Eric, would you like to try on your outfit?" He looks at Eric with stars in his eyes. Eric sure knows how to work the gays.

"Sure." Eric brushes past me and shoots me a grin as he heads into the dressing room, holding what he's picked out. A couple of minutes later he steps out of the dressing room with that same cocky grin he has when he gets what he wants. He's wearing black dress pants, a white tuxedo shirt, and a black bow tie with a black Dolce and Gabbana bomber jacket zipped up half way. He looks like a badass, and he knows it.

"Alright, you look great. You can stop with the shit-eating grin," I say with an eye roll. He puts on a serious face and begins to strut around the store like a male model on the cat walk, checking himself out in every mirror available.

When we finally leave, I turn and ask him how on earth he was able to pull that off without paying.

"Simple!" he says to me. "Everyone in Miami wants to be at the opening of the hottest new club, especially store managers of a place like Dolce and Gabbana. It makes them feel important to be around all of the richest, sexiest people in town, and they want to rub elbows with clients from their store. I offered him a ticket for tonight in exchange for borrowing clothes for the evening."

"But we only have five tickets, whose ticket are you giving him?"

"Don't worry; all of us are going. I'll just have to sneak someone in." *Oh that's wonderful*, I think to myself. Tonight is supposed to be a great opportunity for Eric, and he's already coming up with shifty ideas that will piss off the people running the club.

AT 10 P.M. WE meet the boys in the hotel lobby, and they tell me how pretty I look. I feel hot in my sexy white and gold dress that I paired with gold heels. Carrie Bradshaw would approve. I decided to slick back my hair into a ponytail and wear Momma's diamond earrings and tennis bracelet.

"Well don't you clean up nice, Sunny." Sam smirks at me in the lobby mirror while fixing his tie. "Dare I even ask who Eric scammed to get those outfits you two are wearing?" he sneers with a disapproving look on his face.

"Yeah, and Eric doesn't look bad either!!" Kevin says as he punches Eric in the arm. The boys are wearing nice suits, but Zack and Kevin have on dress shirts with no tie, which exposes their freshly tanned chests. Eric catches me admiring them and squeezes my hand tightly, shaking his head *no*. I look away quickly, knowing we are in for a terrible night if his temper begins to boil.

We pass by dozens of enormous lit-up palm trees as we arrive at the Mondrian. All different colors of Lamborghinis, Maseratis, and Porches are parked along the driveway outside the fabulous hotel. There are two lines: one line full of people waiting with the red and gold VIP tickets, and one line for people who have desperate looks on their faces who are hoping to get in. The strip is sizzling hot tonight, and I can feel the electricity in the air. Eric gets all of us in the ticketed line, and then disappears. Twenty minutes before we are about to walk into the entrance, Eric reappears with Javier from Dolce and Gabbana.

"Sunny, escort Javier, and I'll be inside in a minute."

"What?" I look at him perplexed.

"Just do it!" he yells at me and shoots me a dirty look.

After handing our tickets to the bouncers and showing them my fake ID, I grab Javier by the arm and lead him through the enormous white doors and into the party. The inside of the club is incredible. We make our way past dozens of beautiful people dressed in their sexy suits and tight skimpy dresses. We pass through a long white hallway with soaring thirty foot glass ceilings. I look up and see sharks swimming back and forth in crystal blue water above us. At the end of the hall, there is an enormous circular white room, dimly lit with purple spotlights. In the center of the room is a mirrored, circular bar. Everything is very modern, and the lines of the club are clean and sexy, much like Miami itself. I turn and see Eric talking frantically to the door guys. Sam and the boys are behind us, and Sam asks everyone to pause and says, "This shouldn't take long." He's clearly annoyed by Eric's antics. A few minutes go by, and Eric's in. He struts up to us, looking shifty as ever.

"How did you get in?" I look up at him suspiciously.

"Sam, what was my time?"

"Two minutes, forty three seconds," Sam says with a yawn.

"Ohhhh... that's a new record!!!" Eric laughs at Sam.

"Yeah, whatever. I'm going to get a drink and find Michael, the general manager. You'll need to meet up with me in one hour so I can introduce you to him," Sam says dryly. "Keep an eye on him," he whispers in my ear and walks away.

Kevin and Zack start discussing which girls they want to hit on, and I follow Eric to the bar with Javier in tow.

"Can I get three shots of Patron?" he asks a handsome bartender.

"Eric, I can't drink tequila!" I say to him quickly.

"Ok two shots of Patron and one vodka soda with a lime. Javier, you drink tequila right?"

"Yes, Mr. Eric, thank you!" Javier says excitedly.

I look up at Eric, and he winks at me. I wonder what he's up to now. One thing's for sure; he always has something up his sleeve. Eric asks for another round of shots, then another, then another. He and Javier are definitely starting to get drunk. I'm not sure if I should say anything for fear of pissing him off, but I feel like I have to at this point.

"Eric don't you think you should slow down? You have to meet with that guy soon; it's almost been an hour."

"Yeah, I'll be fine, don't worry. I just want to get some shots in me before we hit the dance floor!!!"

What? The dance floor? He's not even thinking about the meeting, and little Javier already looks like he's three sheets to the wind. Javier whispers something in Eric's ear, and I'm curious as to what they're talking about.

"Ok, Sunny, follow me. We're going to the dance floor for just a minute." Eric grabs my hand and pulls me through the crowds of people. I see Javier in a serious conversation with some shady looking guy, a heavyset, Latin man with a black goatee wearing a gold chain and a suit over a black V-neck. Javier looks over at Eric, nods, and we begin to follow them. What the hell are we doing now? I have a bad feeling about this, not to mention the fact that Sam is going to flip out when we are nowhere to be found. We follow them through a side entrance, and out of the club, leaving the sounds of the bass-pumping club mixes behind, and we are welcomed with the sultry Latin music inside the lobby, and then we head into the elevator. We exit on the fourth floor and follow the shady looking guy into room 406. We enter a beautiful suite with all white furniture, two separate bedrooms, a full kitchen, and a bar. There are a few guys and girls in the suite who look like they've had a lot to drink and barely notice us walk in. The shady guy who Javier finally refers to as Enrique makes himself a drink and asks everyone what they'd like. Eric and Javier both want another Patron shot, which makes eight for each of them. I shake my head in disgust and take a seat on one of the giant white couches. The three of them are talking so low I can't hear what they're saying, and then they begin to head towards the balcony.

When Eric passes me, he puts up his index finger signaling me to wait and whispers to me, "Stay here for one second, I'm going to have a cigarette on the balcony, then we can leave. Ok?" He's slurring his words, and I've had enough.

"No, Eric, absolutely not!!" I hiss at him. "What the hell are we doing up

Here? Why are we not down there for your meeting? That's the whole reason we came!! This is fucking ridiculous!!" I say exasperated.

"I promise, five minutes and we can leave!!" he says with a sweet puppy dog face, then grins and winks. I cross my arms and sit back in a huff on the couch. I watch the three of them slide the glass balcony door shut and move to the right. I'm guessing the balcony must stretch over to one of the bedrooms because I can't see them any longer. Clearly they are moving over so no one sees what they're doing, and now I know something's up. Does Eric do drugs? God, I hope not, I can't be around this shit. Please, God, tell me he doesn't do drugs.Suddenly after a couple of minutes, I hear shouting coming from the balcony. All I can see outside are huge spotlights moving back and forth across the downtown Miami skyline. The shouting gets louder and louder, and then I see Enrique first, then Javier flings open the glass door and runs past me; both have panicked looks on their faces. Enrique is holding Eric's Dolce and Gabbana jacket and shirt. They swing the hotel door open and take off running. I jump up and run to the balcony door and step outside. Eric is nowhere to be found. I run to the next room guessing he went through the other balcony door into the bedroom, but it's vacant. I run back out to the balcony, and it dawns on me. Cold chills run down my spine, and I can't move. I realize how high up we are. Four stories. It takes everything in me to take the three steps to the balcony and look over the railing, terrified at what I'm about to see.

I look down below through the tops of the palm trees, and even though it's dark, the lights from the pool are shining bright. I can see the outline of Eric's half naked body lying on the cement next to it. I'm frozen in sheer horror as I see him twitching the same way a bug does after it's just been squashed. He is slowly dying. I begin to scream bloody murder. I figure the louder I scream in horror, the quicker someone will get to him and call an ambulance. One of the girls from the party runs outside and starts screaming as well when she sees Eric's body. She pulls out her cell, and I hope she's dialing 9-1-1. I turn to see people coming out on the balconies next to the one we're on, and I see people gathering around Eric's body next to the pool. I walk inside and see the other people gathering up their stuff and running towards the door. This is now a crime scene, and none of them want to get caught here; I'm sure many of them have drugs on them.

I make my way to the elevator, then to the lobby, my heart pounding out of my chest the entire time. There are hotel managers and employees rushing out towards the pool area. I walk to the doors and look out and see a huge group of people surrounding Eric's body, and I can't force myself to walk out there and see him like this. I take a seat on one of the couches in the lobby and begin to cry. How God? How can you let him die like this? I'm lost. I want more than anything to call home, but I know I can't. I need to find Sam and the boys, but it is so chaotic in the lobby, I'll never find them with all the people rushing by. The Miami police begin to make their way through the entrance of the hotel along with firemen and paramedics. I can see them pulling out tools to work on Eric's seemingly lifeless body. I put my head in my hands and continue to cry. Please, God. Don't let him be dead. I'm begging you...

I hear a commotion outside, and people begin to scream. I look up, and my eyes cannot believe what they are seeing. Eric zooms inside running at full speed, shirtless, flying through the lobby of the hotel, and police officers chase him screaming for him to stop!! How is this happening? It's not possible!! Then a cop tackles Eric, followed by another cop, then another. I jump up and start screaming.

"He's hurt!! What the hell are you doing? He just fell four stories!!" The police are holding him down like a criminal when they should be treating his injuries. I can't help but scream along with many other hotel guests who seem perplexed as to why this is happening.

The paramedics bring in a stretcher, and it takes six cops and fireman to lift him and tie him down as he fights to get free. They load him in the ambulance, and I run over and tell them I'm his girlfriend, and they pull me in. I take a seat, and he is struggling to get up; he can't talk because they've put some sort of mask on him. We finally make it to the emergency room, and they wheel him into a room. Doctors and nurses frantically begin to work on him, and then something goes terribly wrong. His heart monitor flat-lines, and I hear one of the doctors yell, "He's having a heart attack." I watch in horror as they prep to shock him back to life. At this point a nurse asks me to step into the lobby. I begin to cry hysterically again. I have never been in a situation like this before. After about twenty minutes, a doctor comes out and asks me my name and relation to the patient.

"Sunny," I tell him. "And I'm his girlfriend." Not exactly true but what else am I'm supposed to tell him?

"Sunny, I want you to follow me." We begin to walk back into the emergency room. "We have him stabilized in a room; he had a mild heart attack, but he's ok now. A mix of alcohol, cocaine, and Ritalin. The problem is we can't get him to calm down, so I'm going to let you try. You have five minutes, and then we're going to have to inject him with something to put him to sleep."

"Yes sir," I say to the doctor and walk into the room where three nurses stand. Eric is tied to the bed with all kinds of straps and is wearing a mask that looks just like Hannibal Lector's in *Silence of the Lambs.* One of the nurses reaches over and slowly unbuckles the mask and takes it off Eric's face. He turns his head calmly to look at me, and I see a fire flash in his eyes.

"What the FUCK, Sunny? Why the hell would you let them bring me here!!! Get me the fuck out of here now. How could you do this to me?" he screams at me in rage, spit coming out of his mouth.

"Eric, please listen to me." I run my fingers through his hair and begin to cry. "If you don't calm down, they're going to put you to sleep."

He begins to scream again, and his entire body lifts up off the bed. He spits into one of the nurse's faces and calls her a fat whore, and I hear the doctor say, "That's it, do it." They put the mask back on him and inject him several times. I watch as his body instantly goes limp. The emergency room doctor asks me if he's had a history of suicide attempts or drug use, and I shrug my shoulders and tell him I honestly don't know. He says he'll let me know what they decide to do with him and escorts me back to the lobby. I step through the door, and there stand Sam, Kevin, and Zack. The boys look worried and look at me for a sign of good news, but not Sam. He has a look of pure hatred on his face.

"Well, haven't you just been a wonderful influence, you little bitch," he jeers at me.

"Looks like you're the only little bitch I see around here," I say back and shove past him towards to the waiting area.

It's 1 p.m. the next day, and I'm finishing up some terrible meatloaf and green beans in the hospital cafeteria. I look up to see Zack heading towards my table.

"Hey, Sunny." This is one of the few times I've heard Zack speak. "Um, the doctor said we can see Eric now, but the only person Eric's requesting to see is you," he says shyly.

"Oh...ok. Thanks, Zack," I say, as I hurriedly grab my things and put away my lunch tray. This is going to be a weird conversation. What do I say to Eric? I follow Zack back to the emergency room, and a nurse is waiting for me. She hands me a name tag and requests I follow her. We make our way through one wing and then another, and finally arrive outside huge locked doors that say *Psych Ward* above them. The nurse begins to enter a code.

"He's in the psych ward?" I ask her.

"Yes. They have him under suicide watch and evaluation for mental problems."

Oh my god, this is so scary. It's like being in a movie. The nurse opens the door and lets me in, and there, at the end of a long white hallway, is Eric sitting on a hospital bed with his feet over the side kicking them back and forth like he's a little kid. He's eating blue Jell-O and is wearing a powder blue hospital gown. I see him look at me, and a smile spreads across his face. His whole face lights up. I take a deep breath and walk towards him.

"Hi, Sunny!!" he says very bubbly.

"Hi. How are you feeling?" I try to hug him, but he flinches.

"Sorry, I'm really sore."

"It's ok…so, do you remember what happened, how you fell?"

"Nope. Not a thing. Last I remember, I was with you and that guy from Dolce and Gabbana at the bar."

"Oh, ok well…," I say, hesitant to tell him what happened.

"Do you think you could do me a huge favor and get me out of here? They've been asking me questions all day like I'm a crazy person; they think I jumped off a balcony. Police came in this morning and told me I hit a canopy and that I'm lucky to be alive. Pretty crazy, huh?" He says this as though it were an exciting story he recently heard.

"Let me go ask your doctor what the plan is ok? I'll be right back."

To my surprise, the doctor releases Eric a couple days later. I can't even imagine what he said to the doctor during his analysis, but whatever Eric said, it worked. We make our way back to the hotel, and the silent tension among everyone could not be more awkward. I know Sam wants to chew out Eric, but it won't do any good because Eric couldn't care less and is pretending like nothing happened. The next morning we check out and have breakfast at a little cafe on the strip.

"Ok, so where are we headed to next, Sam?" Eric asks, as he tears into his French toast.

"We have to be in Atlanta soon, so we'll head to the bus station as soon as everyone's done." Sam looks down at my untouched plate of eggs Benedict then up at me and rolls his eyes.

"Look if you have something you want to say to me just say it," I say to Sam as my temper rises.

"Ok, I'll say it. I think you should take the next bus back to Texas," Sam says in a matter of fact tone as he pulls out a Marlboro Light and lights it.

"Fine. That's fine. I did nothing wrong. You can place the blame on me all you want, but it's not my fault he fell off the building," I say unbothered as I sit back in my chair.

"Wait, what?" Eric says, his mouth full of food. "Sam, are you blaming Sunny for what happened? It was my choice to go up there; she was trying to get me to turn around and head back to the meeting," Eric says pointedly at Sam.

"Well either way, you really fucked up big time, and both of you are to blame. I mean, this was the big break you've been waiting for. You've been begging me to get you to the next level, to play mainstream clubs, to be a famous DJ. I hand it to you on a silver platter, and you go and jump off a goddamned balcony!" Sam yells as he stands up, smashing his fists on the table.

Eric stands up towering over Sam, and yells back, "Shut the fuck up, Sam!! If it weren't for me, we wouldn't be playing any gigs at all!! I'M THE TALENT!! Now apologize to Sunny!" They stand there glaring at each other, both waiting on the other to stand down. Sam finally breaks, grabs his Ray-Bans, and marches to the front of the cafe. After a couple of minutes, he returns.

"The bill's paid. Let's go," he says, his words cold as ice. I look over at Zack and Kevin, who both look unfazed, and begin to grab suitcases. I'm guessing this is a common occurrence between Sam and Eric, and they've gotten used to it. It's silent on the way to the Greyhound station and for the rest of the day.

As I look out the window of the bus, I see that we are approaching

Orlando; Disney World is ten miles ahead. Just then, I feel someone sit down beside me; it's Sam. I turn around nervously and see Kevin and Zack several rows behind us in deep conversation, and Eric is spread out across the seats in the back of the bus sound asleep and drooling.

"Ok, so this is not something I normally do, so don't get used to it. I apologize for the way I acted at the hospital. I didn't realize you were trying to help. I just figured you were enjoying yourself and wanted to go party," Sam says to me. I can tell it's really hard for him to get this out.

"I honestly did everything I could to get him to the meeting. I know how much it meant to the both of you," I say honestly. He looks at me intrigued.

"Well it's good to hear you say that. I work so hard trying to keep him on track, and every time it's important, he figures out some way to screw it up. I just took it out on you, and really it's my own fault for not staying with him. I hate playing babysitter," Sam says with a sigh.

"He's kind of his own worst enemy, isn't he?" I say sympathetically.

"You nailed it. You know, I could really use your help. We could do this together if you'd be willing to assist me," Sam says to me hesitantly. I'm pretty sure he's used to calling the shots and rarely asks anyone for help.

"I would be happy to help," I say to him with a smile.

"Ok great. Let me explain to you my long-term plan for him and what the next step will be…" He wants to do publicity for talent and feels that Eric just might be his ticket in the door. He's hoping to land Eric a resident DJ spot in a club in L.A. As I listen to Sam, my wheels begin to turn, and my eyes light up. This just might be my ticket to Hollywood. Maybe fate put me on the wrong bus for a reason. I can't help but think that if I stick with these boys, we will end up in Los Angeles soon, and maybe Sam can help me get where I want to be as well.

"My ultimate goal is to do publicity for the stars in L.A., and if I can turn Eric into a famous DJ, he'll be my stepping stone to Hollywood."

I love listening to Sam plotting out his next move, controlling the next step, and I realize he only puts up with Eric's behavior because he thinks he can make him a star. I'm intrigued by this, but I'm hesitant to tell him my dreams of becoming a star just yet. We sit and talk the rest of the way to Atlanta, and my imagination comes alive thinking about all the things I could achieve with someone as smart as Sam on my side.

CHAPTER THREE
Coast to Coast

SIX MONTHS PASS quickly. We travel from city to city, never knowing where we'll end up. Sometimes we play at amazing clubs, and if they have female dancers, Sam gets me a spot dancing for the night. If not, I stay in the DJ booth and help Eric. Sam chases cute boys, and Kevin and Zack are always in competition to see who can sleep with the hottest girl. Life is a constant adventure; I never know what's going to happen next. What I do know is that eventually we will be in L.A., and I've been saving every bit of extra money I can for when we get there.

Several times over the past six months, I've tried to bail. Eric's mood swings are extremely unpredictable. Sometimes he is the sweetest guy in the world, especially when he wants something from me, mainly sex. He wants sex in elevators, bathrooms of restaurants, and even in the DJ booth with hundreds of people down below. He loves the thrill of possibly getting caught. I often feel as if I don't know which way is up because he is a masterful manipulator. One minute he's funny and comical, the next dark and brooding. He's such a mystery to me, but it keeps me intrigued. I've also learned Eric is a con man. He tells me constantly that everything is a negotiation. He's gotten worse and worse, and he's gone way past negotiating.

He started out doing things like stuffing Walmart or Target bags down his pants, going inside the store, and filling up the cart with steaks, crab legs, gourmet cheeses, and the most expensive groceries in the store. Then he takes the cart to the very back of the store to an aisle where there are no cameras and quickly loads the food into the bags. He heads back to the front, grinning and waving to the unsuspecting store clerks who wave back without a clue. I'm shocked at how often he gets away with it. When we're at a store where he doesn't think he can get away with shoplifting, he simply changes the stickers on the food, making his groceries super-cheap and goes to self-checkout. Eric convinces me that grocery stores charge too much for food and that we need to save money.

Everything in life is a game to him. If we're at a club, the game is to get in for free and see how many drinks he can get bought for him or put on someone else's tab. If we're at a restaurant, it's all about getting the meal for free or charging it to some unsuspecting customer's bill. At the mall, he persuades girls or gay guys who work in the stores that they should let him have free clothes and in exchange he will get them into whatever club he's playing at, but he never comes through on his part of the deal. Once he gets what he wants, he's done with them. And every time, it works like a charm. Often, he's able to fill a shopping bag with pairs of sunglasses that he has stolen from people. New and expensive sunglasses are his favorite things to steal. He walks past people's tables at restaurants and grabs them and runs, or he pulls them off people's heads at the beach and asks if he can wear them for a minute, and then takes off into the crowd. I can't count the times I've heard him yell *RUN*, and we barely escape the police. In my heart I know what he's doing is wrong. Every time I complain about it, he begs me for forgiveness. He gets on his knees and pleads with me, telling me he'll never do it again, and every time I believe him. It has all happened so fast that I never have time to stop and think. Eric gloats to the boys for hours about how good he is at working the system. The last stunt he pulled, however, was the end of the road for me.

A couple of weeks ago, we were at a club in Colorado Springs; Eric was DJing, and I was bored, so I left the DJ booth and went to order a vodka soda from the bar. A very good looking guy came up to me and began to chat. I was as polite as I could be, told him I had to get back to the booth, and let him know I had a boyfriend. He shrugged, walked away, and that was that. A couple of minutes later, I looked out at the crowd and saw Eric in a fist fight with the same guy. Security was scrambling to pull them off each other, and fists were flying. I watched as they pulled the innocent guy to the front door and threw him out on Eric's word. After all, he's the DJ. He came storming up to me, his face dripping with blood.

"Are you happy now? I'm bleeding thanks to you!! Are you fucking happy, you little slut!!" I looked at him in shock.

"Happy? Have you lost your goddamned mind? Why in the hell were you fighting with that guy?" I yelled, exasperated.

"Because he had his hands all over you!! And you were egging him on!! I watched the whole thing from the DJ booth!!" he screamed as his face flashed with fury.

"Eric you are delusional, you know that? I told him I had a boyfriend, and he walked off. You are seriously crazy!!! We need to check you back into the psych ward!!" He glared at me in outrage, and stormed off towards the bathroom.

Later that night when the club was closing, Eric stepped out onto the patio where I was sitting with Zack and Kevin.

"Hey...I just want to apologize for how I acted." Eric looked at me with a tortured look on his face. "I hate that I acted like that towards you...you forgive me?" he asked, looking at me longingly.

"Yeah I do, I just hope you realize I wasn't..."

"Shhhh…" he said as he slid a mint breath strip in my mouth.

"What? Do I smell like alcohol?" I asked him.

"Yeah, you do, and I wanna make out with you when we get back to the hotel. Here, take another one," he said with a sweet tone, grinning. "Anyway, I'm sorry that happened tonight."

"How's your face?" I asked him, glad that were not going to a have a huge over that.

"Let's talk later…" he whispered and bent down to kiss me.

In the cab on the way to the hotel, I started to feel a little strange. I looked over at Eric and didn't recognize him. I had to really look at him to realize it was him. I began to see weird shapes floating around the cab.

"Eric, something's wrong. I don't feel good," I said to him scared.

"You're fine. Maybe you just had too much to drink." We got to the hotel, and he had to hold me up as we walked to the room. I got inside and quickly lay down.

"What in the hell is going on? I'm seeing all kinds of weird shit!" I said to him with fear in my voice. Eric busted out laughing and fell on the floor in amusement. "What is so funny?" I asked him in disbelief.

"Sunny, there's nothing wrong with you. Those weren't breath strips I gave you; it was acid!!" He fell over into another fit of giggles. "Don't worry; I took two hits as well. We're gonna be trippin' all night!!"

I jumped up off the bed and steadied myself up against the wall. I was terrified. I threw open the door and headed next door to Sam's room, knocking in panic.

"What in the hell are you banging on my door for?" Sam said as he opened the door, visibly pissed, wearing a silk robe with a half- naked guy looming in the bedroom behind him.

"Eric…Eric gave me two hits of acid. He didn't tell me what it was; I thought it was those mint breath strips he's always popping in his mouth," I said sliding down onto the floor.

"What?" Sam yelled, as he pushed past me and into mine and Eric's room. "What in the hell is wrong with you, Eric!! You both could die from doing that shit!! What have I told you about doing acid!! And you gave it to her and didn't tell her? Are you out of your mind? You can't trick someone into doing drugs, you fucking moron!!" I lay down in the hallway, which was moving like a carnival ride. "Oh my god, Sunny, get up before someone sees you, the last thing we need are ambulances and police again!!" Sam hissed, pulling me up off the floor. "Now listen. You're going to be tripping on acid till probably sometime tomorrow. You have to stay in your room no matter what. Two hits is a lot. Just...have sex the whole time or something. Your pupils will be huge, and you can't go walking around in public." He walked me back into my room. Eric was sitting up on the bed trying not to laugh. "Don't let her leave, Eric! You don't leave either. I'll bring you food in the morning, although I doubt either of you will be hungry," Sam said and slammed the door shut.

The colors of the room became very intense. Everything began to look as if it were moving, and I slowly lay back on the bed beside Eric.

"Sunny. Listen to me. Take in deep breaths. Don't be afraid of it, just enjoy it. I'm going to have sex with you, and I promise it's going to be amazing." Part of me wanted to fight Eric; part of me felt incredible. I closed my eyes, and it began. I felt Eric undress me and climb on top of me. I smelled the alcohol and cigarettes on his skin, but it smelled more intense than ever. I wanted him. I wanted him badly. Then I didn't want him; I was furious with him. But he's my boyfriend, and he wanted to do this, so I felt I should just do it. No, he drugged me!!! I was so confused. However, minutes later, the acid kicked in, and I was lost in a state of slow-motion sex. I opened my eyes, and I saw Eric. Then, I opened them, and I saw some other guy.

"Where's Eric?" I whispered.

"I'm right here, baby," he said as he went deeper and deeper inside of me.

THE NEXT DAY, I was still seeing strange shapes, pink elephants, and every other weird thing one could imagine. I felt sicker than I had ever felt in my entire life, and there was nothing to make it stop. Sam checked in on us every couple of hours and brought me Sprite and crackers. He told me that the feeling would eventually wear off, which couldn't come sooner. Eric moved around the room in his underwear talking to the TV, the couch, and to himself. I will never ever do acid again for as long as I live.

"You can say anything you want, Eric!! Your bullshit doesn't work on me anymore!! I'm leaving, and that's the end of it!!" I yelled at Eric as I waited in line with my bags at the ticket counter of the Colorado Springs airport.

"Sunny, please!! It was a mistake!! I promise I'll never do it again!! I just wanted to experience sex with my girlfriend on acid!!" he yelled at me desperately.

"Will you shut up!!" I hissed at him as I looked around at other travelers who were wide-eyed and listening to him. "And besides that, you did it to get back at me for what happened at the club, because you got your face bashed in, not because you thought it was something *fun* we could do together!!!" I yelled.

"Sam, tell her! She has to stay!!" Eric looked at Sam hoping he would back him up.

"I don't blame her for wanting to leave. You drugged the poor girl. Had someone done that to you, you would've flipped out, Eric," Sam said with a yawn.

Eric dropped down on his knees and grabbed my hand. "Sunny, you are the only bright thing in my life. If you leave, I'll kill myself, I promise.

I hated my life before you. I honestly was hoping I would die when I fell off the balcony. I know I have a dark side, and I know I'm fucked up in the head. You're the only thing that I have that's good and pure, and that makes me happy. I need you, Sunny." He pleaded with me, as tears rolled down his face. I looked over at Sam who was looking back at me in shock.

"Never thought I'd hear that come out of his mouth," Sam mumbled.

"Sunny, listen. I know you want to get on this plane and go to L.A. We have two more gigs booked, one in San Francisco and then one in Seattle. After that, I promise we will head to L.A. All of us, the whole group, right, Sam?" He wiped his tears and looked at Sam, hopeful.

"Well, I do agree with him, Sunny. You should wait and go to L.A. with us. You don't need to go out there on your own. I would personally appreciate it if you wait and go with us. No matter how mad you are at this idiot," Sam said as he pointed to Eric.

"Fine...but after Seattle, we better be heading to Los Angeles, and you better be on your best behavior or I'm gone, got it?" I scolded Eric, as he jumped up and threw his arms around me.

So I STAY, AND now it's Saturday evening, and Eric is spinning at Badlands, a gay club in San Francisco. Zack and Kevin are asleep in the hotel, so Eric, Sam, and I decide to head to dinner at the Wharf for all-you-can-eat crab legs. We are seated at a table overlooking the San Francisco bay which is beautiful. I look out and see the island where Alcatraz sits, and I get an eerie chill imagining all the prisoners who tried to escape and drowned or were eaten by sharks in the murky bay.

"Hey guys, I have an idea!" Eric says to us cheerfully, startling me out of my thoughts. "We don't have to be at Badlands for a couple of hours. Why don't we go next door to the karaoke place after we eat? I wanna sing!

And Sunny, I might even dedicate a song to you!!" He looks at me and winks and grabs my leg under the table. He has gone out of his way to be as sweet as possible to me since we left Colorado, but I'm still not over being drugged. I give him a faint smile.

"I'm cool with that. Sam?" Sam shrugs his shoulders and shakes his head *yes*.

After dinner, we make our way next door to Crazy Pete's Karaoke bar, which is built over the water. As we walk inside, I smile at the tacky tropical theme. Classy. There's a stage at the back of the bar with fake plastic palm trees on each side and fake parrots sitting in cages that hang from the ceiling. The place is half-full, and we find a little booth pretty close to the stage.

"I'm gonna go grab drinks for us, guys; be right back!" Eric says politely.

"Well, it sure is nice to see him use manners for a change," Sam says to me dryly. "I have to admit, it was hilarious watching you put him in his place like that in the airport. Did you finally just have enough?"

"Well, what else was I supposed to do, Sam? The son of a bitch drugged me!" We both look at each other and laugh about it for the first time.

"Watch, I'll bet you twenty bucks he gets up and sings Ricky Martin's 'Livin' La Vida Loca,'" Sam says rolling his eyes. Sure enough, right after Sam says it, I hear the music begin to play. Eric rushes over to the table trying not to spill our drinks.

"Here guys, grab these!! I gotta be on stage like now!! Didn't know they would play my song so quick!!" He bolts towards the stage, leaps onto it, grabs the mic, and slides into position. He howls out the words to "Livin' La Vida Loca," and I wince a couple of times. He's off-key, and Sam just rolls his eyes with his usual annoyance. Eric makes up for his bad singing with his dance moves, good looks, and flirtation with the audience. People are into it and cheering him on. He ends the song with a wink and a sexy smile. He walks back to the table, head held high, as the clapping begins to die down.

"Well, Sam, I'd say that was one of my all-time best performances! Are you hearing this? The crowd loves me!" He can't help but pat himself on the back.

Crazy Pete, an older man with a short white beard, walks out onto the stage wearing a Hawaiian shirt, white pants, and a boat captain's hat.

"Alright ladies and gentlemen, next up we have Sunny Collins!" I look up in surprise.

"What? You put my name in?" I look at Eric skeptically.

"Yeah!! You're always talking about how you used to perform as a kid, so let's see what you got!" he says with a vindictive smile. He thinks I can't sing and just wants to embarrass me. "Awww… it's ok, Sunny; it was just a joke. You don't have to go up there," he says as he looks at me sympathetically.

"No, it's fine. I'll sing," I say as I scoot out the booth. "Move. They're waiting on me," I say to Eric who looks at me surprised. I glance at Sam who also looks perplexed, and I make my way to the stage as I feel anxiety kick in. It's been a long time since I've gotten up and sang in front of people, and I feel terrible stage fright come over me.

"Do you have 'She's in Love with the Boy' by Trisha Yearwood?" I ask Crazy Pete shakily.

"Well, yes, we sure do, young lady! Coming right up!" he says, and heads back to the DJ booth. I walk up to the mic and stare blankly out at the audience. *Ok, Sunny, Sam hasn't heard you sing. This is your chance to show him what you can do and convince him it's worth helping you when we get to L.A.* My stomach churns, and I sway to the left. *Ok, you have a choice to make. Either stand up here and put on an amazing show, or go sit down and forget about everything you've always dreamed of.* If I can't even get up and sing at a cheesy karaoke bar, I have no business going to L.A.

The thought of working at Walmart in Cleburne, Texas flashes through my mind, and fear slowly washes over me. I can't live that life. I was meant for bigger things than that town can ever give me. It's now or never. I take a deep breath, and the music begins. The country music blasts through the speakers and spreads through the room. I close my eyes and imagine myself on tour singing in front of thousands of people.

Katie sittin' on her old front porch, watchin' the chickens
peck the ground.
There ain't a whole lot goin' on tonight in this one horse town.

I open my eyes and escape into the music. As the song picks up, I start to dance around the stage, and I give it my all, pointing at different people in the audience and singing my heart out. It's been so long, and it feels great to be belting out the words and to be back on a stage. I do a big finish, and the song is over. I look out through the spotlights, and the entire audience is up on their feet applauding. I got a standing ovation! I wave, take a bow, and the audience applauds me all the way back to the table. I scoot back into the booth and look at Sam and Eric. Eric is scowling at me, his arms folded. Sam is wide-eyed and looks like a deer caught in headlights.

"That was awful. You should never get up and sing again, Sunny; you sound like a bird being chocked to death," Eric says in a hateful tone as he gets up and storms away from the table towards the bar.

My heart drops, and embarrassment washes over me. I feel a stab of pain in my gut.

"Sunny...what the fuck just happened? Since when do you sing? Why haven't you ever told me you could sing like that?" Sam looks at me in awe.

"I have told you that many times. Apparently you never listen to me," I say to him looking down at my cocktail.

"You didn't just sing well; it was incredible. And that little performance you just did… who knew you could work an audience like that!" Sam leans back in the booth with a look of disbelief on his face, and I see the wheels in his head begin to turn. After a couple of minutes, he slides over next to me.

"Listen, we need to talk about this. As soon as we get to L.A., we need to get you some representation; I mean, maybe I could represent you. I wonder how good of an actress you are… I need to get a script, get you to read some lines for me… clearly you're not shy, and that's a good thing… who knew you could sing like that!!"

He seems to be more talking to himself than to me. Eric really hurt my feelings, but it feels good to hear Sam's ideas, and I feel a small rush of excitement knowing we are heading to Hollywood soon. I glance over at the bar just in time to see Eric get punched in the face by another guy. Sam and I both jump up and run over to the bar.

"Get the hell outta here!! I didn't say you could put drinks on my tab!!" the man screams at Eric. "Call the police on him, Bernie!!" he yells to the bartender.

All three of us take off running for the exit. Just another normal night with Eric.

THE NEXT DAY we wake up around noon and head to the beach. Sam tells us he's going to go shopping for a new outfit, and Kevin and Zack stay at the hotel because they drank too much last night and are both severely hungover. I have an amazing day with Eric, who, thank God, is in a good mood and fun to be around. Sam tells me to ignore Eric's hateful comments because he was just mad that I got more applause than he did. We spend a couple of hours playing carnival games on the pier, and I beat Eric every time. This, of course, pisses him off all over again, so I promise I'll tell the boys that he beat me. I hand him the stuffed animal and basketball I won, and he goes back to being in a good mood. He honestly acts like a spoiled brat when things don't go his way. Later we head to the Coney Island corn dog stand and get a deep fried corn dog to share. We can't help but laugh at some of the strange tourists. Eric waves at Sam when he spots him walking down the pier.

"Hey, you guys, I'm done shopping. Are you two ready to head back or what?" Sam asks as he puffs away on a Marlboro Light.

"Son, there's no smoking on the pier," a security guard says to Sam.

"Oh fuck off!!" Sam yells at him, as he pitches the cigarette over the side of the pier and into the water, and I can't help but giggle.

"Get anything good while you were…."

"SAM, ERIC, SAM, ERIC!!!!" All of a sudden, Kevin and Zack are running barefoot and shirtless down the pier towards us, screaming, wide-eyed like they've both just seen a ghost.

"Eric…dude…two guys…Middle Eastern looking…with guns…came to the room…looking for you!!" Kevin is trying his hardest to get out the words, and at first I think he's kidding. I look at Zack who's not saying anything, and he doesn't have to because the look on his face says it all. Sheer terror. I look up at Eric.

"Ok… where are they now?" he asks calmly. How is he not shocked by this!!! Sam looks fearfully around the pier.

"We told them you had left for the bus station, and that we were spinning in New York next." Kevin still has no color in his face but is finally speaking in full sentences.

"Ok, good, you sent them in the opposite direction… good thinking… that was smart." Eric looks intense like he's forming a plan in his head. "Sam, we play Seattle tomorrow night, right? Cancel our bus tickets and let's get to the airport as fast as possible."

"Uh, hold on just a second. Are you planning on explaining why the hell there are guys with guns looking for you?" Sam looks up at Eric perplexed.

"It's a long story, bro; I'll tell you later, but right now we need to get the fuck out of this city!! If they know I'm here, you better believe they will be looking for me!!!"

"Don't worry about getting us tickets, Sam; we're done," Zack finally speaks. "We don't want any part of whatever the hell Eric's got himself into this time. We're not getting dragged into another one of his messes. I can't afford to bail myself out of jail again. Thanks for everything, Sam. Later, Sunny."

They both look at Eric, pissed, and turn to walk away.

"C'mon you guys, don't leave!! We'll get out of San Fran, and it'll be fine!!" Without turning around, Zack puts his middle finger in the air and flips Eric the bird.

We get back to the room and quickly start to pack. I am baffled by what just happened, and the thoughts start to swirl in my mind. Who is Eric really? What am I doing with him? This whole time I've probably been in danger and didn't know it. I have to get out of here. I try to think of a way to get Sam alone and ask his thoughts. Eric goes to the bathroom, and I hear him begin to pee. I reach over and pull out his wallet which is sticking out of his backpack. When I open it, four IDs along with a small bag of cocaine fall out onto the bed.

"Holy shit!!" I whisper. "Sam, look at this!!" Sam looks down at the IDs and then up at me. He simply shrugs his shoulders.

"Are you surprised?" he asks.

I read aloud the name from each ID in bewilderment. "Eric Jordan, New York; Eric Argyos, Colorado; Eric Mohammed Hassan, Washington..." The name sounds Middle Eastern, and I know he's originally from somewhere near Seattle, so this one must be his real ID. Eric walks out of the bathroom and sees the IDs and the look of shock and disbelief on my face.

"Who the hell are you, Eric? What kind of danger are we in?" He is enraged.

"Why the hell are you going through my stuff!!! It's none of your goddamned business what I did before I met you!!! Stay outta my shit!!!" he screams.

"Ok, fine!! It was nice knowing you, asshole. Sam, I'm out. I'm done." I start grabbing my stuff and throw it in my bag, and then head for the door. Eric grabs my arm.

"Wait, I'm sorry!! Please don't leave!! I'm just freaked out. I'll tell you anything you want to know! You can't leave me now!!" He has a look of desperation on his face. I roll my eyes and drop my bag on the floor and cross my arms. Even though I'm really mad, I can't help but be curious as to why these guys are after him. Why do they want to kill him and possibly Sam and me just for being with him?

"Alright, will both of you please just sit down for a second?" Eric says as he begins to pace up and down the room, I take a seat on the bed, and Sam, looking rather curious, stops folding clothes and takes a seat. He lights a Marlboro Light, and we both give Eric our full attention.

"A couple of years ago, before I met you, Sam, I was living in New York under bridges and eating out of trash cans. I was totally broke and desperate for cash. I come from a family without a lot of money, and what money I made, I sent home to my mom and brothers. I ended up meeting these guys from Saudi Arabia, and I started hanging out with them a lot. I told them my situation and how I would do anything to make a lot of money fast. They said they were God's people, and I was one of the chosen ones. They told me that because I seemed like a good guy and I was like family because of my Middle Eastern heritage that they were going to help me out with money. They opened up several kiosks at malls in New York and Philadelphia in my name and began to make a fortune and kept all the money in a safe house in Oregon. I was allowed to go there and pull out twenty thousand dollars a month and spend it however I wanted to. This went on for about a year while I was traveling the country helping them open new kiosks at malls that sold women's spa treatments. All of us were making a fortune, and all the businesses were in my name. I was staying in the nicest suites at the nicest hotels, driving a new Mercedes, and sending money home to my mom. I even bought a house and was stashing money in a safe there.

"Ok, so one day I'm at the mall training some of the girls at the kiosk, and someone taps me on the shoulder and asks if I'm Eric Hassan. I told him I was Eric, and the guy tells me he's with the IRS and I have one week to pay $687,000 in back taxes. That entire time I thought they're taking care of the tax part of the business because I knew nothing about it. I jumped on a plane and headed to the safe house as fast as possible, and when I got there all the money had been cleaned out of the safe, several million dollars in cash. So a week later I found myself at the F.B.I. headquarters turning in both of the guys and all of the illegal workers they had brought over from Saudi Arabia. When I turned them in, everyone got deported for being here illegally, except for the ones they couldn't find, and who have been trying to hunt me down ever since. The IRS gave me some slack because I turned in everyone, but because every aspect of the business was in my name, they still want their money, and I have nothing left to give them." He pauses and takes a deep breath. "So now I'm on the run from the IRS as well because I don't want to go to prison."

"Eric, why can't we just go to the police? I mean they're trying to shoot you!!" I say to him exasperated.

"Sunny, it's just not that simple!!" Eric yells at me. "Please, both of you get your stuff packed and let's head to the airport, ok?"

I can tell he's extremely nervous, and I feel like he's probably right; we need to get out of here as soon as possible. Sam calls us a cab, and we head downstairs to wait. When we finally get to the airport, my anxiety is pretty high. Eric was turning around in the cab every five seconds to see if we were being followed, and now I'm doing the same thing while we wait for Sam to purchase our tickets to Seattle. We finally get on the plane, and I feel like I can breathe. When we arrive at the airport in Seattle, it's pouring down rain outside. Sam gets a cab, and Eric directs the cab driver to a hotel in downtown Seattle, close to the Pike Place Market where all the ferries are lined up at port. We make our way to our hotel, and the silence among the three of us is awkward.

"I'm going to take a hot shower," Sam says quietly. I can imagine he is pretty pissed at Eric by the tone of his voice. I don't know what to think. I know if my momma knew I was on the run from people who are trying to kill my boyfriend, she would be furious with me, not to mention disappointed with my choices in men, but then again she doesn't have the greatest track record either.

"Sunny, will you come with me? I want to talk to you about everything that's happened today." Eric looks at me longingly with a sad helpless expression on his face that I can't resist. He takes me by the hand and leads me out of our hotel room, down the hall, and into the elevator. We step inside, and he hits the button for the top floor where the pool and spa are located. "I want to go somewhere quiet so we can just hang out and talk."

I nod to him in agreement and follow him to the spa which is closed. He picks the lock on the door, looks around, and hurries me in. We find a huge room with big plush couches and chairs and floor-to-ceiling windows that overlook the lights of downtown Seattle and the harbor. It's still pouring outside, and the rain is hitting the windows hard. I am, of course, worried security will find us in here, but Eric always seems to get away with this kind of stuff. I lie down on one of the oversized couches and listen to the rain. Eric sits down beside me and begins to speak softly.

"Sunny...I'm really sorry for not telling you about my past. I just didn't want to accept that it's real. I felt like I could jump from city to city and run from it. Today I realized that it's catching up with me, and I put you and everyone else in danger. For that, I'm sorry. I promise tomorrow I'll figure out a new plan to make all of this go away, and you and I can plan a life together. I want to be with you. I don't want to keep hurting you. I think we should finally settle down once we get to L.A." I look up at him, and his eyes are intense and sorrowful. I want to believe him. I sit up and kiss him passionately, and he wraps his arms around me. I feel him slide his hands up my shirt as he pulls it off over my head.

I think back to all the awful things Eric has done since I met him. Theft, drugs, lying, conning, cheating people left and right, and his terrible temper. Then I think about how sweet and amazing he can be, how dashingly handsome he is, and how he does cute little things like surprising me with flowers or a new dress. Do I love him? Do I know what love is? I want to believe I do, and I want to believe Eric loves me. I shut my eyes as his long tan fingers make their way up my sides, caressing my stomach gently. For some reason, he is different tonight. His movements are different; his kisses are a little longer than normal, and he is holding me very closely. This should feel amazing, but my instincts tell me something isn't right. This is not the norm for him. I open my eyes, and his face is dangerously close to mine.

"What is it?" I whisper to him.

"Nothing," he whispers back. "I just never really realized how beautiful you are. I want to remember you like this forever." I look into his eyes, studying his expression.

"I'm not going anywhere," I whisper into his ear, and then lean back and close my eyes as he slowly slides off my shorts. He slides inside me, and I raise my hips to meet him so he's all the way in. He presses his body close to mine as his movement gets faster and faster, until our bodies are in rhythm with each other. I let go of all the worry and doubt and listen to Eric's heavy breathing, as the storm outside grows louder and louder.

I WAKE UP, and the sun is shining brightly outside our hotel room window. Eric is sound asleep next to me, and Sam is reading the morning paper sipping a cup of coffee.

"Morning," he says to me without looking up.

I put my hair in a ponytail and head to the bathroom to shower. Later, the three of us walk down the street and find an IHOP for breakfast.

"So what's the plan for today?" I ask. Neither one of the boys have said anything to each other since we got up this morning. "I was hoping y'all would take me around and show me the sights since I've never been here!" I say trying to sound enthusiastic, hoping we can at least attempt to put yesterday's events aside for now.

"Yeah, that's fine. I want to get out and do something today anyway," Sam says. "I'm pretty familiar with Seattle. We can do Pike's Peak, the first ever Starbuck's is right by it, and possibly go to the Space Needle if it's open today," Sam says unenthusiastically.

"Awesome! I'm excited! Eric, what do you say? Space needle?" I ask hopeful.

"Listen, you guys, it's been a while since I've been to see my mom. I'm gonna take the ferry over to Bainbridge Island. I'll be back around eight, and we can head to the club. Sound good?" Eric says looking out the window at the bay.

"Why can't we come with you? I wanna meet your mom and see where you grew up," I say, studying his solemn face.

"No, Sunny, not this time. She's not doing well and probably wouldn't be happy if I brought visitors to the house. You guys have a good day; show her the sights, Sam," he says, still looking out the window. I look over at Sam who has a skeptical look on his face. After a minute or so, Sam finally speaks.

"Yeah. Ok. Whatever. We'll see you later then."

"Great, I'll meet you guys back at the hotel at eight."

We walk Eric to the pier where the ferries are, and he gives me a kiss goodbye and stares into my eyes for a minute. *What is he thinking?* I wonder. He nods to Sam who doesn't nod back, makes his way up the dock, and boards the gigantic ferry.

"Do you want to tell me why you're so quiet this morning? Are you worried about the Middle Eastern guys coming after us?" I ask him, concerned.

"No...did you see how he stared at you before he walked away? Strange..." Sam continues to stare past me towards the ferry as the fog horn blows, and it begins to make its way out to sea. We see Eric appear on the second story railing and wave goodbye to us. "Something's not right Sunny," Sam says to me, as he takes a deep breath. I've learned to trust Sam's instincts when it comes to Eric, so of course this makes me feel uneasy.

We make our way to Pike's Peak Market, and Sam explains to me that it's one of the most famous fish markets in the world. I can't believe how cool it is as I watch the butchers throw the fish to each other up in the air. There are many tourists standing around watching and cheering them on. Sam says it's a time-honored tradition. We make our way through the marketplace, and get some coffee at the first ever Starbucks. I dig through my purse for my camera and make Sam take pictures of me with the fish and in front of the famous coffee house. We stroll through the rest of the tiny shops, and I think about how much Momma would love to be here and see all of this.

"I'm so excited to go to the space needle later!!!" I tell Sam. Growing up in Texas, I never had any desire to come to a place like Seattle, but it's actually a really cool city.

"Well if you want to go to the Space Needle, we might as well have dinner there, but we'll have to go back and get some cash from the hotel room…" Sam freezes mid-sentence. "The money. That's what he's doing." Sam turns back towards the street and hails a cab as quickly as possible.

"What are you talking about? Who? Eric?" There's no way. Sam is just paranoid. Eric wouldn't do that to us. Besides, Sam keeps everyone's cash, mine included, in a locked briefcase.

We get back to the room, and Sam crawls under the bed frantically looking for his briefcase that he usually carries around with him. It holds all the money from each show and everything we've saved up. He has always taken care of the money and given Eric and me cash when we needed it. He starts laughing as he lies on the floor.

"It's gone!! All of it!! That stupid son of a bitch took everything we have saved up for the past two years."

I look around and realize Eric's suitcases are gone as well. I run to the closet and swing open the doors. All of his stuff is gone. My heart is beating out of my chest, the blood in my head is pounding, and anxiety is rushing through me. This isn't happening. I check in my suitcase where I've kept some of my cash, and it's all gone as well. Eight hundred dollars. I have forty in my purse, and no way to get any more. There's no one back home to call to send me more either. I feel tears begin to stream down my face, and I become hysterical. I hit the floor shaking, and Sam jumps up and puts his arms around me, which is very unlike him.

"What are we gonna do!!!" I scream, my throat closing up with panic.

"C'mon, Sunny, follow me." I drudgingly get up, wipe the tears off my face, and follow Sam out of the hotel room. We make our way downstairs, and he hails another cab. He calmly tells the driver, "The Space Needle, please," then looks lost in deep thought. We arrive in front of the Space Needle, and Sam asks me to pay for the twelve dollar cab ride. *Great*, I think to myself. I have forty dollars to my name, and he wants me to spend twelve of it on a cab.

"Just do it," he says to me when I hesitantly hand it to the driver.

When we arrive, we head to the elevator and take it to the top of the Space Needle. We walk in the restaurant, and it's beautiful. A hostess takes us to a table next to the large windows that overlook the sound. Why the hell are we coming here for dinner? Neither one of us has any money. We should be eating cheeseburgers from the dollar menu at McDonalds.

"Sam...will you please explain to me why we're sitting here at an expensive restaurant after everything that's happened?" I'm trying my hardest not to sound exasperated. Sam, still lost in thought and looking out the window at the ocean, finally looks me in the eye.

"Sunny, I'm about to do some things. I'm going to need you to trust me in everything I'm about to do. It's very important that you don't ask questions, just follow my lead and do exactly as I tell you. You and I have become very close, and I will do what it takes to protect you. The most important thing right now is not to get emotional. We have to think with our heads not our hearts. I realize how hurt you are because you love him, but Eric only cares about himself and is doing what it takes to escape whatever mess he's gotten himself into, even if it means stealing everything you and I have and leaving us in the dust. He'll find another Sam and another Sunny by next week and use them just like he used us until they no longer serve him any purpose. I knew he would pull something like this one day; hell, I'm surprised he didn't do it sooner. Go ahead and decide what you want to eat, get anything you want. It's on me. I'll be right back; I need to make a phone call."

I wrack my brain thinking of ways Sam will try to get money. Ten minutes later, Sam returns to our table. I take a deep breath and try to be open to whatever plan it is he's contemplating. Besides, it's not like I really have any other options but to go along with whatever plan he has up his sleeve. I'm really hoping he will arrange for us to head towards California, but how on earth will we afford it? And how does he plan on paying for this food? God, I hope we're not going to pull an Eric and do a dine-and-ditch because I really don't want to end up in jail tonight.

"Ok, it's all set," Sam says as he slides back into his chair. "I have two seats booked for us tonight. We'll head back to the hotel for our bags and then to the airport as soon as were done eating."

"Where are we going?" I ask him.

"I got us a flight into Shreveport. It's the only thing I could book this late. Then, we'll take the train to Baton Rouge tomorrow morning," he says as he digs into his Caesar salad.

"Baton Rouge? We're going to Louisiana?" I hear the bewilderment in my voice. "That's your hometown, right?" I ask him curiously.

"Mmm hmm." He nods not looking up.

I can tell this is the part where I'm not supposed to ask any more questions. What in the world are we going to do in Louisiana? Another place I've never been. And how on earth is Sam paying for all of this if Eric took all of the money they had made together? After we're done eating, the waitress comes to the table and brings our check. Sam opens his wallet and pulls out an American Express black card. What the hell is going on? Did he steal that? Surely not. I try to hide my expression of shock and take a sip of Coke. So many questions!! Sam gets up and holds out his hand to me.

"Well, Sunny, Louisiana here we come...," Sam says with a troubled sigh.

CHAPTER FOUR
Swamps, Magnolias, and Sweet Tea

I LOOK OUT THE window with curiosity as the train makes its way through rural Louisiana. I feel a little homesick as we pass through a small town called Natchitoches. I remember the name because it's where *Steel Magnolias*, one of mine and my momma's favorite movies, was filmed. I have never seen a place like this before. The further south we go, the stranger it gets. Sometimes we're surrounded by forests of towering pine trees as far as the eye can see, and then we cross bridges that go on for miles with nothing but boggy swamps on both sides. I'm shocked to see alligators resting on the side of the Mississippi River as we pass it.

It's around 3 p.m. when Sam and I arrive at the train station in Baton Rouge, and I don't think either of us could be happier to be off the train after such a long trip. We find our suitcases, catch a cab, and begin to head from downtown Baton Rouge through the most beautiful neighborhoods I have ever seen. Huge, decadent Louisiana homes sit side by side on every block we pass, and there's every kind of enchanting tree you can imagine lining the streets. There are gigantic oaks, towering pines, and huge magnolia trees. I take in a deep breath, and for the first time in my life, I smell the sweet scent of the beautiful magnolias. We finally arrive at the gates of a giant mansion and make our way up the long half circle driveway. I look in wonder at Sam.

"Whose house is this?"

"This is my family home," he says nonchalantly as he hops out of the cab and pays the driver.

It's a big, beautiful, white plantation-style mansion that sits on acres and acres of green, finely manicured lawns. There are huge white pillars across the front of the house and gigantic shade trees throughout the grounds. It reminds of the White House in Washington. I never thought of Sam as being poor, but I also never imagined he grew up as Louisiana royalty, by the looks of this house. I'm even more baffled as to why he has been traveling around with Eric all this time barely scraping by if he comes from a family that is so wealthy. I, of course, am ready to bombard him with questions which I know he won't want to answer. The driver carries our suitcases to the front porch, and Sam gets out his keys and opens the front door. I step inside the house and into the grand foyer. It literally takes my breath away: thirty foot ceilings with chandeliers that hang in the main entryway, a sitting room to the left, and a family room to the right. There are huge paintings of generals from the Confederate Army, and furniture so delicate I'm afraid to touch it. I look at him, bewildered.

"Ok, Samuel LeBlanc, start explaining what is going on."

"Alright, Sunny, sit down," he says, annoyed as usual.

We make our way into the family room, and I sit on one of the enormous couches.

"No one knows this, especially Eric, because he would have tried to make me invest every dollar he could get out of me into one shifty scheme or another had he found out. I come from one of Louisiana's wealthiest families. Our family settled here hundreds of years ago. I graduated from LSU with a degree in public relations in hopes of one day moving to L.A.

I wanted to represent celebrities and live the Hollywood life, but I was so bored with this town, with school, and with my family constantly on my ass about my 'lifestyle' as my mother calls it, so I decided to take some time off before going to L.A. I wanted to travel, and pretty much just blow my trust fund money.

"That's when I met Eric who was DJing in the Boystown section of Chicago. We hit it off well, and I, of course, being the clever control freak I am, took over handling his money and bookings and got swept up in the excitement of being in his life. Eric was just what I needed to shake things up. That is until now, of course, because he took off and left me and you stranded and possibly being followed by these pissed off Middle Eastern guys. I always knew he would disappear someday; that's just the kind of guy he is. Anyway, good riddance. It was time to come home; my parents' patience with me is wearing out. Luckily they will be in Europe for the next couple of weeks, so you and I are going to have some fun."

I stare blankly out the window. Even though my emotions toward Eric change constantly from sad, to furious, to missing him, I can't help but wonder how he could just leave us without a second thought. I can't help but look back and hope I haven't made the same mistakes Momma made with Daddy. Eric is dangerous and didn't treat me well. Either way, I'll miss lying next to him at night and listening to him breathe. I'll miss being on an adventure with him. The chaos of being in his life was comforting. Maybe that's because chaos is all I've ever known.

"Sorry, I didn't mean to bring him up again, Sunny. I know you're still upset, although I can't imagine why considering how he treated you. Let's get you a glass of sweet tea, and I'll give you a tour of the plantation. There are fifteen bedrooms in the west wing and fifteen in the east, and there's also a ballroom for formal parties." I get up half-heartedly, and Sam gently grabs my face. "Hey, chin up. It's over, and we're moving on to bigger and better things. Stick with me, kid, and I'll help you get to Hollywood. I think we can be a big help to each other, Sunny." Sam says, as he smiles, and I smile back at him while thinking of the possibilities.

"Thanks, Sam." I try to hug him, but he pulls away.

"You know I don't do hugs...oh lord, ok, ok," he says, finally giving in. I can't help but laugh. Sam stands and turns to look at me. "Sunny...life is a tricky thing. I have a feeling we'll see Eric again, whether we want to or not. He's like a cockroach. You can't ever get rid of him."

CHAPTER FIVE
The Gemini

"**S**unny, are you ready?"

"Yeah, give me one second. I'm puttin' on my jeans." I run down the stairs and into the foyer and see Sam impatiently waiting for me by the grandiose front door, twirling car keys around his finger. "Ok, let's go." I rush past him and out the door still zipping up my pants. The truth is I'm going stir-crazy in this house, and I'm in desperate need of a cocktail. Sam has been telling me for days how insane the night life is in Baton Rouge. Finally, it's Thursday night, and I can't wait to go out. We get in his mother's big white Mercedes, and haul ass down the long driveway and out the gates.

"Loving the outfit by the way," Sam says dryly as we speed down Highland Road.

"Well, what the hell was I supposed to wear, Sam? It's ninety five degrees in Louisiana, even at night!" I had decided on cut-off jeans, cowboy boots, and a white tank top with my hair up in a ponytail.

It's 11 p.m. when we pull up at Gator Bar, which is built over the water on the banks of the Mississippi River. When we pull into the parking lot, I'm surprised to see a giant two story shack with the murky water below. This must be where all the cool people go, I think to myself. If there weren't dozens of people mingling across the second story balcony, I would think the place were condemned. Giant trees grow along the banks, and long strands of moss hang from their branches. An old rusty sign that says *Gator Bar* hangs in front, and looks like it's been there a lifetime. When we step inside, it's like no bar I've ever seen. There are all kinds of crazy things on the walls: alligator heads, Mardi Gras beads, and gold and purple LSU memorabilia everywhere I turn. In the center of it all is a huge wooden dance floor with hundreds of people dancing like there's no tomorrow. Sam turns and grins at me.

"Sunny, welcome to Cajun Country." A tinge of excitement runs through me hearing these words. What a strange and mysterious place, I think to myself. We head to the bar, order two Grey Goose and sodas, and make our way to one of the tables scattered throughout the place.

"Well, holy shit, if it ain't Sam LeBlanc!!" a guy yells. "Awww, hell!"

The whole table of guys and girls begin to whoop and holler. I wait patiently as Sam walks around shaking hands with people, forgetting to introduce me. Typical.

"Well, stranger, looks like you're back from the dead!!" the prettiest black girl I've ever seen says as she approaches Sam. She's very tall, taller than me at least. Her black silky hair is long and flowing, her skin is the color of caramel, and she's wearing a purple LSU jersey tied into a knot so it shows off her bellybutton. She has on tight, khaki boy-shorts, silver hoop earrings, and brown strappy wedges. She looks like the models in *Vogue* or *Cosmo*, so beautiful.

"Brittany, what are you doing, you crazy bitch?" Sam gives her a hug and turns to introduce me to her. "Sunny, this is Brittany Laveau, she's one of my oldest friends in Baton Rouge, we went to private school together, then to LSU, not to mention she was captain of the Golden Girls while she was in college," he says with an air of pride.

"Hi, Sunny, nice to meet you," she says with a dashing smile.

"Nice to meet you as well. You're really pretty," I say to her, in awe of her beauty.

"Thank you! You're really pretty, too! So, is this your first time in Louisiana?"

"Yeah it is, and I'm excited to be here. It's so different than anywhere else I've ever been."

"Girl you haven't seen anything yet. Anyway how did you meet this crazy guy?" She looks at Sam with a sly grin. "I'll never get the truth out of him, so you'll have to tell me." Sam and I look at each other.

"That's a story for another day, Brit," Sam says to her and downs his Grey Goose and soda.

"Oh, lord, I can only imagine." She rolls her eyes at Sam, as she lights a Marlboro Light. "Alright well I'm gonna grab another Bloody Mary; you guys want anything?"

"You're drinking Bloody Marys at night? How tacky," Sam says to her rather arrogantly.

"Sam, I will knock your ass into next week, son," she threatens as she struts to the bar.

"What on earth is a Golden Girl?" I ask Sam curiously.

"I forget you don't know these things," he says in his usual annoyed tone when he has to explain something to me. "Ok. Being a Golden Girl is everything in Louisiana. Growing up here, girls aspire to be one. They are the pride of LSU When I was a kid, and the fight song would begin, the crowd would go wild because we knew the Golden Girls were coming out to do their signature dance. The history, the pride, and the legacy of being a Golden Girl is something every girl would kill for."

"Oh," I say bewildered. "I didn't realize it was such a big deal."

Sam immediately goes into a tangent about how ridiculously loud the music is tonight, and my eyes wander around the room. Suddenly, I stop. My world comes to a halt. A strange feeling comes over me, one that I've never felt before.

"Sam... Sam... SAM!! Who is that guy looking over here?"

"Where? Oh shit. That's Lance Arceneaux...he plays baseball for LSU He's actually one of the best first basemen we've had in a while. That and he's Baton Rouge's most sought after guy. He's dated every hot girl who's stepped foot on the campus. They never last long, though. He's got a love 'em and leave 'em reputation," Sam says with a sigh.

I look back, and Lance Arceneaux is standing with a group of guys, towering over everyone else. He's wearing a tight gray t-shirt, dark jeans, and cowboy boots. My god he's tall; he's easily six foot four. I watch as he takes a sip of beer, then he looks around the room. His eyes stop as soon as they land on me. I quickly look away, knowing that he's caught me staring. The intensity of his face is etched in my mind, and all I want to do is look at him. *Don't do it, Sunny; you'll look like an idiot.* My heart starts pounding out of my chest, and I can feel him watching me from across the crowded bar. I wait a couple of minutes, and finally give in to my curiosity. Thank God, he's talking to one of his friends. Damn, he's hot. Every time he slightly moves, I can see his ripped muscles move through his shirt. His hair is golden brown and messy, like he just rolled out of bed. His green eyes are wide set and go beautifully with his tan skin.

"Wow, he is really tan," I say to Sam without taking my eyes off him.

"That's because he's a real Cajun. He's from Black Bayou. It's pretty far down south. All the people from that part of Louisiana are French/Indian heritage, so they all have that reddish brown tan." Just as Sam finishes his sentence, I see Lance Arceneaux take a sip of his beer, and then start to make his way through the crowd towards us, never taking his eyes off me. His face is striking. That is the guy I'm going to spend the rest of my life with. Wait, what? I've never even spoken to him! Why did that just pop into my head? *Shit, just focus, stop thinking*, I tell myself.

"Sam, he's coming over here," I say freaking out.

"Jesus, Sunny, shut up. Don't embarrass me, ok?" Sam says overly annoyed.

"Sam LeBlanc, how are ya, buddy?" Lance walks right past me and sticks out his hand to shake Sam's. I'm unbelievably nervous now that he's actually standing next to me. I can smell his scent, which smells like pure sex. As he's talking, I look up and realize how tall and masculine he really is. He has a chiseled jaw line, his face is covered in scruff, and his body is very well proportioned. I have the strangest urge to just reach out and touch him.

"So last I heard you were out on the road livin' the crazy life, man; how's that going?" he asks Sam with a slight southern drawl, an accent I've never heard before.

"Oh, you know, I just needed a little break from this town and from my family, so I thought I'd get out and see the world. I just rolled back into town, and I brought a friend of mine with me who I met along the way. Lance, this is Sunny. Sunny Collins…" I stick out my hand to shake his, but he just looks at me with his intense stare.

"Welcome. How ya liking Louisiana so far?" he asks in a domineering tone.

"Um… I like it…it's pretty hot, though." Shit. I want to impress him, and that's all I can think of to say?

"Oh, too hot for you, huh?" He looks at me amused. "Well here, this will cool you off." He presses his ice cold beer against the back of my sweaty neck, and a shudder runs down my spine. I quickly move away from the beer and look up at him in disbelief. He completely ignores my shock.

"Well, Sam, it's good to see you, man; come over and say hi to the crew before you leave," Lance says with a shifty grin, as he turns and walks away. Did he really just do that? I don't even know what to think! The guy stands there staring at me for five minutes, and then comes over and has the audacity to press his beer up against me!!!

"Shut up, Sam," I say to him as he falls out of his chair laughing.

"Oh damn that was funny! He just totally blew you off!" Sam loves it any time I'm embarrassed. Not one of his greatest traits as a friend.

Brittany comes back with two Grey Goose and sodas, a Bloody Mary, and three green shots.

"Gator bombs, you guys!! We gotta welcome Sunny to Louisiana!!!"

"Thank you. I can really use that right now," I say to her as I take a deep breath.

"Yeah, I saw Lance Arceneaux over here; what was that about?" she asks curiously.

"Oh, Sunny has fallen in love with him just like every other girl who comes into contact with him, but he immediately blew her off. It was highly entertaining, Brit!" Sam retreats into another fit of laughter.

"Yeah, he bartends here on the weekends now, been doing it for a couple months. Girl, don't worry about it, he blows off most girls. If you're looking for a good southern boy, we'll get you one," Brittany says to me sympathetically.

Right here and now, I know I'm in trouble. I don't want any other guy in the world; I want Lance Arceneaux, and I won't rest until I get him. I have never been so attracted to someone in my life, and I sure as hell have never felt anything like this before. I can already tell that pursuing him isn't going to be easy and will pose challenges I have never dreamed of.

"Still thinking about Eric?" Sam grins at me.

"Eric who?" I ask him honestly. I literally couldn't care less about Eric right now.

"How 'bout Hollywood? You still want to leave Louisiana right away?" Sam looks at me smirking.

"Hollywood isn't going anywhere. I'll get there soon enough. I think we should spend some time here, you know, get to know the people."

"Oh, brother...," Sam says rolling his eyes.

The music stops, and the DJ comes over the mic. "Alright LSU Tigers, it's midnight, and y'all know what that means!! Here we go!!!" Sam and Brittany both look at me and grin.

"You ready to see how we do it in Baton Rouge?" Brittany asks curiously.

"What? What's going on?" I ask looking around the bar. Brittany and Sam both get up and head to the dance floor along with everyone else. The sound of a fiddle blasts over the speaker system, and people are screaming with excitement. The few people not dancing head to the ledges around the dance floor to watch. Guys and girls are hurriedly getting in place on the floor, and then the music picks up. I hear the familiar voice of Garth Brooks singing, *I spent last night in the arms of a girl in Louisiana*, and realize it's the song "Callin' Baton Rouge." The entire bar is screaming the words right along with Garth. People have coupled up, including Sam and Brittany who are waving at me as they scoot around the huge wooden dance floor. I wave back at them, and then, trying not to look too obvious, I let my eyes slowly wander around the room for Lance. All of the sudden I feel a tap on the shoulder.

"Have you ever danced with the devil?" There he is standing behind me with a huge grin on his face. *Holy. Shit.* Without waiting for me to respond, he grabs my hand and pulls me out onto the floor. He puts one hand on my waist and holds one hand in his. My hands feel very small compared to his big hands. He pulls me tight up against him and starts to guide me around the dance floor; my heart is beating out of control. *Ok, Sunny, you gotta attempt to be cool*, I say to myself. I look up at him, and his piercing green eyes are looking right back into mine. It's too hard to look at him; his eyes are intense, like he can see right through me. He's not exactly smiling; hell, I can't tell what he's thinking, so I just look straight at his chest which is extremely muscular, and I can once again smell his intoxicating scent. I watch a bead of sweat run down his neck, and I feel a burning deep inside me. He radiates sexiness.

Callin' Baton Rouge...My sweet Baton Rouge!!!

The music ends, people are screaming, and my head is swimming. Wow, that alligator thing I drank is really kicking in.

"Well, thanks for the dance," I say nervously as I turn to look for Sam and Brittany.

"And just where are you going?" He smirks at me, one eyebrow higher than the other. I am at a loss for words. Looking at him is intimidating, so I keep my head down; I've never met a guy so captivating. He pauses for a minute with his arms folded, studying me. "C'mon," he says with a grin as he grabs my hand and pulls me to a table.

"Oh, there you guys are!" Sam and Brittany say as they both pretend they weren't watching our every move.

"Listen, Sam, I was thinking of heading down to New Orleans tomorrow night to see some friends of mine who work in the French Quarter; why don't you come and bring Sunny, here. After all, you can't bring the girl to Louisiana and not show her New Orleans." Lance winks at Brittany who tries to conceal her grin. I wonder what is so funny. Sam looks apprehensively at Lance.

"Uh, well, I'm not sure if she's ready for that kind of excitement just yet, Lance." For Sam LeBlanc to imply New Orleans is bad after all the clubs we have been to in the past year and all the trouble Eric constantly got us into, New Orleans must be really bad. The main point here is that Lance Arceneaux wants us to go, and there's no way I'm missing an opportunity to hang out with him.

"Well I would love to go; I've always wanted to see New Orleans," I say trying not to sound overly excited.

"I'll call you tomorrow if we can make it, Lance," Sam says to him.

"Good deal...And, Brit, your ass better be coming; it's been too damn long." With that he nods at the three of us, winks at me, and takes off into the crowd.

"Well, that's enough excitement for one night, Sunny; let's go home," Sam says gulping down the rest of his drink.

"What?" I see Sam and Brittany wink at each other and give each other a knowing look.

"Well, Sunny, it was great to meet you; hopefully your dad here will let you come tomorrow night," she says sarcastically, hugs me, and heads to the bar. What is with all this winking going on? We get out to the parking lot, and I stop Sam who is making a bee-line for his mother's Mercedes.

"What is your deal? Why did you tell him we can't go tomorrow?"

"Listen, Sunny, New Orleans, Louisiana isn't a place you need to be going. I just don't think you're ready for that yet."

"Sam, I REALLY want to go! Pleeeeeeease!!! It'll be fine I'll be with you; nothing's gonna happen!!" I beg him. He looks at me for a minute.

"I'll think about it... now get in."

I WAKE UP EXCITED even though it's been a really rough week. Life was always so hectic with Eric. My worrying about what I was going to do when I got to Hollywood constantly gave me anxiety. Last night changed everything. The sun is shining, and Lance Arceneaux is all I want to think about right now. I'm not sure what the feeling was that came over me when I first saw him, but it was more than a feeling; it was a *knowing*. When I looked at him, I saw my life flash before my eyes. Who is this guy? Is the universe playing a trick on me? Is it trying to tell me something? Either way, it doesn't matter. I'm screwed. I've made up my mind that I will get him no matter what it takes. There are two things I want in this life: love and fame. And one of the two is right in front of me. If I didn't believe in love at first sight before, I sure as hell do now. My thoughts are interrupted by Sam briskly walking into the guest room where I'm staying; he hands me a cup of what he calls good ole' Louisiana chicory.

"Ok, so I've thought about it, and we will be accepting Lance's invitation to join him in New Orleans this evening."

"Really??" I jump up to hug him, and my coffee spills all over the bedside table. "What made you change your mind?" I'm beaming at him.

"Well, I decided why put off the inevitable? You're going to have to do it eventually, and this way I can keep an eye on you. My little girl is growing up so fast." He gives me a devilish grin as I throw my arms around him again. "I've already called Brittany, and she's coming over this afternoon with some outfits for you to pick from for tonight, and we can all get ready together."

It's 9 P.M., AND Sam has "Like a Prayer" by Madonna blasting throughout the mansion. I look at the clock, and my nerves begin to set in. Brittany has brought over several cute dresses for me to pick from, but it's so hot outside, we both decide on tank tops and cut-off jeans. Brittany helps me flat iron my hair, so it's long, straight, and soft. I pull out my cotton candy scented perfume and spray it in my hair, secretly hoping Lance is turned on by it. The doorbell rings, and I jump.

Brittany, who is finishing up her makeup in the mirror next to me, says, "Don't look at me girl, go open the door!!!" I sigh, throw down my eyeliner pen on the counter, and head for the grand foyer. Is he really here for me, or does he just want to visit with his old friends? He kind of ignored me last night, then swings me around the dance floor without even asking if I wanted to dance, then invites me, well us, to go out with him!! He's already a confusing guy. I wonder what his sign is. God, please don't let him be a Gemini.

I take a deep breath and open the front door. There Lance stands, his intense green eyes staring right through me, wearing a navy blue Ralph Lauren button-up with the sleeves rolled up, dark jeans, and boots. Good god, he's sexy, so sexy that it takes my breath away. His demeanor is stern and demanding, and once again I can smell his sexy scent.

"Um, hi. C'mon on in." I give him a little smile, but, dammit, he's hard to look at!!

"Wow, I didn't really get to talk to you last night. Where's that accent from?"

"Oh… I'm from Texas."

"Really? Where?"

"Um, it's called Cleburne, a small town right outside Dallas."

"Oh. Cool…well, where's everyone at?" he asks uninterested.

"I'll go grab them." Ok, so maybe he's not here to see me. He couldn't care less about what I'm saying.

When everyone is finally ready, we do a shot of Southern Comfort and toast to my first night out in New Orleans. We walk out onto the front porch to leave, and I see Lance's ride: a brand new black Ford truck with shiny rims and a huge LSU baseball sticker on the back window. The license plate reads *LUCKEE*; *very cocky*, I think to myself.

"You get in the front seat!" I immediately whisper to Sam. He rolls his eyes at me and climbs in.

"Um, don't think for a second you're going to break tradition and not stop to get us daiquiris," Brittany yells at Lance from the back seat.

"Do you not see what street I'm taking Brit? Already on my way there," Lance says matter-of-factly. Why on earth would we stop at a bar and drink? Isn't that what we're doing in New Orleans? Great, we're never going to get there. A couple of minutes later, we pull into the parking lot of Tiger Paw Daiquiris. Instead of parking, Lance pulls into the drive-through. This is odd.

"Yeah, give me four large strawberry daiquiris, please," Lance says to the guy in the window. I look at Brittany perplexed.

"In Louisiana, we drink and drive," she says with a grin. Sam hands me a huge Styrofoam cup with two lids and two straws.

"What am I supposed to do with the extra lid and straw? I ask.

"Hold them in your lap in case we get pulled over. Technically you're not supposed to pierce the lid," Sam explains to me. Another Louisiana first.

It's an hour's ride to New Orleans, and there's not much to look at along the way except swamps and pine trees. We go through a lot of small towns whose names I can't pronounce and eventually arrive on a long narrow bridge that stretches twenty miles over what looks like the ocean but is called Lake Pontchartrain. They tell me horror stories about people who went missing or were murdered and thrown in the murky waters and eaten by the alligators.

"Just be careful who you piss of in Louisiana because you just might end up at the bottom of Lake Pontchartrain as an alligator's dinner," Lance says in an eerie tone. This of course terrifies me. Everyone in the car seems to be getting a good laugh except me. When we approach downtown New Orleans, I realize just how big the city really is.

We exit off the highway, and I try to pronounce the name of the exit, which is Vieux Carre (You try to pronounce it!), and Lance, Brittany, and Sam, all correct me at the same time. As we drive through the French Quarter, I can't help but think that this is one of the most interesting places I have ever seen. We find a parking spot on the outskirts of the Quarter and pass a cemetery with graves above the ground that date back to the 1700s.

"Why are the graves built above ground?" I ask shocked at the sight.

"Because the coffins would rise and float away when there are hurricanes. New Orleans is below sea level," Brittany says, nonchalantly as if she were simply describing a beautiful day. I shudder at the thought of coffins floating down the tiny narrow streets in front of us.

"Is that not scary to any of y'all?" I ask mortified.

"We grew up around it," Sam says annoyed as usual with all my questions.

"We'll start at Cafe Lafitte's, and then work our way down to the Bourbon Pub, then to Fat Tuesdays, oh and she has to have a Hand Grenade. Let's show her Preservation Hall for sure..." The three of them are saying so many strange names of places that I can't keep up. Lance and Brittany lead the way, while Sam and I follow behind.

"C'mon you two, y'all gotta keep up!" Lance shouts mockingly, as he and Brittany get further and further ahead.

"Well not all of us have legs as long as you, Lance!!" Sam says irritably. I can't help but laugh considering Sam had the same problem keeping up with Eric.

"Excuse me, miss, can you, please, spare some money for food?" An elderly homeless woman with only stubs for hands and no legs, scoots across the bricked street and holds her stubs out to me.

"Oh my god, how disgusting. C'mon Sunny, get away from her," Sam says as he grabs my arm and pulls me through the crowd. "I see the mayor still hasn't done anything about these ingrates since last time I was here," he says horrified by the woman. My heart absolutely drops. I may have come here with nothing, but in this moment I couldn't feel more blessed to have my hands and legs. Sam will be furious if he sees me give her any money, considering he had to give me twenty dollars just so I wouldn't be walking around broke. I see a small sandwich shop called Quarter Master to my right, but I have to think quickly.

"Sam, hold on a minute! I need to grab some gum."

"Sunny, you don't need gum. Let's go!" he yells at me impatiently through the crowd.

"You may find a cute boy to make out with! You'll be thanking me later!" I yell to him teasingly. I watch as the wheels in his head turn.

"Ok, fine. Get some gum and meet us on the corner," he says as he pulls out a Marlboro Light and heads towards the end of the block. He lights up a cigarette and hands one to Brittany. Lance is leaning up against the wall, towering over the passing crowd. Perfect, they're smoking, and that gives me enough time to do what I want to do. I step into the shop and ask for an Italian sub and a Coke, while pacing back and forth nervously. Defying Sam is never a good idea because I'll never hear the end of it. I pay for the sub and Coke and rush back outside to find the poor woman.

"Excuse me, ma'am, this is for you," I say, not sure how to hand it to her.

"Oh thank you, dear. Can you just put it in my bag?" she asks looking up at me with her sweet weathered face. I open her bag that is slung over her shoulder and place the sandwich and drink inside. She thanks me, and I run to the corner where the other three are waiting.

"Took you long enough," Sam says impatiently as the four of us step out into the glow of the bright neon lights of Bourbon Street.

The first place we go is Lafitte's Blacksmith Shop, the oldest bar in New Orleans. The four of us stand at the bar, and Sam whips out his credit card.

"Ok, guys, what's everyone drinking? I've got the first round."

"You're buying? Well then, Crown on the rocks for me," Brittany announces.

"I'll have a vodka soda," I say to Sam.

"Lance?" Sam looks up at Lance impatiently.

"Oh, I think I'll have a sandwich and a Coke," he says to Sam with raised eyebrows and a slight smirk on his face.

"What?" Sam looks at him confused. Oh shit! Did he really just say that? *Please, don't tell Sam what I did, please!* I beg him in my head.

"Sorry, I meant Captain and Coke," Lance says, as he turns his head to me and winks.

"Two Grey Goose sodas, a double Captain and Coke, and one Crown Royal on the rocks," Sam says to the bartender, still looking at Lance suspiciously. How did Lance know? Who is this guy! He may be tall, but there's no way he could see me hand her food from that far away. Was he keeping an eye on me?

An hour later, we walk into the Bourbon Pub, and I look around at all of the craziness before my eyes. Sam and Eric had taken me to some pretty insane clubs, but they were tame compared to this place.

"Well, hello, kids! Glad to see the old gang is back together!" says a strikingly beautiful Latin woman wearing a black jumpsuit, a chunky gold necklace, and dozens of golden bracelets as she hugs each of the others; she pauses when she sees me. "And who is this beautiful girl?" she asks looking at me curiously.

"Sandy, this is Sunny Collins. It's her first time in New Orleans,"

Sam announces to her in a very formal and gracious manner. She must be important for Sam to speak to her in such a tone.

"Well, Sunny, it's nice to meet you. I'm Sandy, the owner here at the Bourbon Pub."

"Oh, how nice. It's a pleasure to meet you as well," I say trying my best to make a good impression as the other three watch me cautiously. She must be a big deal in New Orleans and an important person to know by the way they are acting.

"Well, enjoy yourself tonight. You definitely came with the right people to party!" Sandy says as she winks at Lance who grins back at her. This of course makes me nervous.

Sam and Brittany head to the DJ booth to say hi to the DJ, and I'm left standing alone next to Lance. He's looking out at the sea of people grinding on the dance floor and drinking his third Captain and Coke. I feel small compared to him; my buzz finally starts to kick in, and I work up the nerve to say what I have been planning to say all day, hoping I don't sound like an idiot. I look up at his beautiful, tan, chiseled face as I twist my fingers behind my back nervously. Finally, I just say it.

"Well, I guess if neither one of us can find someone to make out with tonight, we'll just have to make out with each other."

Without missing a beat and still staring out at the crowd, he says, "Looking forward to it." My heart pounds so fast with excitement that it feels like it's going to burst. My prayers have been answered.

Six vodka sodas, four shots, and two Hand Grenades later, I'm feeling fearless. I have no idea where Sam and Brittany have disappeared to, and I don't care. The moment I've been waiting for has come. I grab Lance's hand, which takes him by surprise, and pull him up the staircase to the second floor of the Bourbon Pub. I push through the huge wooden French doors and out onto the balcony. We're overlooking all of the twinkling lights of Bourbon Street and downtown New Orleans, and there's a strange feeling in the sticky night air. It's magical. The sultry jazz music coming from the clubs below and the smell of the gulf breeze are dazzling. Lance looks down at me intently.

"So...you have me up here...whatever will you do with me?" he asks cocking his head to the side. His eyes narrow and look intensely at me, then flash dangerously.

I push him up against the wall, and an animal-like instinct comes over me. I let it control me. I reach up and grab the back of his head and pull it down to mine and begin to kiss him wildly, and he reaches down and grabs both of my legs as I jump into his arms. It's the most incredible feeling in the world. Everything is spinning. The way his skin smells, clean and sexy, the way his hair smells, even the smell of his breath is intoxicating. This is heaven. He's so tall and strong, and I can't resist wrapping my hands around his ripped muscles. I kiss a bead of sweat on his neck, and the taste is sweet. That same feeling from when I first saw him comes over me, and I feel it bursting inside of me, all around me, and it's even crazier this time. He's an amazing kisser, and the electricity I feel when he kisses me is so intense it could blow out every power line in the state of Louisiana. I stop to take a breath and look into his eyes; they're wild like fire. He wants me, and I want him. This is out of control, and I love it. Here I am in Louisiana, the full moon and glittering stars above us, dozens of people down below, the sound of jazz music playing in the distance, and I am wrapped in the arms of Baton Rouge's hottest guy, who's passionately and wildly kissing me. His tongue is moving across my neck, and I want him more than anything in every way possible.

I wake up and can barely open my eyes. The morning sun is pouring into the room. Wait. Where am I? I'm in a room I've never seen before. I'm wearing a huge gray LSU baseball shirt that I vaguely remember putting on. This shirt smells really great…god my head is killing me…what did I drink last night? I have never felt this sick in my life. I turn to my left, and there lying next to me is Lance, sleeping peacefully. He's still wearing his outfit from last night. Oh my god, please, tell me I didn't have sex with him. I'm not saying I don't want to…, I just…god this cannot be happening. What am I doing here? Why didn't Sam insist I go home with him? I guess that whole over protective big brother act he's been trying to sell me is dead and gone. Dammit. I try to quietly get out of the bed so I don't wake him up, but too late. The wood floor creaks when I stand up. Lance starts to stir, and I watch him open his eyes slowly.

"Morning, trouble." He grins at me. I'm too hungover and my head hurts too badly to feel intimidated by him this morning.

"Ok, tell me what happened…I don't remember anything," I say sounding hoarse.

"Well, let's see, where should I begin? You asked me fifteen times what sign I am, and I told you fifteen times I'm a Gemini, which you were not happy about at all. You absolutely refused to go in Sam's house and demanded I take you home with me. I brought you back here, and you insisted on sleeping in my shirt." He's grinning at me from ear to ear, I'm sure because he knows how embarrassed I am listening to him describe my behavior. "I'm gonna grab you some Aleve and a glass of water. Get dressed and I'll take you to breakfast if you're up for it." I shake my head *no*. There's no way I can eat anything. I just want to get back to that damn mansion, kill Sam for letting me act so stupidly, and throw up about five times. "Ok, well, I'll take you back to Sam's whenever you're ready."

I put on my clothes, then successfully stash Lance's baseball shirt in my purse while he's in the kitchen. I need a souvenir, and it smells so good that I can't resist. We head back to Sam's house and not a moment too soon because I can feel myself getting sicker and sicker. We pull up in the long driveway, and I thank Lance for the ride home.

"Can I take you to dinner tomorrow night?" he asks kindly. I can't even believe he wants to see me again after the way I acted.

"Um, sure why not," I say hoping I don't puke in front of him.

"Awesome, I have the perfect little Cajun place in mind. Maybe we'll have some fried alligator!" He grins at me, knowing damn well I can't think about food right now, and just the thought of anything fried, especially alligator, makes my stomach churn. I fight back nausea as I shut the truck door and head up the steps of the LeBlanc mansion.

"Morning, sunshine!!" Sam and Brittany both greet me cheerfully as they sit on one of the porch swings. They're both drinking coffee and wearing old LSU football t-shirts and shorts while doing everything they can to control their laughter.

"I told you New Orleans might be a little too much for you, Sunny!!"

Sam says gleefully.

"Too much?" Brittany says to Sam mockingly. "Girl, you were out of control!! I thought you were all shy and sweet, but you were crazy last night!! Untamed!! You had dance moves I've never seen before!!" Brittany says to me as I turn red with embarrassment.

"Oh god, please, don't tell me anymore." I shrug past them and into the house, so I can lie down on one of the oversized couches. Brittany goes to the kitchen and comes back with a Bloody Mary.

"Here, drink this. I know it sounds crazy, but it'll make you feel better. Hair of the dog. Later, we'll take you to Raising Cane's for chicken fingers. It's tradition."

"You Louisiana people and your traditions," I say with my face stuffed in a pillow.

"Sunny, sit up. I wanna talk to you about something," Sam says in a serious tone. "Remember when we talked about you getting a job so you'll have some money? Well, I talked it over with Brit, and she said she may be able to get you a job working with her on the weekends in New Orleans. It'll be a quick way for you to make some cash." I sit up and look at her.

"Really? Where do you work?" I ask Brittany curiously. I see Sam wink at Brittany, and I wonder what they are scheming now. The last time I saw that wink, I ended up looking like an idiot.

"I… um…cocktail waitress in the Quarter," she says cheerfully.

"Oh, ok, awesome, I'm sure I could handle that. For now though, can I please get some sleep?" They both pat me on the head as they leave the room. I doze off and dream of making out with Louisiana's hottest Gemini. Boy, am I in trouble.

CHAPTER SIX
Romance and Blues on the Mississippi River

THE NEXT EVENING, Lance picks me up from Sam's at 8 p.m. Luckily, Brittany left me a couple of dresses before she headed back to the Quarter. I am surprised by how many expensive things she owns; Brittany must be the best cocktail waitress in the city of New Orleans. When we arrive at Tsunami, the most exclusive restaurant in town, I can't believe how futuristic it is, especially for Baton Rouge. It sits at the top of an art museum fifteen stories up and is surrounded by old classic French architecture and high-rises. When we step out the elevator, we're in a huge room that's glassed-in from floor to ceiling. Small, intimate tables and a beautiful blue dimly lit sushi bar greet us. On one side of the restaurant is the Mississippi River and on the other are all the glittering lights of downtown.

"Hey, Lance, how are ya man?" says a short rather goofy looking guy at the host stand as he looks up at Lance like he's a god. His eyes are gleaming.

"I'm good, thanks. Can we get a table for two?"

"Sure!! Hey, I gotta tell you, you played great last season; we were all rooting for you."

"Thanks, buddy, I appreciate that," Lance says cool and confidently. He gives me a wink, but his face stays serious.

"Does everyone treat you like that?" I ask him. Lance ignores the question, and the host comes running back, stars in his eyes. It's surreal to see the effect he has on this guy.

"Right this way!!" the little host says enthusiastically. He gives us the best seat in the house overlooking the river below. What a beautiful Louisiana evening.

"Ok, Sunny, so here's the first test I'm giving you to see what kind of girl you are."

"What? What test?" I say with too much surprise in my voice. "Listen, don't think I'm falling for whatever Gemini nonsense you are trying to use on me because it won't work," I say to him suspiciously, as he does his best to hide his amusement.

"What is it with you and Geminis?" He asks calmly as a wide grin slowly spreads across his face. He knows exactly what he's doing, and he's enjoying this.

"What sign are you?" he asks curiously.

"I'm a Leo," I say trying to read his facial expressions.

"A Leo, huh. The lion. You know the Gemini always ends up taming the lion, don't you?" he says as another shifty grin spreads across his face.

"Some lions are too wild to be tamed," I say to him as I break my chopsticks in half.

"We'll see about that," he says, excitement flashing in his green eyes. "Anyway, I'm not worried about it; I'll have no problem figuring you out," he says, quickly changing his attitude as though he's bored discussing it any further. "Now, back to your test. Have you ever eaten sushi?"

"No," I answer honestly.

"Ok, well, why don't you let me order, and let's see what you like and don't like. I love every kind of food, especially sushi, and the stranger the roll, the better. Wait, you're left handed?" he questions as I pick up my chopsticks.

"Yeah, why?"

"Ok, I'm gonna scoot over next to you and show you how to use chopsticks correctly. If not, we'll have sushi flying all over the restaurant, and this isn't *Pretty Woman*," he says sarcastically.

I want to roll my eyes at this, but he just made a reference to my favorite movie, and I can't help but smile. I'm also happy he's sitting next to me; it's not quite as intimidating. Lance smells so good that it's hard for me not to melt into my seat. As he places the chopsticks in my hand, I feel chills run down my spine. His hands are so beautiful and masculine. Mine are minuscule next to his. He wraps his left hand around mine and begins to explain how to properly use the two wooden sticks. My mind, however, is elsewhere as I feel his right hand gently move down and rest at the small of my back. The warmth of his hand pressed up against me makes me crave him even more. I get lost in the thought of those hands all over me, and it's exhilarating.

Everything Lance orders is incredible. Trying all of these new and different pieces of raw fish is surprisingly wonderful. He explains to me what's in each roll and has a story for each one.

"The first time I had this one was with my best friend, Mikey, after LSU beat Ole Miss. We were celebrating and drinking heavily; it became a favorite!" His demeanor changes from demanding to childlike. Lance resembles a little boy as he goes on, excitedly explaining each roll and what's in it. This definitely takes me by surprise. Suddenly, he's not so intimidating. We talk about his growing up in Louisiana and my growing up in Texas, about college life, and about how I met Sam. I leave out huge parts of the story, of course, because I'm afraid of what he'll think, and I definitely don't bring up Eric.

"So you guys have been traveling the country together and ended up in Baton Rouge, huh...sounds like quite an adventure," he says studying me for a moment. He looks at me like he wants to ask more questions, and I realize he knows I've left out part of the story. "Well, anyway, I have a surprise for you. There's a place down the street called Tabby's Blues Bar, and one of my favorite singers is there tonight. Are you a blues fan at all?" he asks with raised eyebrows.

"Well...not really, I mean, I've never heard it, so I don't know if I'm a fan or not. I mostly listen to pop," I say honestly.

"Ok, well now we're definitely going. There's more to life than Britney Spears and Christina Aguilera," he says matter-of-factly. I get the impression he is irked that I listen to that kind of music.

We leave Tsunami and walk along the banks of the Mississippi towards Tabby's, and I feel the gentle Louisiana breeze tousle my hair. I listen as Lance explains the different buildings as we walk past them.

"That over there is the old governor's mansion, and that's another awesome museum." I'm surprised that he knows all of this, considering his reputation for being LSU's biggest playboy.

We get to Tabby's, which is very small and not very nice. The building looks as though it's been plucked directly from the 1950s. An old 7up sign hangs in the front, and the faded name of the bar is painted on the side of the tiny brick building along with the words, *Live blues music every night*. We enter the bar, and I look around as Lance pays the five dollar cover. There are little tables and chairs scattered around a tiny wooden dance floor with candles glowing on each table. Two bars run along the walls to my left and right, and a small stage sits directly in front. There's a five piece band on stage, and a tall, good looking black man wearing a fedora and suspenders over a crisp white shirt is playing a slow, melancholy song on his saxophone. The place is dimly lit with a soft blue glow, and the smell of cigars is floating through the air. I wonder what Lance likes about this place. It's half full, and some of the people in the crowd look like they've come from the rough part of town. Not exactly a place a girl wants to go after a beautiful dinner.

"What do you want to drink? Vodka soda?" Lance asks me as I follow him to the bar.

"Sure," I say wondering how long he will want to stay here.

After we get our drinks, Lance finds an empty table to the left of the stage, which he tells me is his favorite spot. I look around the room, bored. Why on earth does he like this place? The walls are peeling in places and look like they haven't been painted in years. The chairs and tables are battered and broken and definitely need replacing. The drinks aren't that great, and the crowd isn't exactly friendly. I want to leave, but I don't dare tell him that. I look over and watch him watch the saxophone player. His face is so beautiful to me: the shape of his nose, his thick eyebrows, and his sexy lips. I think about what an amazing kisser he is, and I remember why I'm going to sit here and pretend to like this.

"There she is," Lance whispers to me excitedly as he nods to the right of the stage.

A beautiful heavyset black woman is making her way through the crowd and stops to visit at one of the tables. She is wearing a sparkling champagne colored gown that lights up every time she moves. Her silky black hair is wrapped in a tight bun on top of her head with a long ponytail flowing from the middle of the bun down her back. She makes her way from table to table, greeting friends and customers, flashing her beautiful smile to each new person she sees. She begins to walk past our table but suddenly spots Lance.

"Well, hi, sugar pie! I didn't know you were comin' in tonight!" She greets Lance with a warm and smoky voice.

"Do I have to have a reason to come see the most beautiful woman in the state of Louisiana?" Lance is beaming as he stands to give her a hug. I'm perplexed by what's happening right now. "Besides I haven't seen you in a while, and tonight I'm on a mission. I brought my friend, Sunny here, who hasn't ever been to a blues bar." Lance looks at me disapprovingly for a moment, and then a cute grin spreads across his face.

"Well, hi there, baby! I'm Trixie, Trixie LaDoux." She turns to me, and I stand to greet her.

"Hi, it's so nice to meet you," I say dazzled by her charming smile. She reaches for my hand and puts it in hers.

"Don't worry about it being your first time, baby; tonight were gonna teach you everything you need to know about the blues." Her smile is endearing, and I feel myself blush. "Now I gotta go. I'm up next, but you let me know if this guy gets out of hand, and Momma will come deal with him!" she says playfully as she brushes Lance's cheek and gives me a wink. Lance and I sit back down, and I look at him puzzled.

"How do you know her so well?" I ask him.

"I come here to unwind some nights after baseball practice or an exam. It takes my mind off things," he says watching the band.

"By yourself?" I ask a little too quickly. His eyebrows furrow at the question, as he continues to watch the man on the sax. I shouldn't have asked that. I look to the stage as a man helps Trixie LaDoux up the steps, and the music begins to fade. She looks out and flashes her beautiful smile to the crowd.

"How's everybody doing this evening?" she asks after a round of applause dies down. "It's another beautiful night here in Baton Rouge, and it makes me think about a beautiful and dangerous thing called love. What we'll do to get it, what we'll do to keep it, and what we do to get it back once it's gone." She looks out at the audience with a serious expression on her face.

The band behind her begins to play slow, seductive music. The piano, the bass, and the sax all come together as one as I watch Miss Trixie enthralled. It's as if though she's thinking back to a great love in her life whom she's lost, and the pain of it slowly sweeps across her face. Then, she begins to sing. I've never heard anything like it. Not just because she's an incredible singer, but the sound of the pain and longing in her voice sends chills up my spine.

"This song is called 'Ain't No Way' by Aretha Franklin," Lance whispers in my ear. I look up at him, and his face is lit up. He's in heaven. Who would have ever known at first glance that blues is something he would enjoy so much. I have a feeling he will continue to surprise me again and again.

I look back to the stage as Trixie LaDoux belts out the haunting song. A strange feeling comes over me; I feel the music reach inside my soul and tug at my heart. Just then a single tear rolls down my face. Why am I crying? I think of home, I think of Eric, and I think of Hollywood. Somehow this music has brought everything that I've been trying to suppress straight to the surface. I feel hot tears begin to roll down my face, and I quickly grab a napkin and wipe them away. I look at Lance out of the corner of my eye, who thankfully is too mesmerized by the music to notice I'm crying. As I look at him, I take a deep breath. All of that is in the past and sitting right next to me is the future. This gorgeous, interesting, complex man sitting next to me is all I should be thinking about right now. I feel a weight lift off me, as I let the sultry voice of the beautiful blues singer wrap around me like a velvet blanket of soul.

An hour and three Grey Goose and sodas later, the whole place is alive with Louisiana decadence. People are clapping, dancing, and hollering as Miss Trixie belts out a rendition of "Mardi Gras Mambo."

"C'mon, let's dance." Lance stands up, removes his jacket, and takes off his tie. I watch as he unbuttons a couple of buttons on his shirt revealing his tan chest, and I feel fire ignite inside me. He holds out his hand and pulls me up next to him. His breath smells like Captain and Coke, and his chest emanates his signature sexy smell. I feel the fire run though my veins, down through my fingertips, and to my toes. Being this close to him feeling his touch is a rush. We begin to move around the dance floor, as people clap and cheer us on. I turn red from embarrassment, but I'm smiling from ear to ear. Lance is clearly having a blast and doing most of the work, so I follow his lead and let loose. We go round and round on the dance floor faster and faster, as Lance spins me out and then back in again.

"Who knew you could move so well, you little country girl!" Lance yells at me over the lively jazz music. As the song ends, he spins me out again, and I fall into his arms laughing as he grins down at me. Who knew tonight would end up being this much fun.

As we pull up in front of Sam's beautifully lit plantation, Lance reaches for my hand.

"I really would like to spend more time with you, Sunny. How do you feel about that?" Lance looks at me intensely. I want to jump out of the car and do a happy dance on the finely manicured lawn right through the sprinklers.

"I'd like that, too." I try my best to sound calm and collected. He leans over and kisses me. His kiss sends heat searing through my body again. Lance's kisses are passionate, blissful, unstoppable...I feel the sparks begin to fly all around us the second his lips press against mine. I could live in this moment forever.

CHAPTER SEVEN
Life is Like a Circus

I'T'S A SWELTERING Saturday evening when we arrive in New Orleans. It takes an hour to find a parking spot in the French Quarter because most of the streets are narrow and packed with cars. I step out of Brittany's gorgeous white BMW and feel the sticky night air against my skin. I can smell a mixture of spicy crawfish, puke from the drunken tourists, and a distinct odor, one that reminds me how old this city really is.

"C'mon girl, let's do this." Brittany flashes her pretty white smile at me, and we begin to make our way through the tiny streets of the Quarter.

"I hope my outfit's ok. You think your boss will like it?" I ask nervously.

"Trust me, Sunny, it's not your outfit he wants to see."

We finally get to Bourbon Street, and there are thousands of people walking the streets wearing Mardi Gras beads, drinking Hand Grenades, and dancing to the music. The sound of live Jazz bands and the bass of club music are pumping through the air.

"Alright, we're here," Brittany says after we push our way through the crowds for what seems like an eternity. I look up and see *The Circus* in dazzling gold and red letters. We skip the line to get in and head to the VIP line. "Sunny, this is Big Louie," Brittany says, introducing me to a giant bouncer.

"Hey girl, how you doin'? Nice to meet ya!!!" he says cheerfully in a deep New Orleans accent.

"Hi there." I giggle at him. For the biggest, most intimidating black man I've ever seen, he sure is friendly.

"Louie does security here at the Circus," Brittany says to me. "This is Burt and Larry. They take money at the door and sometimes perform in the show," she says while waving at them as they both sit behind a counter taking money.

Larry and Burt are identical midgets, and Larry has a cigarette hanging out of his mouth. They're dressed exactly alike in circus-themed outfits, which I'm guessing they're not happy about because they're both frowning. We walk through a long dimly lit hallway that has white and red stripes painted across the ceiling to resemble a circus tent. We exit into the main room, and my eyes are wide with curiosity. Like most of the eccentric places I've seen so far in New Orleans, this place is even more ostentatious than I could ever have imagined. The ceiling soars upward three stories and becomes a beautiful dome painted blood-red with all sorts of golden creatures on it. I can barely make out the shapes of evil little winged devils in the dimly lit dome. It's not a terribly big place, and Brittany tells me it was an old opera house in the 1800s. There are little tables and chairs throughout the mezzanine that seat approximately two hundred people. A giant balcony wraps around the entire second floor, and everything in the whole club is covered in gold paint or wallpaper: the walls, the statues, and even the railings, but most of which is either tattered or falling off. The winged cherubs that line the stairs creep me out.

"They remind me of the carvings of children in the movie *The Haunting*," I tell Brittany.

Between each of the golden pillars that surround the first floor, there are red velvet curtains draped in between. In the center of it all, there is a wide ramp coming from the curtains and a huge circular main stage which is amazing, and has black and white diamond-shaped tiles painted on it. There are beautiful spotlights that go all the way around the front of the stage and up the ramp that are constantly changing colors with giant jets from fog machines shooting out smoke from in between each light. I look up at the ceiling above the stage, and there are three gigantic circular rings suspended from the air that hold hundreds of spotlights.

"The show should be starting any minute. Let's go grab a seat," Brittany whispers to me. We end up standing in the back because every seat in the house is full including the entire balcony.

"Is it always packed like this?" I ask her.

"Yeah, pretty much. Which is a good thing. How do you think I paid for that BMW!" she says.

I look around the room, and I suddenly realize the audience is all men: some young college guys, a lot of middle-aged men and older men, but no girls except for the ones bringing drinks to the tables.

"Brit, what kind of show is this exactly?" I ask warily. As soon as I say this, the lights dim, and the crowd goes wild. Men are cheering from every corner of the theater. A man's voice comes over the speakers, and spotlights begin to swirl over the audience.

"Ladies and gentlemen, boys and girls, welcome to... THE CIRCUS!!!" he screams. "And now we present to you, your favorite mistress of the evening, the queen of the Quarter, and, yes, she's been around since God was a boy, the spectacular, the phenomenal, the dazzling, the beautiful, MISS LISA BEAUMANN!!!"

The applause is so loud that I have to cover my ears. The lights dim, and a heavy fog pours off the edge of the stage. The gigantic red curtains at the back of the stage slowly lift to reveal a staircase. Four ripped and shirtless male dancers wearing nothing but skin tight black leather pants, black army boots, and rhinestone covered suspenders strut out onto the stage, circle once, and stop and throw their hands in the air as though they're praising the sky. The room goes so silent that you could hear a pin drop. Suddenly I see a swing covered in black sparkly velvet descend from the ceiling, and there in the swing she sits. Miss Lisa Beaumann. She's wearing the most over-the-top beautiful sparkling diamond gown I have ever seen. Never in my life have I seen someone so glamorous. She has a certain elegance about her, a grandeur. The look on her face is coy, as though she has secret that she's keeping from the audience. She's in her late forties or early fifties, and her hair is dark brown and styled like a Southern Belle's straight from the plantation. Her eye makeup is dark and cat-like, and reminds me of Elizabeth Taylor in *Cleopatra*. She lands on the stage and looks out into the audience. She's ready to share her shifty secret. The four male dancers bow to her as one of them hands her a microphone; she taps him on the head with it and purrs into the mic,

"Down boy..." The crowd goes wild again, and she and the dancers go straight into a musical number. They shimmy and shake through a medley of "Hello Dolly," "Don't Rain on my Parade," and they finish with "Diamonds are a Girl's Best Friend." I know all of these Broadway classics and movie musicals from seeing them performed every night when Momma worked at the theater in Dallas. As soon as the applause finally dies down, she addresses the crowd.

"Well, boys, you're all here once again; you must have enjoyed yourselves last time! And your wives must not have gotten ahold of your credit card statements!" Another roar of laughter and applause erupt. "And, now, gentlemen, your ringleader extraordinaire!" Lisa and the boys exit, and a ring of fire ignites along the edges of the stage.

"She is stunning," I whisper to Brittany.

"Yes, she is, and can you believe, she used to be a man?" Brit says.

"What?" I look at her in disbelief.

"Yeah, she's transgender. She has boobs, but I think she still has the man parts, too. That's the rumor anyway. Who knows, maybe she had the little operation. Either way, she's one hell of a woman." Brittany looks at me and smiles.

"That's crazy; she's more glamorous than most women," I whisper in shock. A panel slides open from the middle of the stage floor, and a man dressed like a ringleader begins to rise. He's heavyset and has jet black hair and a thin line for a mustache. He's wearing a bright red topcoat, black knee-high boots, a gold bow tie, gold gloves, and red coattails covered in sparkling red sequins. He waves a golden scepter at the crowd, and both ends burst into flames.

"Welcome to my circus!! Be cautious because here you won't find lions, tigers, or bears, but instead a wide variety of freaks of nature!!! Ahahahahahhaha!! But best of all, my mistresses of the night!!!" He instantly vanishes. Three silver shiny poles descend from the ceiling as six girls, two on each pole, slide down topless. The music begins to pound through the speakers.

"BRITTANY, THIS IS A STRIP CLUB!!!" I cannot believe that she or Sam didn't tell me.

"Sunny, it's not a strip club; it's a burlesque show. Haven't you ever heard of burlesque? Sam said you wouldn't come if you knew it was topless. I wanted to show you what we do here before you said no. Besides that, Sam said you're broke, you don't have a car, and we both know he's not going to carry you for long. This is a fast way to make money," she says miffed by my reaction.

"Brittany, there is no way I can do this; I'm not getting up in front of all these people naked!!" I say as my heart pounds out of my chest.

"Listen, you haven't met the ringleader yet; he might not even let you dance since you don't have any experience," Brittany says as another wave of anxiety washes over me. "Look, Sunny. I know you want to move out to

L.A. eventually. I know you want to get a car so you don't have to depend on anyone else. I know you want to be able to go on dates with Lance and wear outfits you paid for instead of borrowing mine." She looks at me intently. "If you get hired here, it will give you the freedom to do all of those things. Sometimes we make a thousand dollars in one night. You're never going to make any money working at a Waffle House." I know Brittany's right. I can't even afford food right now without Sam paying for it, much less a car or new clothes. "Let's just go back stage and talk to the ringleader. You don't have to make a decision right now," she says sympathetically.

"Ok, fine. Let's go talk to him," I say half-heartedly. Brittany grins at me, and I follow her backstage. What would Momma think if she knew what I was about to do? We walk into the backstage area where people are running around getting ready for the next act.

"Sunny, this is the ringleader and also the owner of the Circus."

"Well, hello, my dear! How very nice to meet you! And my, what a beauty you are!" he says as he looks me up and down, and then raises his eyebrows at Brittany.

"Thank you." I smile back at him nervously. Seeing the ringleader up close freaks me out. His outfit is somewhat tattered, and his makeup is smudged. I see white powder, which I assume is cocaine, caked inside his nose.

"Is it fair for me to presume you are here for a job? You know I have many girls come to see me every week, and I turn down almost all of them! But, if Brittany here says you would fit in with us, I, of course, trust her judgement!" he says in a creepy, dramatic tone.

"I saw her dance at a club in Baton Rouge the other night; she's got the moves. I'll work with her and show her the routines for the show," Brittany says to him pointedly.

"Fine. She starts tomorrow evening. If she's awful, it'll be her last evening!" He belts out a strange laugh that gives me chills, then swiftly turns and begins to head up a flight of stairs. "Good night, ladies. I have a show to do!!" he says, and then he stops midway and turns to look at me. "Oh, and Sunny...welcome to the Circus!!"

LAST NIGHT I SLEPT at Brittany's apartment in the French Quarter and dreamt of home and Momma. I dreamt of Lance Arceneaux and how excited I am to see him again, but right before I woke up, I dreamt about being on a round stage in front of hundreds of men butt-naked. I sit up drenched in a cold-sweat.

Around noon, Brittany and I get up and go to Cafe du Monde for beignets and chicory. The streets of the French Quarter are bustling with people, mostly tourists. That unfavorable smell is always present but is a little more fragrant in the heat of the day.

We head back to Bourbon, amidst the clean-up crews who are picking up trash from the night before, the bums begging for money, and the tourists taking pictures. When we get inside the Circus, it looks quite different from last night. There are people milling around sweeping the stage and restocking liquor. Brittany heads up to the DJ booth to put on some music. Madonna's "Vogue," which I love, is the song we're opening with tonight.

"We gotta work on this till you get it. It's an easy chair routine, so I'm thinking you'll catch on pretty fast," Brittany says as she goes backstage and pulls out two black cabaret chairs and begins to show me the steps that we will work on for hours.

At 8 p.m. we rehearse the number with the rest of the girls, and I'm feeling pretty confident that I have it down for the most part. At 8:30, in walks the ringleader. He seems frantic and is yelling at his two assistants.

"WHERE THE HELL IS LISA!!!!" We hear from the back of the theater.

Forty minutes later, right before the doors open to let in the hundreds of men waiting in a line down Bourbon Street, Lisa Beaumann walks in. She is wearing a white silk blouse, dozens of strings of pearls, black satin trousers, very high heels, and oversized black Chanel sunglasses, even though it's dark outside. Following Lisa are the male dancers who were on stage with her last night.

"Where the hell have you been? You know you are supposed to be here at seven for rehearsal!" screams the ringleader.

"Oh, I'm so sorry, Herman," Lisa says very blasé. "The boys and I were having a cocktail down at the Bourbon Pub." She glances over at the bartender. "Franko, the usual, dirty martini, extra olives, dear. Anyway, we went down to the Bourbon Pub to have a drink, and you want to hear something hysterical? The owner, Sandy, offered to pay me double what you pay me to perform!! Isn't that just the funniest thing you've ever heard?"

Everyone in the theater goes quiet, and I see the ringleader, Herman as Miss Beaumann calls him, turn bright red. His blood is boiling judging from the color of his face. He mumbles something too ugly to mention and storms out of the theater towards the dressing rooms.

"And now to the bigger and better question of the evening, who, might I ask, are you?" Lisa is staring right at me and so is everyone else in the theater.

"Um… hi…I'm Sunny, Miss Beaumann. Tonight's my first night here." I hear a couple of the girls behind me snicker, and suddenly I feel like I'm at Cleburne High School all over again.

"Is that so? Well, I hope you know what you're getting yourself into, dear," she says to me in warning and heads towards a door hidden under the staircase that leads to her dressing room. "Boys, get ready to rehearse my number!!" she yells from the back.

Brittany introduces me to all of the boys who are all good looking, sweet, and extremely talkative. As we head backstage, I tell Brit how much nicer the guys are than the girls.

"Yeah, well thankfully they're all gay, and you don't have to worry about them hitting on you," she says with a smirk.

It's ten minutes before show time, and my nerves are shot.

"Brittany, I can't do this; I'm freaking out," I say to her as anxiety weighs down on my chest.

"Yes, you can do it, and you better. Don't embarrass me after I went out on a limb to get you a job here. Plus, you gotta pay rent if you're going to stay with me, you've got to get a car, and you gotta have some money to spend on yourself if you're gonna keep dating Lance. Here, drink this; I drink one before I go on at night. It'll help you relax." She hands me a shot of Grey Goose as she applies fake eyelashes.

"How did I get from little Cleburne to a strip club in New Orleans?" I say aloud, lost in my thoughts "I'm supposed to be in Hollywood right now, not dancing topless at a club." I take a deep breath and drink the vodka in one gulp. Brittany stops what she's doing and looks at me.

"Listen, I have no doubt that you will make it out to L.A. one day, but tonight you're on stage at the Circus. You have a job to do, so don't let me down." Her tone is serious, and I know she's right; I'm grateful she is helping me. I pick up the lacy black body suit and slip it on along with the long black gloves and heels. It's show time.

The show starts, and once again Lisa Beaumann descends from the ceiling. She and the boys perform a splashy Liza Minnelli number. When we step out on stage with our chairs, I look out to the crowd, and it's even more frightening than I thought it would be. The music begins, and the other girls hurry to their spots. "Vogue" is playing full blast, and the girls hit their marks perfectly. Luckily I'm behind Brittany and can watch her if

I mess up my dance moves. Half way through the song, I make a decision: I don't have any other options right now, and I need the money, I need to just breathe and perform the best I know how, so I close my eyes and pretend I'm dancing for an arena packed with twenty thousand screaming fans. They're here to see me because they love me, not because I'm half naked. I feel the music pulse through me and let fantasy take over, just as I did when I was a kid. The part in the song comes where we have to rip off our tops, and I'm mortified. I do it anyway and try to keep imagining myself as a big star, not just some topless nobody. Finally, the song is over, and I turn to walk off the stage. I wait and let the other girls go in front of me, but as I'm exiting, the ringleader appears, grabs my arm, and pulls me out to the front of the stage.

"Gentlemen!!! I have a treat for all of you this evening!! This is our newest addition here at the Circus. Her name is Dixie Daniels, and she's a wild little cowgirl from Texas. She's here to rope and ride you and whip some of you into shape!!" The crowd of men goes wild, and I jerk my arm out of the ringleader's grasp.

"What are you doing?" I shout at him over the applause. He shoots me a sinister glare.

"Don't you dare defy me, girl," he hisses out of the corner of his mouth. To the boisterous crowd he says, "Now, gentlemen, you can make your way to the lap dance room if you would like a dance with this sassy cowgirl!!" The lights dim, and the ringleader grabs ahold of me even tighter and marches me backstage. I almost trip and fall several times because I can't see, and he is literally dragging me at this point. I'm terrified and pissed off all at the same time, but I can't get out of his tight grasp no matter how hard I try. When we finally get to the giant doors of the lap dance room, Lisa Beaumann is standing outside.

"Explain to her what to do," he says and shoves me towards Lisa. "Defy me in front of my fans again, and it'll be your last," he says to me heatedly, and then storms off.

"You gave me quite a laugh out there, darling," Lisa says as she studies her fingernails. "Tell me, what on earth is a girl like you doing in a place like this? I have a feeling there's a story there. I mean, you clearly don't fit in, but I guess that's none of my business, is it?" she says smiling but also looking very coy. Lisa Beaumann is a bit intimidating, and I'm not sure what to say, so I say nothing. "Let's go inside. I'll give you the rules of the lap dance room."

She opens the doors to reveal a small intimate room that is dimly lit and circular with golden pillars in between each small compartment. Each nook consists of a red velvet bench and pillows with red velvet curtains that are kept partially open so the huge bouncers can look in to make sure the guys aren't getting to handsy with the girls. There's a bar along the back wall with one female bartender, and slow, entrancing music plays in the room. Lisa quickly explains the rules of the lap dance room, and then whisks back outside to greet the men getting in line to enter. Several guys ask me for a lap dance right away. I could kill Brittany for not telling me we have to do this. Some burlesque club! I've never heard of burlesque dancers having to give lap dances in a secret room. My first customer is somewhat good looking, a college guy visiting from Lafayette. I'm definitely pulling out my acting skills and pretending to care what he's telling me. We talk for a while, and he buys me a double Grey Goose on the rocks at the bar.

When I begin dancing, I have no idea what I'm doing, but I don't think he notices my inexperience because he's so drunk. If it weren't for the alcohol I drank, there's no way I could do this. I close my eyes and picture Lance. Seven customers in a row. I've never done anything so terrible or degrading in my life. By the end of the night, I make eighteen hundred dollars. More money than I've ever seen at one time.

CHAPTER EIGHT
Pursuit of a Gemini

"**S**UNNY, GET YOUR ASS up! You can't sleep all day. We've got a big night ahead of us!" I hear Brittany shout from her kitchen.

I wearily open my eyes and search for my phone. Two p.m. Great. Working at the Circus is so exhausting, and I hate sleeping all day. Just then, Brittany enters the living room.

"Ok, so we need to take showers and get ready. We're gonna go eat at Raising Cane's, then head back to Baton Rouge. Chad Beauregard is throwing a party tonight, and everyone who's anyone is going to be there."

"I'm so tired. Do I have to go?" I ask her, rolling over to stuff my face back into my pillow.

"Oh, you're going back to sleep? Ok, totally fine," she says in a vexed tone. I hear her footsteps as she briskly leaves the living room. "Don't be pissed that you didn't get to see Lance Arceneaux when I drive off and leave your ass here," she shouts perkily down the hallway. A smile spreads across my face. It's been almost a week since I've seen Lance, and I'm dying to see him again.

The last time I saw him he said he wanted to see me soon. I haven't heard from him once. Sam told me that's typical of Lance. Typical, huh? Well, guess what? Lance Arceneaux will think twice about ignoring me after tonight. I'm going to make sure I look as hot as possible. I jump up and run to the bathroom where Brittany is doing her makeup in the mirror.

"Ohhh, well looks like I know how to get somebody up out of bed from now on."

"Whatever, Brit," I say smiling. "Just tell me what the plan is for tonight, and who is Chad Beauregard?" I ask, dying to hear every detail.

"Ok, so Chad's dad is a senator, and the Beauregard family were early settlers in Louisiana. He comes from old money like Sam, but his family is much wealthier. We're talking extreme wealth. You think Sam's house is huge? Wait till you see Chad's. It's literally the biggest house in Baton Rouge. I think it's worth something like eighteen million. Just wait, you'll die. It's insane," Brit explains to me as she carefully applies mascara. "Every time his parents are out of town, Chad throws these badass parties, and you have to be on the A list to get in." She looks at me and smiles a cocky smile. "Luckily you know me." I roll my eyes at her.

. "Ok, so you think Lance will be there tonight?" I ask her nervously.

"Oh he'll be there alright. Lance and Chad are good friends, and he never misses Chad's parties."

"Shit! I have to find something to wear! I have to look hot tonight; Brittany, can I please borrow something?" I plead with her.

"Seriously, Sunny, it's annoying that you're even asking me at this point. Get your ass in my room and start pulling out outfits. When I'm done, I'll come show you what's appropriate for an LSU party."

"Hurry up and get in!! It's starting to sprinkle!" Brittany yells out the window of her BMW at Sam who is pacing back and forth on the porch of the LeBlanc mansion and talking on the phone. "He works my nerves sometimes," Brittany says as she lights a Marlboro Light. When Sam finally finishes his phone call, he makes a run for it and jumps into the back seat.

"Where the hell have you guys been? I told you to be here by nine," Sam yells from the backseat.

"You can blame your friend Sunny here who changed fifteen times. Then we hit traffic on I-10," Brit says to Sam, frustrated.

"Why was she changing? Oh, because you told her Lance would be there tonight?" he asks amused.

"Yeah, how else was I supposed to get her out of bed?" Brittany says puffing away on her cigarette as we exit the magnificent gates.

"Oh. Well sorry to burst your bubble, Sunny, but I just talked to Chad, and Lance isn't coming tonight," Sam says in mock sorrow. I feel my heart drop into the pit of my stomach. Great. That's just great. I stare out the window watching the rain drops hit the glass.

"Just kidding; he's there. Chad said they were all about to do Gator Bombs," Sam says gleefully from behind me. Sam and Brittany both begin to chuckle, and I immediately turn around to slap Sam.

"Don't do that to me!" I yell at him.

"Aww, Sunny, what were you gonna do? Pout in the car all night? You are getting way too wrapped up in that boy. It's not gonna be pretty when he drops you like he does every other girl," Brittany says to me. I stop hitting Sam and turn to look at Brittany.

"Well luckily, I'm not every other girl," I say with a confident smile.

As we pull into Chad Beauregard's plush neighborhood, I see one gigantic mansion after another. Each property is massive and is beautifully lit. Some houses are enormous plantation style homes similar to Sam's, and some are more modern. We turn on to Magnolia Lane which dead-ends. As we approach the end of the street, there is only one house, if you can even call it a house. We are still a block away when I see enormous lit up palm trees lining the main driveway. We pass through the gates, and I see the mega mansion in the distance.

"Holy shit, that's a house?" I blurt out in disbelief.

"Yep. I told you it was huge," Brittany says matter-of-factly.

The first thought that pops into my mind is that it looks like a Mediterranean palace. The house is built with cream colored stone and has towers on both ends, topped with red terra cotta tiles. There are different sized towers throughout the gigantic structure, which just keeps going and going. We park on the grass on the side of the long half-circle driveway where hundreds of other Mercedes, Porches, and trucks with lift kits are parked. As I step out of the car, I take one last look at my outfit in the window of Brit's beamer. I settled on a sparkly black halter top with a faded jean skirt and black strappy heels. I put my hair in a high ponytail so it wouldn't be hot on my neck in the Louisiana heat.

"You look fine, Sunny," Brittany says to me, still aggravated that I changed so many times.

"Brit, you look cute as well," I say mockingly. Brittany is wearing a long flowing orange skirt and matching halter that reminds me of the sunset. Her wavy, beautiful hair is long and flowing down her back.

"Of course I do! When do I not look hot, bitch?" She teases back.

As we get closer to the house, I'm surprised to hear "Gangsta's Paradise" blasting from inside.

"Hell yeah, I love this song!!" I turn to Sam and begin to dance.

"Chad has this thing for 90s hip-hop. You'll be sick of it by the end of the night," Sam says dryly.

We make our way up two sets of stairs surrounded by beautiful tropical plants and pass by an enormous bubbling fountain with a ten-foot tall mermaid perched in the center. There are dozens of LSU students everywhere I look, all drinking, dancing, and having a blast. Everybody I see is gorgeous. As we pass through the oversized wooden front doors, I feel as though I'm walking into a beach resort. There are courtyards encased by giant arches, plush sitting rooms, and a long hallway with thirty foot ceilings that run through the middle of the main house. We pass by a movie theater, a grand ballroom, and finally, the kitchens, which span the entire back of the house. The huge glass walls across the back of the kitchen are slid open to reveal a tropical paradise. Palm trees line an Olympic-sized pool to the left and tennis and basketball courts are to the right. Directly in front of us, where dozens of people are mingling, is a large open veranda that leads to the bank of a lake. We make our way through the crowds of people to the inside bar and get drinks.

"Now, Brit, let's remember our southern manners and find the host of the party before we say hi to anyone else," Sam says sounding like a snob, as Brittany rolls her eyes at him. After a couple of minutes of searching, we find Chad who is at the DJ booth in the main living room.

"What's up you guys!! It's about time you got here!" Chad yells over the music to Sam and Brittany. "Let me find this next song, then I'll come talk to you guys," he shouts. Chad Beauregard is tall, around 6'1", has a nice tan, and spiky, white-blonde hair. His haircut reminds me of Sonic the Hedgehog. He's wearing a tight green t-shirt that says *Gangsta4Life* and tattered jeans. Are all the guys in Louisiana good looking? It must be in their genes. Just then, the song "Crossroads" by Bone Thugs-N-Harmony comes on, and the crowd goes wild. Chad steps down from the DJ booth and hugs both Sam and Brittany.

"Chad, this is Sunny Collins; she's visiting Louisiana," Brittany says, introducing Chad and me.

"Damn, Sunny, you are cute as hell!!" he says, mesmerized, as he takes my hand and guides me in a slow turn.

Just then, a feeling comes over me. I look across the crowd, and making his way through an archway is Lance Arceneaux wearing a purple Ralph Lauren polo and khaki pants. His hair is swept to the side, and he looks breathtakingly handsome. He's headed this way, but stops to talk to a group of people. Suddenly, I feel Chad Beauregard pull me close to him and begin to grind on me.

"Hell, yeah!" he shouts from behind me, as I feel him put both of his hands on my waist. I quickly pull away from him and look over in Lance's direction just in time to see him leave the room. Great. I immediately give Chad a go-to-hell look.

"That's all I get? Oh, I see, you have your eyes on Lance, huh…Another one bites the dust," he says with an eye roll. "Fine. I need another drink anyway. C'mon Brit," Chad says as he and Brittany head towards the bar.

"Well that was an interesting move you just made, wasn't it? Tell me, when did you decide to jump on the express train to pissing off Lance? Did it come instinctually to you? Or have you been plotting that one all week?" Sam says sarcastically.

"What are you talking about? Chad just grabbed me; that wasn't my fault!" I say trying not to get riled up.

"Hmmm. Not your fault indeed," he says back skeptically. "Now think really hard, Sunny. Do you think grinding on one of Lance's best friends in front of him was the best idea?" he asks condescendingly. I stare blankly at Sam, as he takes a deep breath. "Not only was it generic, basic, and an obvious move, but you have yet to realize you're playing a game with someone who's better at it than you are. Even if it wasn't your fault, Lance won't see it that way. What's worse is that you just yelled 'your move' with your actions, so now it's his turn. Big mistake," Sam says, finishing his analysis.

"Ok, well you may be right, but he didn't see it anyway," I say to him unconvincingly, praying Lance really didn't.

"For my sake, let's hope he didn't. I'm exhausted just thinking about listening to you complain about Chad Beauregard all week."

An hour later I step out of one of the many bathrooms throughout the house. It took me ten minutes to find one without a line of bubbly LSU girls gossiping outside of it. I head down the stairs into the grand foyer to look for Sam and Brittany, and I see dozens of people making their way outside through the glass doors in the back. The music has stopped as well. I make my way through the crowd, curious to see what on earth is going on outside. I step out onto the giant veranda several yards away from the dimly lit lake and spot Brittany.

"Well, Sunny, if you wanted to see some crazy shit happen during your time in Louisiana, I guarantee you're about to see it," Brittany says grinning.

"What are they doing?" I ask her trying to see over the crowd.

"Well, Lance and Chad you know, and the dark haired guy is Danny Knight." The three of them together look like an Abercrombie ad. "They have this tradition of jumping in the lake and taunting the alligators at Chad's parties, but really it's just a chance to show off their bodies in front of everyone," Brittany says with an eye roll as she sips her cocktail.

I finally see what everyone is talking about. Lance, Chad, and Danny are all three stripping off their clothes. I can't take my eyes off Lance; I'm mesmerized. He pulls his polo over his head, and I see the tight rippling muscles of his bare torso for the first time. He waves to the crowd of people and flashes everyone a shit-eating grin. I watch as he unzips his jeans and slides them off revealing his tight black boxers. His dark tan, beautifully defined torso, and long muscular legs remind me of a Greek god. I feel myself blush, hoping no one around me notices. Lance and the other guys run into the water splashing and taunting the alligators in the distance. I put my hands over my face unable to watch, and then I feel someone brush up beside me.

"Oh great, this old stunt again," Sam says dryly, shaking me out of my train of thought. "Here, I brought you a Grey Goose and soda," Sam says, as he hands me a red Solo cup.

"Thank god, I needed this," I say as I gulp down half the drink.

"Have you said hi to him yet?" Sam asks me impatiently. I shake my head *no*.

The boys start yelling and come flying out the lake as the alligators begin to approach them. The crowd cheers even louder. I watch Lance come up out of the water, his magnificent body glistening with rivulets of lake water. He takes both of his hands and wipes the water out of his eyes, and then he spots me in the crowd. He looks at me with his piercing green eyes and studies me for a second. I feel the fire deep inside me ignite. He knows I've been watching him the whole time, and I can't take my eyes off him. I wait for Lance to flash his sexy smile at me, but instead he curls his lip and shakes his head in disgust. I wonder what that was about. Just then a girl walks over with a towel and begins to wipe it across Lance's chest, patting him dry. He stands there letting her and looks over at me with his eyebrows raised. His face says it all. *You don't have a problem with this do you?* he says with just a look. And then I realize it; he totally saw Chad grinding on me, and he thinks I was ok with it. Now I'm going to have to suffer the consequences. In his mind I made a move, and now he's making his. Checkmate. *Bitch, get your hands off him,* I think to myself. I watch the girl as she looks up at his beautiful face with adoration in her eyes. I have the urge to charge over and knock her into the lake with the alligators. He grabs the towel, thanks her, and wraps it around his waist.

"Brothers and sisters of LSU!!" Chad yells as he makes his way through the crowd holding a lit torch. "I give you, our fearless leader, Lance Arceneaux...The Gator King!!!"

The crowd goes wild as Chad raises the torch to the sky. People then start to push past me, and the party resumes as TLC's "No Scrubs" begins to blast through the speakers. Then, I lose sight of Lance altogether.

Should I go and say hi first or wait for him to find me? Clearly we are playing chase the Gemini, which I'm happy to do, but I just hope that idiot Chad Beauregard didn't screw everything up for me. After all, Lance hasn't even bothered to call me in a week. Why should I feel bad? Hold on. Remember, Sunny, you're chasing him; he's obviously not chasing you.

An hour later, I have made my way around the entire house and yard trying to find Lance. As the party starts to clear out, I make my way to the front yard, the only place I haven't looked yet. I pass through the enormous front doors and step outside just in time to see his big black truck peeling out of the driveway. Several people are hanging out of the windows of his truck, but I can't make out if they are guys or girls. Anxiety shoots through my veins; he left and didn't even talk to me once. All I got was a disapproving look or two, not a secret make out session in one of the many beautiful bedrooms, not a stroll around the lake with comments about how hot I look tonight; hell, I didn't even get a cute little wink. All I've managed to do tonight is piss him off. Is what happened with Chad really that big of a deal? Is it always going to be a guessing game with Lance? I suddenly realize that this is going to be way more difficult than I could have ever imagined. The rules of the Gemini's game are complex, and this is going to be a long hard road. I may have to spend the rest of my life trying to win him over. The thought of this makes me crazy...and unfortunately makes me want him even more.

CHAPTER NINE
The Fighting Tigers

"SUNNY!!!" SAM SCREAMS as he comes running down the hallway of the west wing of his parents' mansion. The bedroom door bursts open, and Sam comes flying in. "Ok, we have to talk. I just got off the phone with my mom. She and my dad are coming home from Europe early, and they just landed at the airport in New Orleans. They'll be here in—WHAT IS THAT ON THE BED??? MUSTARD?"

"Yeah, I accidentally spilled some," I say sheepishly. Sam storms out of the room and into the guest bathroom. He comes back with a wet towel and a terrified look on his face.

"We have to get this out before my mom sees it. She will murder you and me both."

"Why are they coming home early?" I ask, trying to change the subject.

"There's a gala tomorrow night that they can't miss. My mom is on the TAF Women's committee," he says as he frantically rubs the wet towel on the comforter.

"What's TAF?" I ask sounding more curious than I really am. Anything to keep his mind off of the mustard.

"It stands for Tigers Athletic Foundation. It's an independent booster club funded by alumni that raises money to support LSU's athletic department. At the gala they auction off football and baseball players as servants to the highest bidders." I suddenly come out of my daze.

"Baseball players?" I ask as my wheels start turning. Sam stops scrubbing and looks at me suspiciously.

"Oh no, don't even think about it. You are not going. My parents spend twenty thousand dollars for a table, and there is no way my mom is going to let me bring you, so just find another way to fulfill your Lance Arceneaux fantasy."

This news automatically puts me in a good mood. I've been wracking my brain since the party with ways to see him, and I haven't thought of anything; I have to figure out a way to go to that gala.

"Sam, we're home," Mrs. LeBlanc yells from the foyer.

"Ok, Sunny, remember, be on your best behavior and don't say ANYTHING about how we met and what we've been doing the past year...Got it?" Sam says to me pointedly.

"Oh my god, Sam, I've got it; you've said it five times!!" I say to him exasperated.

We make our way from the kitchen into the grand foyer. Mrs. LeBlanc is standing at the bottom of the staircase scrolling through her cell phone, and Mr. LeBlanc is helping a driver unload Louis Vuitton suitcases from a Cadillac Escalade parked in the driveway.

"Um...hello, Mother. How was the French Riviera?" I've never heard Sam's voice crack before. He has told me in the past that his mother is the one person he's afraid of, but seeing him like this is kind of comical considering she doesn't look mean to me at all. She does, however, look every bit the aristocrat southern woman. She's wearing a baby-blue pantsuit with white heels, her honey blonde hair perfectly coiffed. She has on a huge sparkling cross necklace encrusted with diamonds (which I'm sure are real) diamond studs earrings, and a diamond tennis bracelet. Not to mention, her wedding ring is the biggest I've ever seen. She's a little shorter than I am, and her fingernails are finely manicured with French tips. She has a kind face but has definitely had work done.

"Oh, you know, if you've seen one part of France, you've seen it all," she says in her southern Louisiana accent, rather bored. "Your father, of course, was mesmerized by the naked women on the beach. I had to drag him by his tongue back to the Ritz Carlton in Cannes," she says still texting away on her phone, never looking up. It seems very odd to me that she is not the least bit interested in Sam or me, and it's even more odd that she hasn't hugged her son whom she hasn't seen in over a year. I suddenly feel sorry for Sam.

"Mother, I want you to meet a friend of mine...This is Sunny, Sunny Collins," Sam says quietly as if she may not hear him.

"Hi, Sunny, it's a pleasure, I'm sure," she says, texting away.

"Sunny's from Texas, Mother; this is her first time in Louisiana. I've been showing her the sights since we arrived."

"That's nice, dear. Go help your father bring in the rest of the luggage, Samuel; you know he has a bad back," she says dryly.

"Yes, of course, Mother." Sam hurries out the front door towards the Escalade.

"Um…. Mrs. LeBlanc? I just wanted to tell you thank you so much for letting me stay at your home. It's the most beautiful place I've ever seen. I especially love the art work and the rose gardens," I say, hoping to make some sort of good impression. Mrs. LeBlanc rolls her eyes and looks up at me for the first time. Suddenly her face changes from annoyed to bewildered. She studies me for what seems like an eternity, looking me up and down. Then, the sweetest, friendliest smile I could imagine spreads across her face.

"Sunny, did you say? How wonderful to meet you. How pretty you are!" she says as she reaches for my hand which she holds in hers. She is warm and enduring.

"Ok, that's the last of the suitcases, Lynne," Mr. LeBlanc states as he shuts the enormous front door.

"Crawford, dear!" Mrs. LeBlanc says sweetly, turning to look at her husband. "This is Sunny, Sam's friend who is staying with us!" She looks back at me in adoration.

"Oh, well any friend of Sam's is a friend of mine," Mr. LeBlanc says as he pats me on the back. Mr. LeBlanc must be of Cajun descent as well. He has the same deep reddish tan as Lance, silver hair, and is very tall. His eyes are bright blue and gleaming. He's wearing a purple LSU polo shirt with khaki shorts and a beautiful silver Rolex. "Honey, I need a drink; I'll have one of the maids take everything upstairs later," he says as he makes his way down the hall towards the bar.

"When does he not need a drink?" Mrs. LeBlanc whispers to me with a wink. "So, Sunny, tell me, what all have you been doing since you got here? I want to hear everything. You know, we have some very handsome men here in Louisiana," she says leaning in as though she's letting me in on a secret.

"Well, we've done a lot of fun stuff since I got here; we went to Gator Bar, and then to Tsunami which was really nice, and I've been to New Orleans several times which was quite an experience," I say to her excitedly. "Oh, and well, speaking of handsome men, I met the most amazing guy. His name is Lance, and he plays for the LSU baseball team."

"Lance? You mean Lance Arceneaux?" She looks at me inquisitively.

"Yes ma'am. Do you know him?" I ask surprised. The strangest look comes over her face for a moment; the same one that comes over Sam's face when he's contemplating something. Then, her face quickly shifts back to pleasant.

"Why of course I know him. We religiously follow all of the best athletes around here! Not to mention, he has been over to the house several times for parties when Sam was still in school. Well, he is quite the catch from what I hear around town. Do you think he likes you?"

"Oh, I'm not sure; we've only been on a couple of dates," I say to her with a sigh.

"Have you now..." she says sweetly, yet I think I see her eye twitch just barely.

"Yes ma'am. I was hoping to see him at the gala tomorrow night, but Sam said it's all sold out," I say sadly. Hey, it can't hurt to let her know how badly I want to go. Just then Sam comes through the front door looking at the two of us in shock.

"Sorry, I had to take a call. You two getting along?" Sam asks cautiously.

"Well, of course we're getting along, Samuel!!" She looks at him grinning. "My question is why on earth did you tell Sunny the gala was sold out?" She turns to look at me beaming. "Of course you can come tomorrow night, sunshine. Don't you worry; I'll arrange everything."

"Mother, Sunny didn't exactly bring a gown with her to Louisiana." Sam looks at his mother in disbelief.

"Oh well, then I'll just have to take her shopping tomorrow, won't I? Now if you two will excuse me, I have to go get ready for dinner. Why don't we all go out? The chef didn't know we would be back today, and he didn't prepare anything. I'm thinking Fleming's Steakhouse. That's your favorite, right, Sam?" Sam is speechless, but nods slowly. "Sunny, go change into something cute: we're celebrating your arrival in Louisiana tonight!" Mrs. LeBlanc says, as she makes her way up the sweeping grand staircase looking every bit the southern belle. I look at Sam with a wide grin on my face. I can't help it; for once I've outsmarted him.

"What in the hell did you say to her?" Sam asks, his face a mixture of rage and worry.

"I didn't say anything! I just told her where you've taken me since we got here and that I met Lance and…" He puts his finger up interrupting me mid-sentence.

"Sunny, I have never seen my mom act like that much less offer to take a friend of mine shopping. I never even got to go to Fleming's for my birthday dinners growing up. That's the most expensive place in Baton Rouge, and the only time my parents go there is when they are entertaining clients from their law firms," Sam says exasperated.

"Law firms? Your parents are lawyers?"

"My mom is a partner at McLean and Calvin, and my dad is the district attorney for East Baton Rouge Parish," he says his eyes drifting off in thought.

"Wow, that's so cool," I say impressed.

"You have no idea what you've done, Sunny. You are a young pretty girl, and you just challenged a wealthy southern woman. She is a lion, and you are the prey," he says looking at me with fear in his eyes.

"Oh, Sam, stop it. Just because you have issues with your mom doesn't mean she hates me. As a matter of fact, she couldn't be any sweeter. Anyway, I get to go to the gala tomorrow and look amazing; that's what really matters here. Just be happy for me and let's go get ready for dinner," I say finally hitting my breaking point with this nonsense.

"Be happy for you?? Ok, you know what? You're right. I am happy for you. I won't say another word about it. Let's go get ready," Sam says with a forced smile, gritting his teeth.

The next morning I wake bright and early, get dressed, and head downstairs for breakfast. I walk into the enormous gourmet kitchen where the chef has prepared a beautiful array of eggs Benedict, brioche French toast, eggs scrambled with andouille sausage and cheese, and fruit bowls filled with strawberries, blackberries, and raspberries. I couldn't be happier. Sam's parents are back along with the help and considering Sam and I have been eating fast food or ordering pizza, this meal is a welcome surprise.

I can't believe rich people wake up every morning to such an exquisite breakfast. It's like living in a palace or in a Martha Stewart catalog. I make a plate, grab some coffee, thank Maurice the chef, and then head out the back door onto the terrace overlooking the rose gardens. The Louisiana morning air is dewy and sweet, and the sun is shining brightly through the giant oak trees that surround the plantation. A smile slowly spreads across my face as I think about tonight. I finally get to see Lance again, and Mrs. LeBlanc is going to help me look amazing. Lance won't know what hit him!

"So...are you sitting out here plotting your game plan to win over Lance tonight?" Sam says from behind me, as he comes over and pulls out a chair next to me.

"Why, yes, I sure am!" I say cheerfully. "With a little help from your darling mother, of course."

"Mmm. Right," Sam says sarcastically as he sips his morning coffee.

"Why are you being ornery this morning?" I ask annoyed.

"Oh, I'm not ornery; I'm just still reeling over how my mother showered you with compliments last night at dinner. You really have no idea how bad this is going to get, do you?" Sam says warning me.

"Sunny, dear! There you are!" Mrs. LeBlanc says as she comes out of the house onto the terrace. I turn around, and there she is, the ultimate southern woman. She's wearing a black and white polka dot dress, pearls, and a shiny black ribbon in her hair. She exudes kindness with her sweet southern charm.

"Good morning, Mrs. LeBlanc!" I say to her excitedly like she's my new best friend.

"Sunny, dear, whenever you're finished with your breakfast, let's head to town. We have to make sure you are a spectacle tonight!" she announces and heads back into the house.

"A spectacle indeed...," Sam mutters.

"Oh will you shut up! If she picks out something horrible, I just won't wear it!" I yell at Sam, and then head into the house. I'm so excited about getting a dress for tonight that I can't even finish my breakfast.

As we cruise through downtown Baton Rouge in Mrs. LeBlanc's gleaming white Mercedes, I listen curiously as she talks on the phone to one person after another about tonight's events. She is, after all, on the committee for the gala, but I had no idea how much work and planning go into these things. I turn around to look at Sam who is yawning in the back seat and looks bored out of his mind. We finally arrive at LaRoux's Dress Shop, and I can't wait to look at all the beautiful dresses.

"Sunny, this is Miss Milly; his real name is Miles, but we call him Milly around here. He helps with all my ball gown needs," Mrs. LeBlanc states. A heavyset and very flamboyant man wearing a caftan and dozens of glitzy rings walks out to greet us.

"Well, hi there, Mrs. Lynne!! I didn't know you were gonna be back from Europe so soon!!" he says in a high-pitched southern twang, as he and Mrs. LeBlanc air kiss on both cheeks.

"Yes, Miss Milly, well, you know we had to come home early because of the gala! I just forgot all about it!" She laughs her sweet laugh. "Anyway, this is Sam's friend Sunny who is visiting, and she's coming with us tonight. I need to get her the perfect dress. After all, she has her eye on a certain LSU baseball player who will be in attendance tonight." She looks at me and winks.

"Girl, I'm right there with you; I get the baseball calendar every year, and those boys just drive me wild. Come on, Sunny, let's get you fixed up!" Miss Milly says to me with his sassy attitude. "What about this Mrs. Lynne? She would be the belle of the ball wearing this!!" Milly says as he holds up a slim-fitting sparkly gold dress.

"Oh, the belle of the ball indeed!!" Mrs. LeBlanc states. "But we need the *perfect* dress for tonight. After all, tonight is a traditional dress gala. No, she needs something classic…like this!!" Mrs. LeBlanc heads over to a wall of dresses and pulls out a velvet purple ball gown, with a giant hoop skirt underneath it. "Sunny, this is gorgeous, don't you think?" she asks expectantly looking at me wide eyed. The dress is nice, but it looks like something the women in one of the paintings from the 1700s that hang on the walls of the LeBlancs' mansion would wear.

"Yes ma'am, it's very pretty; is this appropriate for the occasion? A more traditional dress?" I ask honestly.

"Oh yes, dear, this is very appropriate," she says nodding.

"Ok… well, let's do it! Thank you so much, Mrs. LeBlanc. I couldn't be more grateful."

"Oh dear, you are more than welcome! And by all means, call me Lynne!!!" She purchases the dress, and I can't believe how much she pays for it, and then Miss Milly loads it into the trunk of the Mercedes. The bottom of the dress is so big that it barely fits.

"Well, what do you think of the dress? Pretty, right?" I ask Sam excitedly.

"It's absolutely beautiful, Sunny. I'm sorry I doubted you. Your power of persuasion over my mother is uncanny," he says with a snarky grin.

AT 8 P.M., I HEAD down the grand staircase of the LeBlanc family home in my enormous purple velvet gown and take a seat on one of the giant plush couches. I sit staring at the detailed portraits of the generals that line the walls and think about my plan for this evening. I wonder who will bid on Lance. God, if I only had the money, I would do it. Actually, I should just be happy I get to go. A smile washes over my face thinking about how I

outsmarted Sam.

"Well, don't you look every bit the belle of the ball," Sam says sarcastically as he briskly enters the living room wearing a black Ralph Lauren tuxedo, fiddling with his cufflinks.

"Here, let me help you," I say sighing. Sam holds out his arm, and I begin to fix his cufflinks.

"Do me a favor and for once don't do anything crazy tonight, Sunny. All of Baton Rouge is going to be at the gala tonight. My family is brilliant at avoiding scandals, and the last thing I need is an 'I love you Lucy' moment from you," Sam says looking both nervous and frustrated.

"Well, I'm glad that's what you think of me, Sam. At least give me some credit. You act like I was raised in a barn," I say offended.

"Were you not? Sometimes I can't tell," he says rather snobbily.

"Well, my dears, shall we head out?" We both turn to see Mrs. LeBlanc slowly making her way down the grand staircase wearing a long black beautiful mink coat. She is stunning. "Your father is meeting us there, Sam... Come on! Our limo waits!" she says, and we both follow her out the front door.

We make our way through the LSU campus and finally arrive in front of the alumni building which is beautiful with thousands of white lights wrapped around all of the enormous oak trees, and the front of the building is lit up purple and yellow. Our driver opens the door, and three of us step out of the limo and into the street where dozens of other limos and town cars are letting out guests. Hundreds of gala attendees pass us as they make their way inside. I begin looking at other women's dresses, and horror washes over me. I see dozens of short sexy cocktail dresses, long, sleek, sparkly dresses on the older women, and tight sexy mini dresses on the girls my age. What the hell is happening? Our limo pulls off before I can turn and jump back in it. I look at Sam in panic, and he is helping Mrs. LeBlanc take off her long black mink to reveal a super-short, sexy, black and silver cocktail dress with high shoulders and a plunging neckline that exposes so much cleavage she is almost bursting out of it. She's wearing shiny black Louboutins; I can tell because of the blood red bottom.

"Sam, dear, hold on to my mink until we get inside. I've got to walk over and say hi to Dr. Dupree and his wife," she says in her sweet southern drawl as she flashes me a triumphant grin and begins to make her way through the crowd.

"I am mortified, Sam LeBlanc!!! How could you let me wear this knowing damn well I was going to look like a fool!!!!!!!" I yell at Sam

"I don't want to hear it. I tried to warn you, but you're smarter than I am, remember? Now let's go." Sam turns and swiftly begins to make his way up the stairs towards the front doors of the alumni building. I have no way to get back into the LeBlancs' house if I take a cab back there. Brittany's already inside looking fabulous, I'm sure. I have no choice but to walk into this building in this hideous dress. Everyone is going to be staring, and worst of all, Lance is going to think I'm a lunatic. I got myself into this; now I'm just going to have to face it. This is what I get for thinking I could outsmart these shifty Louisiana people: total humiliation. I pick up my enormous dress so I can walk, make my way up the steps, through the front door, and into the gala.

After searching forever and almost knocking down several people with the circus tent I'm wearing, I find Sam and Brittany sitting at the empty LeBlanc table. The table is set beautifully for dinner and is located next to the enormous stage. Sam is deep in conversation; I'm sure he's explaining to Brittany the happenings of the past couple of days. Suddenly Brittany notices me and covers her mouth as she looks me up and down.

"Oh you can say it, Brit; nothing at this point is going to make a difference. The whispers and stares have said it all," I say to her annoyed, as she sits in shock wearing a one shoulder, gun-metal grey cocktail dress.

"Oh my god, Sunny, I've seen some Louisiana women do some crazy shit, but this takes the cake."

"Yeah, well I deserve it, right Sam? For not listening to you? Isn't that what you were telling her before I walked up?" I say, my temper rising.

"Um, yeah, pretty much," Sam says looking up at me, nodding his head in agreeance.

"You're such a Capricorn, you know it, Sam? Sometimes I wonder why I'm even friends with you," I say, pulling out a chair and plopping down next to Brittany.

Mr. and Mrs. LeBlanc finally arrive at the table with ten other guests whom they've invited to eat with them, none of which acknowledge I'm there. Sam is still pissed at my comment, so he's not speaking to me, and Brittany went to join her family at their table. I make my way through the pan-roasted salmon and fingerling potatoes, and then begin to down glasses of champagne as the music of Sammy Davis, Jr. flows through the hall. At 9 p.m., the lights on the stage dim, and a single spotlight begins to follow a heavyset woman wearing a bright pink beaded mermaid-tailed dress across the stage. She's met with roars of applause.

"Ladies and gentlemen, please, welcome the president of the LSU Alumni Association, Mrs. LuAnn DuBois!!!" The crowd falls into a hush.

"Well, hi y'all!!! How's everyone doing tonight? I'm sorry we couldn't get Coach Holly to host tonight; he's on vacation," she says with a sinister grin. This is met with a mixture of *boos*, shock, and laughter. "Quite the scandalous year we've had in the athletic department here at LSU!! But as always, the current staff, faculty, and students, as well as the alumni, rise above and come back better than ever!!" she says as the crowd once again bursts into applause.

"Coach Holly was fired for sleeping with students...male students,"

Sam leans over and whispers in my ear.

"Oh, are you speaking to me now?" I whisper hatefully back, as he simply turns and looks back at the stage ignoring me.

"Ok, so tonight is about charity, and we have the perfect way to get you to whip out those checkbooks ladies and even a couple of you gentlemen!!" The crowd rumbles with laughter. "Please, welcome the men of LSU, some of our greatest athletes. Football players Jermaine LeBeau and Reagan McDonald, basketball player Danny Knight, and baseball players Lance Arceneaux and Chad Beauregard!!" The crowd begins to rise, and the cheering is so loud I almost have to cover my ears. I look up and see each of the boys walk out one by one. Last but not least is Lance. He struts out onto the stage with a cocky grin on his smug face and waves to the crowd who once again goes wild. The orchestra plays "Cheek to Cheek" as the boys, all wearing tuxedos, wave and flirt with the crowd.

"Well here they are everyone!" LuAnn DuBois shouts as she makes her way past each of the men on stage. "Remember, everyone, what you spend tonight goes to the Baton Rouge Children's Hospital Charity Fund, and you'll have a gorgeous man at your disposal for a whole day! You can have him wash your car, trim your hedges, or even unclog your pipes... if you know what I mean...," she announces with a salacious grin as the audience roars with laughter. "Let's start with our first handsome hunk, Quarterback Jermaine LeBeau!" Mrs. Dubois makes her way down the line, one by one, auctioning off each athlete until finally she reaches Lance. "Ok everyone, you know I always save the best for last. Here he is, LSU's very own, Lance Arceneaux!!" He gets more cheers than any of the other guys, who have all exited the stage. "Now, Lance, tell me, are those rumors true about you being the biggest playboy on campus? I mean after all, you look just as sweet as you can be, but I hear you are just a heartbreaker!!!"

"Aww, well I hate to break it to you, Mrs. Dubois, but I'm looking for love just like everyone else," Lance says in his charming Gemini way, grinning towards the audience.

"Well ladies, you heard it here first!! Should we start the bidding at two thousand?" LuAnne Dubois looks at the crowd expectantly. Dozens of women begin to shout out dollar amounts.

"Cougars in heat," Sam whispers in my ear. I watch in fascination and am finally distracted from the ridiculous dress I'm wearing. Suddenly out of the corner of my eye, I see Sam's mom stand up.

"Ten thousand dollars," she shouts out like a lion roaring in the jungle. I hear gasps all around me from the crowd, and then slow claps turn into a standing ovation.

"Sold! To our very own Mrs. Lynne LeBlanc!!! Why, that's the biggest donation in our auction history! Thank you, Lynne!" Luann Dubois says, praising Sam's evil mother who is grinning from ear to ear as people walk over to the table to congratulate her.

"It's for charity!" she purrs with fake kindness to people, giggling at all the attention she's getting as she shakes their hands. I look over at Sam who is sitting with his elbows on the table and his face buried in his hands. He finally looks up at me wearily.

"Well, this just gets better and better." The music starts up again, and the party resumes. I look to my left and see Lance making his way through the crowd. Aside from everything else, I can't believe how dashing he looks in his tuxedo. He is absolutely beautiful, and I have to stop myself from looking at him as he reaches the table.

"Mr. and Mrs. LeBlanc, I just wanted to come over and personally thank you. That was quite the donation. I know the hospital will be extremely happy with what we raised tonight," Lance says as Mrs. LeBlanc reaches for his hand and clasps it with both of hers.

"Oh, Lance, you don't have to be so formal with us, dear; we've known you so long that you're like family to us!" she says looking up at him, her eyes gleaming. I watch as Mr. LeBlanc simply smiles at Lance, and then turns to make his way into the crowd. It's clear who wears the pants in that marriage. "So, are you available tomorrow? I only have a couple of things I'd like you to do around the house," she says sweetly still holding Lance's hand.

"Yes, of course, if you need me tomorrow, I will be there at noon," he says politely.

"Fabulous! Oh, and don't forget to bring dinner clothes to change into; I'm making a true southern dinner tomorrow night," Mrs. LeBlanc says while leaning over to let her cleavage hang out.

"Sounds great; I'll see you then," he says as she finally releases his hand. He glances over at me quickly, and then makes his way back through the crowd.

Wow! Couldn't even say *hi* to me. Shocking. I guess he's still mad about Chad's party, or he's just lost interest. Maybe he's just too embarrassed to be seen talking to the girl wearing the giant circus tent. I down another glass of champagne, and then dig through my purse for my phone. I need to call Brittany, who's already left, and get her opinion on tonight's events.

"Why did Brittany leave so soon?" I ask Sam. "She could have at least told us goodbye."

"Well, I should probably let Brittany explain the situation to you, but her father is a pretty famous lawyer, and she and her dad have always had a tumultuous relationship. Since we were kids, she has done everything she could think of to defy him. He's honestly not a bad guy; he's just very strict with her and her brother. Her brother actually took off when he turned 18 and hasn't come home since. Mr. Laveau was even more rough on him than he is on Brittany. I think her parents count their blessings at this point that she stayed in school as long as she did."

"So is that why she started working at the Circus? To defy her dad?" I ask curiously.

"I would say so. And the fact that she loves the men, she loves the attention, and she loves the money helps…but pissing off her dad is her favorite thing to do."

I tap my screen and see that I have one text. It's from Lance Arceneaux. Oh shit! I take a deep breath and open it, dying to know what on earth he's texting me.

LANCE: You planning on going to a cotillion later? Let me know what plantation it's being held at. Maybe I'll saddle up my horse and head over… ;-)

"What the hell's a cotillion?" I ask Sam quickly.

"It's an eighteenth century dance that was brought here by the French. The dress you're wearing would actually be perfect for it," Sam says dryly.

"Oh," I say throwing my phone back in my purse. I could not be more ready to go back to Sam's and lock myself in my room while I die from embarrassment.

CHAPTER TEN
Dinner with the Devil

I WEARILY OPEN my eyes, and the morning sun is pouring into my room. I hear the birds chirping and see the giant oak trees swaying in the gentle breeze. I replay last night's horrific events in my mind, and all I want to do is go back to sleep. Sam was right; his mother was out to get me the moment she laid eyes on me, and I looked like a complete idiot in front of Lance last night. I close my eyes, and all I can picture are the other girls at the gala staring at me and snickering, just like high school all over again.

I take a deep breath, throw the covers off me, and make my way to the bathroom to make myself presentable. In order to avoid Mrs. LeBlanc at all costs, I creep out of my room cautiously, and then tip-toe down the hallway towards the grand staircase. I don't want to give her a chance to humiliate me even further, even though I'm not sure that's even possible at this point. The coast is clear, and the house appears to be silent, so I slowly make my way down the stairs but freeze in place halfway down. I glance out the enormous windows that run floor to ceiling across the front of the house, and see Lance washing Mrs. LeBlanc's gleaming white Mercedes in the driveway. Shirtless. I can't take my eyes off him no matter how hard I try. I watch as he plunges a sponge into a bucket of soapy water and scrubs the roof of the car, his ripped, tan, upper torso showing off every muscle with his slightest move. His tight jeans accentuate his cute butt, and his hair is hidden under his purple LSU baseball cap. I feel fire ignite like a small flame in the pit of my stomach, and a longing comes over me. That is the guy I'm supposed to be with. I know it with every fiber of my being.

"Enjoying the view, dear?" I'm startled by the sound of Mrs. LeBlanc's voice from behind me. I turn and look right into her eyes. She looks back at me with a sinister grin.

"I was just...I...," I stutter as I try to think of a quick lie.

"Yes, I realize what you were doing, dear." She looks back out at Lance. "Beautiful, isn't he...Yes, he will make a fine catch one day to a beautiful Louisiana girl no less..." I watch her pretend to be deep in thought, knowing she knows my feelings for him. "Now run along and find Samuel; he's been waiting for you to wake up. You know, Sunny, I'm worried about you," Mrs. LeBlanc says in a mockingly worried tone. "You sure do sleep late, and that's a sign of depression, you know. You're not depressed, are you?"

"Um... no ma'am. I do, however, need to go pack. I think Sam is taking me to stay the week with his friend Brittany in New Orleans." More like *forever*, I think to myself. This is the only thing I can think to say to get away from her. I don't want to spend one more minute around this woman.

"Oh no dear, did you forget? We are having a formal dinner for our guest of honor this evening!" She waves her hand towards the window gesturing towards Lance as her eyes gleam with adoration for him. "No, you and Sam will both be at my dinner table tonight. I wouldn't have either of you miss it for the world!!" she says with an eerie laugh, and then sweeps past me down the staircase and into the foyer. This woman is relentless. Now I know what Sam was talking about, and why she's the only one he's truly afraid of. She's like a predator in the jungle who kills for sport. I glance out the window at Lance and can't help but think that I'm in deep shit.

"Yes, Sunny, I realize you want to go to Brittany's, but there's nothing I can do about it at this point. We are eating dinner with the 'guest of honor' and that's that," Sam says with a hint of disgust in his voice as he paces back and forth in the vast rose gardens of the plantation while I sit pouting on a cement bench. "You know, we wouldn't be in this Lance Arceneaux mess if you didn't have this ridiculous obsession with him!!" Sam says Lance's name with despise. "My mother wouldn't have thought twice about him or even bid on him last night at the gala, if you would have kept your goddamned mouth shut in the first place!! She couldn't have cared less about some two-bit Cajun from Black Bayou until you gave her the perfect opportunity to play the game she's playing," Sam says exasperated, still pacing back and forth.

"But why, Sam? Why is she doing all of this? Doesn't she have something better to do than meddle with a bunch of young people's lives?" I say in a higher than normal octave. Sam stops and looks me dead in the eye.

"That's just it, Sunny; she doesn't have anything better to do," he whispers. "She has everything she wants; her life is boring. Exhibiting power makes her feel alive again. Showing everyone she is the queen is the only thing she truly enjoys, and you have given her exactly what she loves most."

I sit in silence for a minute, thinking back about what a bad idea it was to tell Mrs. LeBlanc about meeting Lance. All I could think about was getting my way and getting into that stupid gala to see him. Look at where that got me. I feel like I've been pushed in the river by this woman and swept downstream, further and further away from Lance.

"Well anyway, you wanted to be around him; you got it. It reminds me of the old saying, *be careful what you wish for...*," Sam says grinning for the first time today.

"It doesn't matter now; I'm sure he thinks I'm a total idiot after showing up in that dress last night," I say with a sigh.

"True, but in public relations they teach us that the one thing of the utmost importance is that what happened yesterday is yesterday's news. As long as you look hot tonight at dinner, Lance won't even think about that awful dress. And the only person you truly care about impressing is him, right? Besides, any publicity is good publicity, and you had everyone talking about you at the gala," Sam says with a triumphant smirk.

"Yeah, but not by choice," I say still pissed.

"Ugh, ok. Well if you're going to make it in Hollywood one day, you've got to have thicker skin than this. Let's go in and find a dress for tonight. Brittany left one that I think will be perfect. Besides, I've always dreamed of beating my mother at her own game; maybe tonight is my chance. She's done everything she can to sway Lance's opinion of you. Let's see if we can change that."

"Cocktails in the drawing room, Miss Sunny. Oh my goodness, girl, you look good! Well if I was thirty years younger and fifty pounds lighter, I'd wear that dress myself!!" Loretta, the LeBlancs' housekeeper, says to me as I stand in front of the bathroom mirror putting the final touches on my hair.

"Thank you!! Do you really think it looks ok, Loretta? Did you see the tall guy downstairs? I'm praying he likes it as much as you do," I say longingly.

"Well yes ma'am, I saw him, and I must say, he is one fine young man if you ask me!" she says wide-eyed and grinning. "You go on and break you off a piece of that!!" Loretta snaps her fingers at me, and I can't help but bust out laughing.

I take one last look in the mirror at the dress Sam has picked out for me. If I can say one thing for Sam, he knows how to dress a girl. I feel incredible. My dress is Versace, black lace, with a nude fabric underneath. The bottom is long and flowing, but still sexy and shows some leg. It's off the shoulder and has long sleeves that go all the way to my wrists. I flat-ironed my hair, sprayed on some Euphoria by Calvin Klein, and finished the look with gold heels. Sam said they looked terrible, but I thought it was a Carrie Bradshaw move. Definitely a bold statement to say the least. I look in the mirror and feel really sexy and confident. I mean business tonight. *Sunny, you can handle anything Mrs. LeBlanc throws at you; just keep your mouth shut and your head held high*, I say to myself.

I make my way through the long hallways of the mansion as Michael Buble's "Feeling Good" fills the house through the speaker system. I approach the drawing room with caution; Gerard the butler stands outside the doors in his black tux and tails. I look at him and sigh. I don't want to walk in the room, and he knows it.

"You look amazing. That's all that matters tonight. Take it in stride, Miss Sunny." He flashes me his beautiful smile, winks, and opens the doors.

I enter the room, and see Mrs. LeBlanc, Lance, and Sam standing by the bar. Sam is wearing a fitted navy blue suit with a black tie and is pouring his mother a drink. Mrs. LeBlanc is wearing a shimmering gold and black beaded mermaid dress with a flowing tail that sweeps the floor. Great, we match. Her honey blonde hair is swept up high onto her head, and long, shimmering chandelier earrings dangle from her ears. She is deep in conversation with Lance, who is wearing a black satin suit with a crisp white shirt that's open and exposes his tanned chest. I catch a glimpse of his small gold cross necklace resting on his neck. I take a deep breath as I watch him. He's as dashing as ever. Lance finally notices me from the corner of his eye, stops talking midsentence, and stares at me. His expression is hard to read, but he's a Gemini; of course he has on his poker face. As usual I have no idea what he's thinking. Although, Mrs. LeBlanc is another story; I know exactly what she's thinking because it's written all over her face. I see her eyes flash with hatred towards me and a look of jealousy because she thinks I'm young and pretty, and she thinks she isn't.

I feel sorry for Mrs. LeBlanc in this moment. If only she could see how beautiful she really is. I know women who would give anything to look like her. Hell, I would do anything to be as beautiful as she is when I'm her age, yet she is punishing me for no reason. Mrs. LeBlanc glances up at Lance, and her facial expression changes quickly. She flashes a beautiful smile as though she's just stepped out on stage to play the delightful version of herself. I realize the shit show has begun.

"Oh Sunny, dear, what a beautiful dress! Well you should have worn that to the gala instead of the one you picked out. This one is much better," Mrs. LeBlanc says in her sweet southern accent. The gloves are off; it didn't take her any time at all to throw the first jab of the night. The dress I picked out, huh? What a bitch.

"Thank you," I say, standing in the doorway awkwardly.

"You remember our guest of honor, Lance Arceneaux, don't you?" Mrs. LeBlanc asks, looking up at Lance with admiration in her eyes.

"We've met," I say looking Lance in the eye, as he looks right back at me with an unreadable expression. Mrs. LeBlanc glances at me, then up at Lance, quickly wraps her arm through his, and begins to pet him on the chest. Lance and I continue to stare at each other, and I'm lost in the moment. I love everything about this man. I only wish I knew if he felt that same strange spark I feel when we're in the same room together. Mrs. LeBlanc removes her arm from Lance's and claps her hands together loudly. She squints at me and purses her lips. She thinks I'm challenging her by staring at Lance, and I can only imagine what ridicule is coming next.

"Well, darling, from what I hear you've met soooo many male suitors since arriving in Louisiana; I just wanted to clarify," she says sweetly as she looks up at Lance out of the corner of her eye. Lance raises his eyebrows, which surprises me. He knows that's not true, yet he seems to be playing into her little game perfectly.

"Well in that case, let me introduce myself," he says calmly as he makes his way across the room and sticks out his hand. I barely shake it, as I look him in the eye for some sign of acknowledgment. I get nothing, not even a small wink. He is very formal and somewhat cold. Where is the Lance I know? Who is this guy? It must be his evil Gemini twin.

"Oh Lance, what a gentleman you are!! You were brought up right!!" Mrs. LeBlanc praises him as he turns and makes his way back towards the bar.

"Ok, well I definitely think it's time for another drink," Sam finally speaks up as he pours Grey Goose into his crystal glass, clunking ice loudly into it and splashing vodka everywhere. I feel somewhat sorry for Sam because his mother acts like he's not even in the room, but, at the same time, I can't help but think how rude he is for not offering me a drink which I could really use.

"Well Sam, where are your manners?" Mrs. LeBlanc says scolding her son. "Didn't I raise you properly? Make another drink for our guest of honor here!!" she says motioning towards Lance, as her dress sparkles in the light from the huge chandeliers that hang from the high ceilings of the sitting room.

"I wouldn't know; I was raised by my nanny," Sam mutters back as he loudly makes another drink for Lance, slamming ice into a glass and pouring Captain Morgan over it.

"Lance, don't mind him; he gets his crudeness from his father," she says winking at Lance like it's a secret between the two of them. Just then the doors open, and Gerard enters the room.

"Madam, dinner is served," he says as he steps to the side of the doors. Mrs. LeBlanc once again wraps her arm around Lance's.

"Shall we?" she says in a baby voice, looking up at Lance giving him a flirty wink. Lance escorts her through the doors as she sashays back and forth like a cat in heat.

Sam and I follow his mother and Lance out of the sitting room down several hallways to the foyer. I glance over at Sam as we walk, who looks back at me with his eyebrows furrowed. He is definitely used to saying exactly what's on his mind. We finally arrive at the main dining room which I've only seen in passing but have never been inside. Gerard opens the giant doors, and the view is breathtaking, and I feel as though I've been transported back to the 1800s. The ceilings in the room soar up two stories high and are completely covered in thousands of ornate gold fleurs-de-lis. The walls are covered in glittering red velvet patterns and enormous oil paintings of Louisiana generals, governors, and both King Louis XVI of France and his wife Marie Antoinette. Three giant chandeliers covered in gold trimming hang from the ceiling and rest over an enchanting dinner table that seats twenty-two. Down the center of the table are all sorts of intricately placed red roses with three-foot tall golden candelabras, the tops flickering with candle light.

"I, of course, will be sitting here," Mrs. LeBlanc says in her cutesy voice, as Gerard pulls out the enormous golden chair covered with blood-red satin at the head of the table. "Lance, you'll be on my right," she says smiling and gesturing to Lance as he takes his seat. "Sam, you will be here to my left," she says nonchalantly, never taking her gaze away from Lance. "…Oh and Sunny, you're over there," she says with a hint of annoyance in her voice, frivolously waving her hand in the direction of the chair on the other side of Sam.

I take my seat and look out the floor-to-ceiling windows that run the length of one wall, overlooking the giant oak trees that are lit up in the soft glow of dozens of tiny golden lights on the west side of the plantation. Wow, she has really gone all out to impress Lance. I can't even begin to imagine what her plan is, but how will her husband react to this?

"Will Mr. LeBlanc be joining us soon?" I ask politely.

"Golf game, running late as usual," Mrs. LeBlanc says as she shoots me a look of hatred. Is she trying to seduce Lance because her husband's not here? Would he ever go for her? Surely not. I feel anxiety building in the pit of my stomach. "Lance, I think you'll enjoy tonight's menu; our chef makes the best Tasso and pecan-crusted duck," Mrs. LeBlanc says brushing her finely manicured fingers over Lance's rough masculine hand. He smiles at her politely.

"I can't wait; I'm a huge fan of duck." Just then the doors open, and Gerard enters with a bottle of red wine followed by Loretta and a young maid both carrying salads.

"Jumbo lump crab and avocado salad, everyone," Mrs. LeBlanc announces. "Gerard, go ahead and pour the wine before we begin." Loretta places a salad in front of me last, and I pick up my fork to dig in.

"Thank you, Loretta, this looks amazing," I whisper looking up at her. Her eyes grow wide, and she shakes her head no at me vigorously. All of a sudden Mrs. LeBlanc slams down her fist on the dinner table.

"Sunny, this is a Christian household!!" she says exasperated, glaring at me. "We pray before we eat!!" I slowly set down my fork and sink back into my seat, not sure of how much more I can take. The point of this entire evening is for her to turn Lance against me for good while also throwing jabs at her own son, making him feel like he can never live up to her impossible expectations or to the almighty Lance Arceneaux. "Lance honey, would you mind saying the prayer?" Mrs. LeBlanc says to him in her sweet baby voice.

"Of course," he says, as everyone bows their heads. I glance over at Sam, who looks beyond fed up with this evening's events.

"Lord Jesus, as we eat, help us to remember your provision and goodness.

May this dinner be more than food to us. Let it be a time to remember your ultimate sacrifice, a time to dwell upon helping others. As we eat let us keep in mind those who are less fortunate than us and work to help those same souls with thankful hearts. Amen."

Wow. I wasn't expecting that from Lance, but then again what should I expect from a Gemini? I keep my eyes closed a second longer and say a little prayer of my own. *God, please help me through this situation. My life has been so crazy since I left home, and now I feel like I'm in over my head. Please guide me and help me make good decisions.* I open my eyes to see Sam and his mom already picking through their salads. Lance, on the other hand, is staring at me with his head cocked sideways. I quickly grab my fork and dig into the chilled crab meat on top of my salad.

"Lance, that was a beautiful prayer!" Mrs. LeBlanc says in awe.

"Thank you. My grandmother taught it to me. We always said it growing up," he says reminiscing.

"So how do you feel about next season? We've sure got some good new players this year...," Mrs. LeBlanc says, obviously bored with his talk of home life. She then trails off into a story about LSU baseball and statistics, and my mind wanders because I know nothing about sports.

"More wine, Miss Sunny?" Gerard begins to top off my glass, as Mrs. LeBlanc stops talking and glances over at me.

"Sunny, you must be enjoying the wine much more than that bottom of the barrel stuff Sam has you drinking every night in the bars." She finishes with a snicker.

"She drinks Grey Goose, Mother, and I don't have her in bars every night," Sam says as his temper grows. Mrs. LeBlanc turns to look at Lance completely ignoring Sam's outburst.

"I'm sure with your palate, you are enjoying it, Lance; we got it at a vineyard in France."

"It's delicious, Mrs. LeBlanc; thank you," he says lifting his glass to her before taking a sip.

"We Louisiana folk have a much more delicate palate than you Texans," Mrs. LeBlanc says to me, changing back to her sweet southern accent and finishing with a chuckle.

As the dinner goes on, beautiful courses of food keep arriving until finally the duck makes its grand entrance on a cart with wheels; Gerard slices up the duck and serves it to us at the table. By this point, Mrs. LeBlanc has had several glasses of wine and is starting to slur her words.

"Samuel, dear, I wish you had as much drive as Lance, here; it'd be so nice to see you do something with your life."

"Well, Mother, maybe you should have had Lance as a son," Sam says cutting into his duck breast violently.

"I just want you settle down, Sam; that's all," she says baiting him, knowing she's struck a cord and loving it. Sam drops both his knife and fork on the table loudly and slumps back into his chair. He's finally at his breaking point.

"Well, Lance, when do you plan on settling down exactly? I mean after all, you've dated more than half the girls at LSU, and I'm only a year older than you. Do you plan on settling down the second you graduate?" Sam says challenging Lance, which in all honesty isn't fair, since he's not the one looking for a fight.

"At least he's not wasting his trust fund money by scurrying all over the country in search of the next boy-toy he can sleep with," Mrs. LeBlanc says heatedly at Sam, throwing her napkin down on the table.

"Listen Sam, don't cross the line, buddy," Lance says rising up to his full height in his chair. "I go on a lot of dates because I just haven't found the right girl." I immediately look up from my plate at Lance. *I'm right in front of you*, I think to myself. "Besides that, you've been known to be quite the party animal yourself. I don't see you settling down anytime soon either," Lance says bringing up a valid point, even though I can't help but feel like Sam's under attack.

"You know what, Lance, how about you just don't worry about MY lifestyle!!!!" Sam screams at Lance from across the table, sliding to the edge of his chair.

"YOUR lifestyle!!!" Mrs. LeBlanc shouts at Sam, and then turns quickly to Lance as her dangling chandelier earrings swing around and hit her in the face. "Who on earth do you think pays for HIS lifestyle!!!"

"BACK OFF HIM!!!!" I yell as I feel my anger go through the roof, and then realize what I've just done. All three of them stop and look at me. I've just yelled at the queen of hearts… at her own dinner table. I almost expect her to yell, *off with her head!* I feel my throat closing up and my skin growing hot. What have I done? I glance at Sam, and then at Lance, who are both wide-eyed. I finally look at Mrs. LeBlanc, whose eyes are ablaze with rage. She turns and looks at Sam.

"The worst part of all is your bringing this Texas trailer trash into my home to disrespect me!" I slide my chair back behind me and abruptly stand up.

"I've had quite enough of your rudeness, Mrs. LeBlanc. I see how much you like to bully your son, but luckily, I'm not related to you. Excuse me." I can't believe the words that have come out of my mouth, but I can't sit through this any longer. I storm out of the room, my heels clicking on the cold wooden floor. Gerard swings open the giant doors, looking at me with shock and a hint of admiration as I rush past him.

I hurry towards the grand foyer, up the stairs, and into one of the guest bathrooms. The entire way I can hear Sam and his mother still going at it, and at this point they are both screaming at the top of their lungs. After wiping my face with cold water, I stare at myself in the mirror for a long time. What am I doing here? I've had several chances to go to L.A., yet I stay here and put myself through this craziness, all over a guy, a guy who after tonight will never talk to me again. I make up my mind right now that I'm leaving because there's no reason for me to stay here, not if I can't have Lance. *Maybe it just wasn't meant to be*, I think as I slowly make my way to the bathroom door. A single tear rolls down my face, thinking about being a thousand miles away from him, but I have to face the fact that nothing's going to happen. I step out of the guest bathroom, and to my surprise, Lance is leaning against the wall across the hall from me. I'm shocked. A cocky grin is spread across his face.

"Well, hello there, Miss Collins," he says playfully. "I've been waiting to get you alone all night." His green eyes burn through me intensely.

"Oh please, you might want to get her lipstick off your collar before you go back to dinner," I say rolling my eyes as I brush past him down the hallway.

With his catlike reflexes, he reaches out and grabs me before I can get out of reach and pushes me up against the wall. He presses his entire body against mine so I can't get away. I feel the length of his erection through his dress pants, and I melt inside. He places his hand on my cheek, and then runs it slowly down my face to my neck. The rough texture of his fingers brushes across my neck slowly, and then he closes his hand around my throat. His nose is close to mine, and his breathing picks up as his hand tightens, slightly choking me. The flame inside is me is not only ignited, but it bursts into flames as his hand gets tighter and tighter.

"Look at me," he says, his voice changing from playful to frightfully serious. I look into his eyes which have grown dark and are flashing wildly. *Damn it, Sunny, stay mad; he's been an asshole all evening, all week even.* I take a deep breath, and his smell is intoxicating. I'm completely disoriented by the Gemini seduction, and I realize there's no escaping him. "Follow me," he whispers in my ear in a dark tone and grabs me by the hand pulling me down the hallway. This shakes me out of my drunken state.

"What? Where are we going? Have you lost your mind?"

He continues down the hallway without answering me and swings open the master bedroom door. I look around the room in surprise. It's dimly lit; the walls are covered in black and gunmetal gray striped fur fabric. The floor is sparkling black tile and is covered with an enormous white bearskin rug. There are two white overstuffed couches facing each other with a mirrored coffee table between them. The entire wall behind the couches is mirrored, and there's a fireplace in the middle. The enormous black sleigh bed is covered with dozens of decorative pillows, some covered in black velvet and diamond-encrusted, some black and white cheetah print. Mrs. LeBlanc's black mink coat lies on top of the gray chinchilla fur comforter. The fact that this is the sexiest bedroom I have ever seen is not helping the situation. Lance reaches behind me and quietly closes the door and locks it.

"We cannot do this here," I say to him, knowing what he is about to do.

"Oh, we're doing this. Right here, right now. She's been playing games with us all day, and now it's our turn," he says in a vengeful tone as he makes his way to the bed. He picks up her long black mink and stares at it intently.

"We cannot mess that up, Lance; put it somewhere else," I say, hearing the desperation in my own voice. He turns to look at me.

"Put this on," he says to me with his head cocked sideways.

I cover my face with my hands, not even able to imagine the repercussions of what's about to happen. He walks slowly towards me and makes his way around to my back. He places his hands on my shoulders, and then, with the tips of his middle fingers, makes his way down my arms. I feel the electricity begin to sizzle through my body. He sweeps my hair to one side and brushes his cheek against my neck. He wraps his arm around me and places his hand on my stomach while pulling me backwards towards him, his massive erection pressing into me. His other hand wraps around my neck, slowly tightening. I tilt my head back, and he begins kissing me. His mouth tastes amazing. The minute he slides his tongue in my mouth, I feel flames begin to shoot through me. I take both hands and wrap them around his strong wrist, and his fingers wrap tighter and tighter around my neck.

"Do you want me to keep going, or do you still want to leave?" I open my eyes and turn to look at him.

"Now I have a choice?" I look at him in disbelief. He just stares back at me with a shit-eating grin.

"I want to hear you say it," he says seriously. I take in a deep breath. Of course it's a game; he's a Gemini. He puts the decision in my hands, so he can blame me if we get caught. Damn it. I want him so badly that I can't stand it. I go in to kiss him, but he stops me.

"No. I want to hear you say you want me. Right now. In this bed. Wearing this fur coat." His grin is absolutely seductive, but his game is infuriating.

"Fine, Lance, I want you...while wearing this fur coat...Happy?" I say exasperated. His face lights up. He's in control, and he's making me beg for it.

He reaches around and unzips my dress and slips it off me. I'm standing in just my black lace bra and panties, while he's still fully clothed. This is incredibly erotic to me. He pulls me up next to him, kissing me wildly and caressing my naked body with his hands. I begin to unbutton his shirt, and he stops me. He decides when his shirt comes off; he's running the show. Lance stops, picks up the long silky black mink coat, and slides it over my shoulders. He scoops his hands underneath me and tosses me onto the bed. My naked skin feels amazing up against the soft fur coat. He climbs on top of me, and I feel his full weight press down on me. I feel safe underneath him, protected. He licks my neck, and then bites into my flesh, which makes me come up off the bed in ecstasy. This makes him bite me even harder, and I writhe underneath him uncontrollably. He takes both of my hands and presses them to the bed under his so I can't move them, and then places both of his knees in between mine, spreading my legs wide open. I'm pinned to the bed and can't move. He presses his erection against me, down there, and slowly begins to grind into me, faster and faster. Every time he grinds his hips, I feel him press deeper into me. I want his pants off now. I want to touch his naked muscular torso. The thought of this is driving me beyond crazy, and I do everything I can to wiggle out of his grasp. He looks at me and grins, knowing I'm no match for his strength. He's teasing me by keeping his clothes on, and he knows it. He releases my hands, and then starts to make his way down my breasts and stomach with his tongue. He stops at my pelvis and kisses the inside of my thigh slowly. I'm praying he keeps going, or else I'm going to burst. Just then I feel his middle finger slip inside of me, slowly at first, then faster and faster. I look into his eyes and see them flash. He is enjoying this as much as I am. Then his tongue slides into me, and I come up off the bed, clutching the fur in my hands. He takes both of his hands and wraps them around my legs so I can't move, as his tongue goes deeper and deeper inside me. He knows exactly what he's doing, and he's amazing at it. I tilt my head back and feel the fire that Lance Arceneaux is creating run through me from down below. The silky texture of the black mink is all around me as I clench it with both of my fists; then out of nowhere I hear screaming again.

"LANCE, WHERE ARE YOU?" Lance jumps up off the bed and looks at me in a panic.

"Where is the yelling coming from?" I look up at him in fear. He walks closer to the bedroom door and bends down.

"It's coming from this floor vent; she must be heading up the stairs. Shit." Lance begins to pace back and forth, and my heart is beating out of my chest. "Ok, Sunny, get under the bed."

"What??" I hiss back at him.

"Now!!" he yells in a whisper, his eyes wide with fear and anger. I scurry off the bed and climb under it as fast as possible, just in time to see the bedroom door swing open, and Mrs. LeBlanc storms into the room.

"What on earth are you doing in my bedroom?" she says exasperated.

"I'm sorry; Sunny was in the guest bathroom, so I came in here to use yours. I'm sure you don't mind...," Lance says, and even though I can't see him, I know he is seducing Mrs. LeBlanc with his sexy voice and a seductive look. This pisses me off.

"Well... of course I don't mind, dear. You are welcome in this room, anytime." Oh, you have to be kidding me! There is no line this woman won't cross.

"Ok, well, I'll keep that in mind, Lynne." Great, now he is using her first name. "Shall we head back down to the sitting room? I would love another cocktail and then maybe a swing around the dance floor with Baton Rouge's sexiest lady." Lance says to her, as I do everything I can not to scream in protest.

"Well, that sounds like the end to a perfect evening to me!!" she says, squealing in delight. "Just one moment, let me grab my mink from the floor. However did it get down here?" I feel terror rush over me like I've been hit with ice water. I'm lying on top of the mink!

"Uh no, I'll get it!!" Lance yells, and then his face appears under the bed. He swiftly lifts me up, pulling the coat out from under me. "Shall we?" I watch as the two of them exit the room arm in arm. *FML*, I think to myself.

After about ten minutes, I figure the coast is clear, so I climb out from under the bed and dust myself off. Still a little shaky and afraid of getting caught, I slowly open the door and peer out into the hallway. Coast is clear. For now. I run as fast as I can to Sam's room. The door is locked, and Beyoncé is blasting inside. He's obviously still pissed, so I decide not to knock. I get to my room unnoticed and change into my pajamas. I climb into bed and turn off my bed side lamp, close my eyes, and pray I can fall asleep. As I lie in the dark, tonight's events flash through my mind. Seeing Lance in his black satin suit, his cold demeanor as he introduced himself, listening to him lead the prayer, and finding him waiting outside the bathroom door. The feeling of the mink up against my naked skin. My eyes pop open. Lance grinding into me. I jerk the covers off me. The thought of him biting into my thigh. I jump up out of bed. It's still too vivid in my mind. I race to the door and head out into the hallway. Anxiety runs through me. I panic and run down the long corridor towards the back part of the mansion. The thought of Lance being somewhere in this enormous house with Mrs. LeBlanc's hands all over him sends me over the edge. I find the servants' staircase that leads to the kitchens and race down them. The kitchen is dark as I run through it towards the doors that lead out back. I open the doors, and the entire grounds are lit up with sparkling lights as far as the eye can see. The gentle breeze blows my hair to one side as I run out onto the veranda. I head down the steps and keep running until I get to the rose gardens.

As I make my way past the thousands of beautiful flowers, I feel a tear run down my face, then another, and then another. How am I supposed to feel? How do I know if I'm making the right decision when it comes to Lance? Momma always said trust your gut instinct, it will never guide you wrong, but I feel so confused. I get to the giant gazebo in the middle of the gardens which is lit up beautifully and has roses growing all over it. I take a seat and go over tonight's events again in my mind. Just then, music begins to play. I don't recognize it, but it's slow and seductive. I look around and realize there are speakers throughout the grounds. Who turned on the music? I peer through the distance and can make out a figure heading down the stairs towards the garden. As the figure gets closer and closer, I realize it's Lance. He walks towards me with a frightening look of determination on his face; his stride is fast and forceful. A man on a mission. Without saying a word, he grabs me by the hand, pulls me up into his embrace, and kisses me wildly. I feel showers of sparks all around me. Lightning flashes through the sky, through me, through him. I feel like I'm on the world's most terrifying roller coaster, never knowing what's going to happen next. Lance ends our kiss with a gentle bite on my bottom lip. I open my eyes and look up at him, as we both sway back and forth to the music. He looks down at me with desire, his green eyes lit up by the sparkling lights of the garden. He cocks his head sideways and stares at me curiously, as though it's his first time ever seeing me.

"You know, you have the bluest eyes I've ever seen on a person. Not blue like the sky, but deeper blue, like the Caribbean," he says, looking at me intently. I'm not sure what to say, so I say nothing at all. He seems to be in a strange mood, examining me in a weird way like he's making a decision.

"Where is Mrs. LeBlanc?" I can't help but ask. A smile flashes across his face.

"It only took one more drink for her to pass out. I escorted her to her room," I quickly look up at him, searching for a sign he's kidding. "Don't worry; I just helped her into bed. I knocked on your bedroom door only to discover you weren't there. Luckily I saw you out the window...I won't even ask why you were running."

"Good," I answer back, not wanting to tell him I was having an anxiety attack and convinced myself he was going to get it on with Sam's mother.

"Walk with me," he says gently.

I put my hand in his and follow him back through the grounds and into the kitchens. I wonder if we are we going back upstairs to finish what we started. God I hope so. Lance says nothing as we make our way through the long hallways to the grand foyer. I turn to head up the stairs, and he pulls me back.

"I have to go," he states matter-of-factly.

"But..."

"No, Sunny. Walk me out," he says, stopping me before I can protest.

I follow him out the front door and onto the porch. He reaches down and kisses me on the neck, behind my ear, and finally he presses his lips softly against mine. A shudder runs down my spine with his every touch. I can't believe he's leaving. He takes a single finger and brushes my neck, and whispers into my ear, "You know, they say the strongest drug for a human being is another human being..." I open my eyes and look up at him in disbelief. Does he feel that way about me? Does he know that's how I feel about him? I'm always left with so many questions!!! The further this goes, the more confusing it gets. He takes one last look at me and heads down the steps towards his truck. I sit down on the top step and watch his truck until he pulls out of the mansion's gates and speeds away. There's no way I'm getting any sleep now.

CHAPTER ELEVEN
Black Bayou

BRITTANY AND I spend a lot of time watching movies like *Showgirls* and *Strip Tease* to prepare me for the large audiences at work at the Circus. We also spend several hours a day learning how to work the pole and memorizing the vigorous dance routines that the girls perform. Sam, Brittany, and I devise a plan to keep Lance from finding out what I was really doing, so I only work at the Circus on the same nights that Lance bar tends at Gator Bar in Baton Rouge. We tell Lance I am cocktail waitressing with Brittany at an upscale restaurant in the French Quarter, and he seems to be pleased with the idea.

During the week, Lance attends classes at LSU, and I stay with him at his apartment. I learn quickly that he has a very serious nature about him. People in Baton Rouge don't mess with him, and he commands respect. He is able to control any room he's in with the tone of his voice or even a look. He also has a playful side that most people don't know about, but I only see it when he lets his walls down a bit. I begin to learn very quickly that Lance does not tolerate bullshit. He is unyielding, which is hard for me considering I'm good at making bad choices sometimes. I'm constantly afraid that he will find out I'm working at the Circus; I don't want everything I've worked for to go up in flames.

When we hang out, he always has something new and exciting planned for us. He takes me to places like Six Flags Dixie Land, alligator tours in the swamps, the beautiful Louisiana governor's mansion, and the Oak Alley plantation. One of my favorite things to do is visit Mike the Tiger, who resides in an outdoor glass habitat right outside Tiger Stadium. When I'm in Baton Rouge, I bring Lance lunch at school when he's working on projects. It's so exciting to visit the LSU campus and see what college life looks like. Not to mention, we find broom closets or lock ourselves in empty classrooms to make out because we can't keep our hands off each other. Watching Lance work on his school projects is pretty impressive. When he's focusing on his school work, nothing else matters. Not even me. He's intent on getting the job done, and he's actually very smart and creative. He's definitely not a dumb baseball player who talks girls into doing his projects for him. When he comes to see me in New Orleans, he takes me on little adventures, and I'm never bored with him. We go on the haunted city tour, which tells of legends about vampires and ghosts who have inhabited the city for hundreds of years, or the New Orleans Aquarium which is amazing. He really enjoys showing me Louisiana's historic places, and I'm always very surprised how much he knows about the history of his state.

I eventually make enough money to get a car, a white Mustang convertible which has been a dream of mine for a while. Ever since the first day I rode in one at Cleburne High School, I have wanted one so badly, and I am finally able to come up with the money to get it. I hate lying, but I tell Lance that my aunt in Texas sent me some money for a down payment. I am able to pay cash for the car after only a month of working at the Circus; one of my regulars gave me five grand to put down on it.

IT'S A CHILLY FALL afternoon as I make my way down Nicholson Drive, and I see Tiger Stadium in the distance. Even when it's empty, I feel like I can hear the roar of the crowd. When I get to the LSU baseball complex parking lot, I glance around quickly hoping Lance won't be anywhere in sight. I had mentioned the other day that I wanted to come watch him practice, and although he didn't say no, he didn't exactly looked thrilled by the idea. I can just imagine how hot he looks in his baseball uniform, and I want to see it for myself, even if it's only for a moment. I park my car far away from all of the players' cars that are parked close to the entrance. I put on an old ball cap and sunglasses, and then head cautiously towards the entrance. The place is as dead as a ghost town, but I can hear voices coming from the field. I creep through the hallway until I get to the seats and make my way up the steps. I see all the boys warming up in their practice gear, and I realize I don't even know Lance's jersey number. Even though I'm almost sure he is the tallest, I still can't see because I'm too far away, and I can't be obvious without getting caught. Damn. I'm gonna have to get closer. I head back down the stairs and make my way to the first level of seats closest to the field. Just one look and I'll leave. There's no way I'm gonna get caught. I turn and see a small hallway that leads out to the seats closest to the field; I slowly make my way in that direction, just enough so I will be able to peek out. I search the field for what seems like an eternity, watching guys run back and forth, but I don't see Lance anywhere. I take a deep breath and realize it's time to go. I normally wouldn't give up so easily, but I don't want to risk it. I turn around to leave and *bam*!! I run right into a guy's chest, and my sunglasses smash into my face. I look up and gasp.

"Well, well, well, look who it is." Chad Beauregard looks down at me with a smirk on his face, his arms crossed.

"Chad...I...What's up?" I say a little too chipper, not sure how I'm going to lie my way out of this.

"And just what are you doing Miss Collins? Come to watch me play?" he asks with a raised eyebrow.

"Um, no... Brittany...um... asked me to meet her here. She was going to drop in and watch you guys practice. She told me to meet her," I say trying my best to sound convincing.

"Is that so? Well, where is she then?" he questions, looking at me curiously.

"That's a good question! If you'll excuse, me I'm gonna go find that crazy girl right now!!" I say as I breeze past Chad and back down the hallway.

"He's sick with the flu, you know; that's why he's not at practice today... Funny that you two are so close, and he didn't bother to tell you that," Chad says as I stop dead in my tracks. "Hope you know what you're in for with him, Sunny. And by the way, he hasn't ever let any of the other girls come to watch him practice. I wouldn't try this little stunt again if I were you," Chad says from behind me.

As much as I would love to turn around and chew him out, I start walking slowly, and then faster and faster until I'm finally back to my car. I get in, take a deep breath, and sit back in my seat. What an asshole Chad is. The other girls? I'm not just some other girl. I belong with Lance, and I'm going to prove it.

"Ha!" I say out loud. I know exactly how to start. I need to show him how much I truly care about him.

I put my Mustang in drive and peel out of the baseball complex. Ten minutes later, I walk into Whole Foods, find a shopping cart, and begin to load up. I find the best of everything to make turkey sandwiches, choosing only organic foods. I know how much he loves turkey. I grab two bottles of everything down the water aisle: Pellegrino, Fiji, Evian, and Perrier. I head to the pastries section and grab six different slices of cheese cake, not knowing which one he will be in the mood for. Next up is the sushi counter; I get one of everything. Lance loves sushi. Oh and soup, he'll need chicken noodle and lobster bisque. This goes on and on as I make my way through the grocery aisles. When I finally get to the checkout, I realize I might have gone overboard. The sales girl tells me the bill is two hundred twenty five dollars. Oh well, he's sick, and I have a point to prove. On the way to his house, I stop and grab flu medicine that will help him sleep and a couple of movies.

As I make my way towards Lance's house, I am pretty impressed with myself. I smile and think how brilliant my plan is. When I pull up, I see his truck parked in front. I get out and carry everything to the front porch and set it down, and then ring the doorbell. After a couple of minutes of waiting, I walk over and try to peer into the windows. Nothing. No sign of him. He must be upstairs. I look up at his balcony that leads to his bedroom on the second floor. There's only one option. I grab ahold of the branch of the magnolia tree next to the front porch and begin to climb my way up. I finally get up high enough to where I can grab the railing. I jump, but unfortunately, I'm not close enough, and I slam into the side of the balcony, and I'm barely able to hold on. I use all my strength to pull myself up and over, and then I tumble onto the wooden floor of his balcony. I get up and brush myself off and peer through the glass door.

Lance's room is a mess, and his bed is empty. What the hell? His truck is here; where is he? I reach down and turn the handle which of course is locked. Why would he lock this door? Who on earth is going to climb up here? Oh. Well, it is different when I do it. I climb back over the ledge, but this time I grab the column and slide down. I stand on the front porch looking around, thinking what to do next. Rain clouds slowly begin to move in from the east, blocking what's left of the afternoon sun. Just then, an idea hits me. Those three Golden Girls who Brittany introduced me to at Chad's party live across the street, and they seemed sweet. I wonder if they can help me. I head across the street and quietly knock on the door, hoping this is a good plan. After a minute or so, Andrea opens the door wearing LSU workout clothes.

"Hi there! Wait, where do I know you from?" she asks looking at me curiously.

"Hi, my name's Sunny; I actually met you at Chad Beauregard's party," I say to her feeling a bit nervous.

"Oh, that's right… you were with Brittany Laveau! Well what's up?"

"Ok, so I know this is going to sound super weird, but I heard that Lance across the street is sick, so I bought a bunch of groceries for him, and now I can't get him to answer the door…I know you girls are friends with him, so I thought maybe you could help me."

"Oh my god, that is so sweet!! Meagan! Alex! Come here!!" Andrea turns and yells into the house. A couple seconds later the two girls appear at the door.

"What's up?" Alex says looking at Andrea then at me.

"This is Sunny, Brittany's friend who we met at Chad's party…She heard Lance was sick, and she brought him a bunch of food. How sweet is that?"

"Well that's a relief; his mom called this morning and told me he had the flu and asked me to go check on him, but I had practice and didn't have time," Meagan chimes in still wearing her Golden Girl outfit.

"Oh wow, I didn't realize how close knit y'all are with Lance," I say taken aback.

"Yeah, we all kind of stick together around here; all of our families know each other pretty well," Meagan says with a smile.

"Wait," Alex says looking at me suspiciously. "It's clear how all of us know Lance, but what's unclear is how you know him…Why are you bringing him stuff when he's sick? Didn't you just move to Louisiana?" Oh shit. I can't say I'm his girlfriend, but I can't look like an idiot either.

"Well...We...," I say looking around nervously.

"Wait are you guys dating?? How does the whole town not already know this?" Andrea says to me gleefully.

"No... no... It's still kind of new. We've just been hanging out, and I wanted to do something nice for him. I...never mind, I'm just gonna go," I say getting flustered and feeling like I've just opened a can of worms.

"No, wait!!! I know where his spare key is; his mom told me it's under a rock next to his porch!!" Meagan yells excitedly.

"Aww... I think it's really sweet that you're doing this for him!!" Andrea says longingly.

"Well, I think it's a dumb idea," Alex says, as the other two turn and look at her.

"Alex!!" Meagan yells scolding her.

"What?" Alex says looking back at them. "I mean, clearly, she doesn't know Lance at all; he won't appreciate what she's doing," Alex says, looks me up and down, and then storms back inside the house.

"Just ignore her, Sunny; she dated him for a couple weeks our freshman year and...Let's just say it didn't work out. She never got over him," Andrea whispers to me.

"Oh, ok...That makes sense," I say, ready to leave.

"Ok, well good luck, and I'm glad we could help!" Meagan says changing the subject. "Go get the key and surprise him!"

"Ok. Thank you, girls, I really appreciate your help," I say to them as I turn to walk back across the street.

"Hey, next time we have a party, you and Brittany better come!!" Andrea yells. I turn and wave to at them, grateful for their help.

My plan is working out perfectly. I get all of the groceries from the trunk, find the rock with the key hidden under it, unlock the door, and tiptoe in quietly. As I make my way through the living room, I freeze in place. There on the couch wrapped up in a blanket is Lance snoring away.

All six foot four of him. His feet hang off the end of the couch; he's so tall. Even when he's sick as a dog, he still looks as beautiful as ever. I take all of the food to the kitchen and get it unpacked. I spend half an hour making sandwiches, cutting up fruit, and setting up everything beautifully so that when he wakes, it will all be ready for him. Thank god for the Circus; I would never have been able to afford all of this without my new job. I find a piece of paper and a Sharpie and write him a sweet note:

Hey Lance,
Heard you were sick and wanted to bring you some food, medicine, and a couple of movies.
Get well soon,
Sunny.

I place the note on the door of the fridge and head towards the living room. I tiptoe to the front door, and then turn to look at him. He is going to be so impressed that I did this. I hope he understands how much I care about him, even if he is difficult, confusing, unpredictable…and just amazing; I smile to myself.

"What do you mean you climbed over the balcony??" Sam yells at me in the highest pitched voice I've ever heard him use.

"I'm not done with the story, Sam; will you just let me finish? So anyway, I walked across the street and talked to those Golden Girls, and…"

"Oh my god. Stop right there," Sam says bewildered. He puts his face in his hands and says nothing for a couple of minutes. I look around his bedroom annoyed, not sure why he won't just let me finish telling him what I did and how clever I am.

"Sunny. Do you just not realize how bad of an idea that was? Do you really think that he is not going to blow a gasket when he wakes up and realizes you climbed up his balcony, conned his neighbors, then creeped around his house while he was asleep?" he says this with as much patience as he can muster.

"Well...no...why would he?" I say honestly, trying to imagine Lance furious.

"Sunny, you told me you were sneaking into the baseball complex to see him in his uniform. I told you that wasn't a good idea. Why on earth you thought this was an even better plan is beyond me," Sam says this in a whisper, and now I'm starting to worry. The more I think about it, the more I realize I did it because I wanted to prove something. I wanted to prove Chad Beauregard wrong. I wanted to show Lance I'm not just another girl like all the rest.

"Sam, I left the front door unlocked. Would you mind going over there with me so I can grab the stuff and just pretend this never happened?" We look at each other for a moment; then both of us jump up at the same time and haul ass down stairs and out the front door of the LeBlanc mansion.

As soon as we get to the end of Lance's street, I slam on the brakes. Sam and I stare at what's in front of us in horror. There in the front yard is Lance wearing sweats and looking pissed as Alex animatedly tells him, I'm sure, our entire conversation, while Andrea and Meagan stand behind her nervously.

"Oh. Shit," Sam says horrified. We watch as Lance turns and walks back into the house and slams the front door. I look at Sam who is looking out the window. "Sunny, I don't even know how to get you out of this one. I mean, my mind is running ninety miles an hour trying to think of what to do, and all I can think is that you're just going to have to face the music."

I feel chills go down my spine just as my phone vibrates in my pocket. It's buzzing even more violently than normal. I pull it out and show the screen to Sam. *Lance Arceneaux calling.*

"Answer the damn thing and get it over with!!!" Sam yells at me. I answer and hit speaker phone.

"Hello," I say hesitantly barely able to get on word out while looking at Sam.

"So…let me get this straight," Lance says in a deadly tone, and then takes a deep breathe. "You showed up at baseball practice after I asked you not to…Then you buy all these groceries and convince my neighbors to tell you how to get into my house…Then you make a huge mess in my kitchen and leave a sink full of dirty dishes for me to clean up…All while I'm sick with the flu and sound asleep…Sunny…Please tell me, what part of this was a good idea?" he says, trying his best to keep his voice steady.

"Well…I…I just thought…the Golden Girls said it was a good idea." It's the only thing I can think of to say.

"We will talk about this later…I'm going back to bed." There's a long pause but he doesn't hang up. "…By the way…I enjoyed the cheesecake." *Click*. He hangs up without another word. I slowly turn to look at Sam who is staring back at me.

"Well…at least he liked the cheesecake…," I say, covering my mouth and trying not to laugh.

"You know, sometimes I wonder what on earth goes on in your head, Sunny," Sam says as he takes a deep breath and rubs his forehead. "Now drive me home. I need a Xanax after that."

As the days and months go by, I try my hardest not to do anything else to piss off Lance. Brittany and Sam both make me swear to run my bright ideas past them first before I make a move concerning the Gemini. Today I woke up early thinking about Momma and home and decide to write her a quick note about my time in Louisiana and send her some extra spending money.

Dear Momma,

Things are crazy here in Louisiana. I've seen things I never could have imagined. Walking down the street in the French Quarter is an adventure in itself. There are drag queens, midgets, psychics, and even a blind man who is led by a parrot on a leash. I also met someone amazing, and I think I'm in love with him, Momma. His name is Lance, and he plays baseball at Louisiana State University. I can't tell you how amazing he is and how wonderful I feel when I'm with him. He's six foot four and a Gemini. I try not to hold that against him. Lol. Hopefully you will meet him someday. I'm enclosing a picture of us standing on Bourbon Street. I've also enclosed a thousand dollars for you. Don't worry about me; I have plenty of money saved up, almost enough to head to L.A. I love you more than anyone else in the world. Please take care of yourself.

Love,

Sunny

Lance calls me early in the morning and says he wants to take me somewhere, and it's a surprise. Excitedly I make the long drive from Brittany's apartment in New Orleans to Lance's in Baton Rouge. When I get to his apartment, he is waiting for me outside dressed in his signature style: purple and green plaid shirt with his sleeves rolled up, khaki shorts, Ralph Lauren boat shoes, and his LSU baseball cap. When I walk up to him, he smells amazing.

"You ready for some fun today?" He grins at me with a shifty smile on his face.

"Why won't you tell me where we're going? You're being a shifty Gemini, and I don't like it."

"You just don't worry about it...You look really nice; did you bring an overnight bag like I asked?"

"Yes, Lance, of course I did; I just want you to know it's hard for a girl to pack when she doesn't know where she's going."

"Alright get in; we gotta get on the road. I hope you're hungry. And what is it with you and Geminis? Don't you know we're the best sign of 'em all!!'"

"Louisiana people are freakin' crazy...," I mouth off at him as I stare out the window shaking my head.

"Yeah, no shit, and I'm the ringleader of them all..." I slowly turn to look at him, and I see the cocky grin on his face.

I shudder in my seat. He can't know; there's no way. If I know anything about this man, I know one thing: my working at the Circus would not be a laughing matter. He turns on the truck, and immediately the radio starts blasting the song, "I'm in love with a stripper" by T-Pain. I am mortified and sink back into my seat as Lance starts singing along and doing little dance moves. The irony of this moment is astonishing.

Almost two hours later we arrive in Black Bayou, Louisiana in Cameron Parish. Louisiana has parishes not counties, and I have to continuously remind myself of this. We drive another thirty minutes south of town and end up on a long gravel road which leads to a nice little house sitting on a lake; there are fifteen to twenty cars parked up and down the driveway.

"Whose house is this?" I ask him.

"C'mon, no time for questions," he says matter-of-factly as he steps out of his truck.

We get to the front door, and Lance opens it and walks in. *How rude, he didn't even knock*, I think to myself. As we make our way through the house, I hear voices out back and jazz music playing. I look at the pictures on the walls as we pass them, and sheer terror comes over me. I see Lance as a kid, Lance as a teenager, and Lance in his LSU baseball uniform. He has brought me home to meet his parents and has given me no warning, no time to think about what I'm going to say, and no time to think about how to make a good impression. Meeting his parents won't even be the worst of it; I bet you anything his Maw Maw will be here. *She's my heart and soul, and means more to me than anyone else in the world*, I remember him saying at our first dinner so long ago at Tsunami. This, of course, terrifies me. Look at what I'm wearing!! Why would he do this to me? I know why he's doing it; it's another test. This is how he works. I always have to prepare to be tested by him. It can't ever just be easy. This isn't just any test though, this is freaking huge! Shit...ok, he wants to play this game? Let's play. It's sink-or-swim time.

We get to the backyard, and there are cousins, aunts, uncles, church members, and even the postman sitting at wooden picnic tables covered in red and white plastic tablecloths, and twinkling steel lanterns are strung through the air. The whole scene reminds me of *Steel Magnolias,* a real southern bayou party.

"That's my Uncle Jett's band over there." Lance points to the group of men who are playing a trombone, a trumpet, and a guitar; his uncle, who is the lead singer, has a tambourine, and there's even a fiddle player, all set up on a small stage in the corner. I recognize one of Momma's favorite songs, "When the Saints Go Marching In." We make our way through the crowd greeting people until we finally get to his mom and dad.

"Sunny, this is my momma and daddy, Connie and Jim Bob Arceneaux."

"Hi, it's so nice to meet you; I had no idea we were coming here or I would have brought food!" I try to say as upbeat as I can to his mother who is a sweet middle-aged woman wearing an apron with little alligators all over it that matches her husband's.

"Oh, don't worry about it!! We just glad ya here, girl! We was so excited when Lance said he was bringin' a girl home for the first time; we couldn't stand it!! Oh don't shake my hand, young'un, get over and give me a hug!!!" she yells as she grabs me and gives me one of the best hugs ever. She smells sweet like honeysuckle and is very warm and inviting. Wait, I'm the first girl he's brought home? Sam told me he usually dates LSU cheerleaders and sorority girls. I really hope the reason I'm the first girl to come home with him is because he really trusts me. If that's the case, I'm the first girl he really trusts, and I'm lying to him. That's great. Just freaking great.

"Hey there, Sunny. I'm Jim Bob, Lance's Daddy. I hope you hungry cuz we got plenty to eat!!" He waves at me from behind a huge tub of something boiling that smells spicy, and he's wearing a tall white chef's hat. Connie and Jim Bob both have adorable Cajun accents.

"Hi, nice to meet you!! What is that you're cooking?" I ask. Everyone starts laughing when I say this, and I have no clue why it's funny.

"Sunny, this is a crawfish boil. I forgot that you don't know about these things. It's where family and friends get together and celebrate," Lance explains to me.

"Ok, Lance, your Maw Maw's over there with her friends, and she's been waiting on you to get here all day," his mom says. I feel my heart sink to the pit of my stomach. Oh my god, what if she hates me? Lance turns to walk through the crowd, and I glance over at his mom in fear. She winks at me and grabs my hand and puts it in hers.

"Don't worry, baby; she's tough, but she's fair...Just be yourself!!" She gives me a little pat on the butt and scoots me through the crowd towards Lance. He's not hard to find since he towers over everyone else in the yard. I make my way to his backside, peek around him, and there sits Maw Maw. She's a tiny woman with long white hair, and glasses, and she's wearing her LSU baseball cap with pride, Coke in one hand, cigarette in the other.

"Well look who decided to join us!" she says to me with the same sarcastic tone that Lance normally has.

"Well, now we know where Lance gets it." I can't believe I just said that. She hates me.

"Well, well, well!!! She's got a little sassiness to her!! Thank heaven!!" she quips. I can't help but giggle. I look up at Lance who rolls his eyes, and then they begin to gang up on me. Maw Maw laughs at what I'm wearing, makes fun of Texans, and even makes a blonde joke. Lance is egging her on the whole time. I try my best to come back at them, but I have nothing.

A little while later, Lance's mom comes up and whispers in my ear.

"Trust me, ya passed. You wouldn't still be standing here if she didn't like ya, and you wouldn't be here at all if he didn't...Imagine how often they team up on me!"

"Thank you, you're my new best friend," I whisper back.

After all the food is ready, they put newspaper down on the tables, which I find odd, and Lance's dad starts dumping food on the newspaper and people begin to dig in, sucking the brains out of these little guys and eating their tails. I have to admit, I only tried the crawfish to impress Lance, but they taste unbelievable. The crawfish boil consists of crawfish, new potatoes, corn on the cob, sausage, and spices. I can't even begin to explain how amazing all of it tastes. There's a long table on the back porch with even more food on it, and Lance tells me that most of the dishes are traditional Louisiana recipes that go back in his family for many years. There's seafood gumbo, jambalaya, alligator, frog legs, crawfish étouffée, deer sausage, dirty rice, and a turdukin, which is a turkey stuffed with a chicken stuffed with a duck. Yes, this a real thing!! I laugh to myself.

After everyone is stuffed, the afternoon becomes evening, and the party rolls on until around 10 p.m. Lance and I have several Abita beers before we head inside and call it a night. I lie in his bed waiting for him to take a shower and look around his old room trying to imagine him as a kid growing up here and how nice it must have been to have a good man for a father who treated his wife and kids well.

"Hey, babe, whatcha doin'?" He walks in wearing only a towel and his small gold cross necklace that glistens on his tanned chest. He leans his arm on the wall and looks at me with his smoldering eyes. His body is so ripped, and his deep Cajun tan is gorgeous. "Maw Maw won't stop talking about you, and she said you better keep your promise to come over and help her redecorate her house. I told her at least you were good for something," he says in his usual tone, then looks at me and winks. I feel myself turning red and give him a small smile.

"I've been sitting here looking at all your old baseball trophies...How was your shower?" I feel a little tipsy from the beer.

"It was good. Get up; I wanna show you something." Lance puts on a pair of basketball shorts, and I follow him out the front door.

As we walk around the side of the house, I hear the band playing a slow sexy jazz set on the other side of the fence. I look up at the full moon and think how much brighter the stars are out here in the country. We head towards the lake where there's a long dock with a small boat house at the end. Lance grabs my hand and pulls me close to him.

"C'mon, we're not there yet."

The warm wood feels nice on my bare feet as we enter the boathouse. I'm surprised to see a bed made up and hundreds of glowing candles lit all around the room. Lance walks over to the bed and sits down. He looks out the window for a minute, and then looks at me like he is just realizing I'm here.

"Sunny...I used to sit in the boathouse for hours as a kid, dreaming of finding a certain kind of girl one day. It's something I wanted more than anything. A girl I really feel something for, a girl who understands me. I had this image in my head for so many years. When I moved to Baton Rouge, I thought for sure I would find her. I'll be honest; I've taken dozens, maybe hundreds of girls on dates." This isn't great to hear; I feel a tinge of jealousy, and the look on his face is so hard to read. He's a little boy lost, meets a man searching for an answer. Where is this going? "I had gotten to the point where I had given up. The same day, I met you actually. I was done. I went out that night to drink and forget about it. Forget everything. Then, I look across the room and see you. You're exactly who I've always been looking for. You're perfect to me. I don't have to pretend to be something I'm not with you."

He looks at me longingly, and then that look suddenly changes to dark and brooding. I don't know what to say, so I just stand in place awkwardly directly across from him. He pauses for what seems like an eternity. Everything suddenly goes into slow motion. He motions to me with two fingers to come towards him. I do, and he leans back and pulls me into his lap so that I'm straddling him. I look into his eyes; they are ablaze with fire. I feel the heat radiating off him. His face is dark and serious. The candlelight around the room flickers as the shadows dance along the walls. Lance smells incredible, and it's intoxicating. I press my hands on his bare chest and feel his hard muscles. This makes me want to touch him everywhere. I run my hands across his neck bone, his shoulders, and down his bulging arms to his wrists. He watches me patiently, like a lion watches his prey. I lean into his neck cautiously, brushing his cheek with mine. His scruff sends chills down my spine. I take in a deep breath, and his amazing smell lights me on fire.

I feel a searing heat run through my veins. He closes his eyes and slowly tilts his head sideways, and I know I have permission to keep going. I bite into his neck, and it's ecstasy. I can't get enough of the way he tastes, so I make my way around his neck, biting and licking him, as I feel his body shudder. He says nothing, but I know he enjoys it or he would stop me.

I feel his hand run up my side and up the back of my shirt, which he pulls over my head and pitches on the floor. It's his move now. Checkmate. He's always in control, and his moves are always calculated, apparently even in bed. The anticipation of what he will do next turns me on like nothing else. Without taking his gleaming eyes off me, he wraps his massive arms around me and flips me over onto my back. Excitement surges through me. He leans back onto his knees, rising to his full height, my legs wrapped around the back of his. He looks down at me, his eyes flashing dangerously, and the light from the candles dance across his tanned chest, his small golden cross gleaming. He wraps his hand around my neck, slightly choking me. I love it. He's showing his dominance over me. He releases my neck and places the tips of his fingers on the small of my neck. He runs his hand slowly down the length of my body until he reaches my panties. He reaches inside the cusp, takes his other hand, and *snap*; he rips them in two and throws them on the floor, never taking his eyes off me. I try to sit up thinking it's my move. I can't wait any longer; I want him now. He grabs both my hands and slams them back onto the bed. I feel his full weight press up against me. I feel so small and helpless underneath him. I love it. He has complete control over me. Apparently, it's still his move. The pressure of his hips pushes into me making my legs tighten around him. He leans back, watching me so I don't try to move again, and slides off his basketball shorts and tosses them on the floor. His naked body is ripped and glistening in the Louisiana heat. He looks incredible, like a Greek god seducing me. The fact that he's made me wait this long to have sex is driving me crazy, but we both know this is his rodeo, not mine. He's calling the shots, and I'm at his mercy. He takes each of my legs in his massive hands and presses his lips against my thigh, kissing me gently, and running his tongue dangerously across my skin. I've been good. I've been patient. And he finally gives me my reward. I feel him slide slowly inside me, teasing me, and then he slams all the way in. I gasp in pain because he's so big, and he's so deep inside.

"Shhh...," he whispers.

The pain goes away, and eventually it feels incredible. He pulls me close up to him so that I'm wrapped around him, and we both begin to find our rhythm with each other; my whole body shutters as he slides in deeply and out. The music from the jazz band fades away, and I begin to hear a symphony playing so loud it could fill Tiger Stadium. But not just any symphony, the music is dark and seductive, a temptress seducing both of us beyond belief...I'm entranced and so is Lance. For the first time, I see him lose control, and we both let the fire between us take over. His breathing is heavy, and mine matches his. We are in sync. He looks into my eyes, and I'm lost in his. The explosions go off all around us. I hear the shattering of glass. The light around the room gets brighter, and the fire begins to run up the walls until the entire room is set ablaze, and the electricity between us is creating it. I reach around to the back of his head running my fingers through his soft beautiful hair and pull it hard as I feel my entire body begin to explode all around him. I feel him explode deeply inside me as he lets out a deep moan. It's pure ecstasy.

"Sunny!!! Sunny!! Open your eyes!!!" Lance booms at me. I open my eyes and sheer terror and disbelief wrack through me. The boat house has actually caught fire. Lance grabs his shorts and throws my clothes to me. He runs to the door, but it's already too hot to open. "Get your clothes on; we're going out the window," he yells to me over the roar of the flames. I do what he says while I watch him grab a chair and smash the window that faces the lake. I barely get my shirt and shorts on when he grabs me and pitches me out of the window and into the murky water. I push up to the surface as I hear his huge splash next to me. He pulls me to the bank, and we both climb out gasping for air. I look up and see dozens of people running towards us from the house.

"Lance, what in the hell happened, son?" I hear Lance's dad call out.

"I don't know, I...I don't know. I had candles lit, and they must have caught one of the curtains on fire." I can tell that Lance is embarrassed and mad at himself.

"And just what were you two doing in there that you didn't realize the place was on fire?" I hear Lance's Maw Maw chuckle.

"Not now, Mother!! They are scared out of their minds!!" Lance's mom says exasperated. I can feel myself turning beet red. Thankfully it's dark outside; the only light is from the burning boathouse. The entire party has come out to watch the remains of the boathouse burn down. Everyone knows what we were doing. I don't think either me or Lance could be more embarrassed.

"Dad, I will pay for the materials to fix the boathouse, and my baseball buddies will come over and help me rebuild."

"Nonsense!!" his dad says. "We been hoping a hurricane would take it down so we could claim it on insurance!! Y'all just got us a brand new boathouse."

His dad grabs his mom, and they do a little dance. The band sets up on the back lawn and begins to play, while people toast to the remains of the fire, singing along to "Louisiana Saturday Night." I have never seen anything like this in my life, and it makes me want to be a part of this family. As we sit on the bank watching the flames, I feel Lance put his arm around me and pull me close into him; and I smile, content, happy, and shocked. How could any girl ever forget her first time with a boy when it is so good that the place burns down!

CHAPTER TWELVE
The Spirit of Louisiana

THE NEXT DAY we wake up and have a Cajun breakfast with Lance's parents, including gator sausage patties and grits and grillades. As are leaving, we hug everyone goodbye and head for the front door. Before we can walk out, the door swings open and in walks Maw Maw with her signature Coke in one hand and cigarette in the other. She has a coy look on her face. No one has said anything about the fire this morning, mainly because everyone knows Lance is deeply embarrassed. He is pretty private, and everyone knowing his sex life is something he doesn't want to discuss.

"Well, bub, are ya off?" Maw Maw says to Lance.

"Yes, Maw Maw. LSU is playing Ole Miss tonight. I'm taking Sunny to her first game."

"Ok, well you two be careful driving back." She gives us both a hug and a kiss and tells me I'm a pretty girl and to stay out of those tanning beds because there's nothing wrong with the real sun. We turn to walk out the when we hear, "Don't you two get frisky and burn down Tiger Stadium!!!!" Maw Maw shouts with triumphant glee. Lance freezes in place and shakes his head.

"She just couldn't resist, could she?" I hear him mumble as I watch him turn red and make his way to the driver's side of his truck.

On the way back to Baton Rouge, Lance explains to me that Ole Miss is LSU's biggest rival, and tonight will be a fierce game. I'm curious about what the big deal is with LSU football. People in these parts talk about it like it's a religion or something. I text Sam and Brittany who both tell me they are going to the game tonight as well. Sam tells me we are welcome to join him in his family's private suite at Tiger Stadium to watch the game. Unfortunately we won't get there in time for tailgating which starts early in the day, and I'm disappointed that we're missing it. Apparently the tailgating is as important as the actual game.

As soon as we get back to Baton Rouge, Lance stops at a sports shop and buys me a jersey. He's adamant that I can't go to the game without wearing one. He, of course, is already wearing his jersey along with his LSU ball cap, dark jeans, and boots. When we arrive, we head over to find Sam's parents' suite. When we enter the stadium, I'm shocked at how giant it is. I look up and see an enormous sign that reads, *Welcome to Death Valley*. Chills run down my spine. I have a feeling today is going to be pretty intense. When we finally find the LeBlancs' suite, Sam and Brittany are already there chatting about football statistics, and I have no idea what they are talking about. Brittany knows more about football than most boys, which impresses me. Sam pauses from the football talk and introduces Lance and me to Andy, the new guy from Shreveport he's seeing.

"Lance, Sunny, this is Andy. We met at Splash last week." Lance and I both shake his hand.

"Hi, nice to meet you both," he says shyly. Andy is thin, tall, attractive, and has impeccable blonde highlights. A *twink* as Sam would call him,

Sam's favorite type of guy.

"Andy has never been to an LSU football game, so I told him to come down and join us in the suite tonight," Sam says smugly. If I know Sam, he is using this as a ploy to sleep with this guy.

"Well, Andy, you're lucky; there's no better way to experience a game at Tiger Stadium," Lance assures him. "This is Sunny's first game as well."

"Is it?" Andy asks curiously.

"Yeah, it's my first time, too. I guess we'll find out what the big deal is, won't we?" I say to him with a smile.

"My mother told me she doesn't mind if I bring a boy to her box; he just better be attractive," Sam whispers to Lance and me.

"Yeah... speaking of your mom...where is she? I'm going to try my best to avoid her," I say to Sam while scanning the crowd of friends and family members in the LeBlancs' box.

"Oh, she's up there with her friends, I'm sure. Don't worry about it; I doubt she will say anything to you since you came with Lance. She pretty much knows she lost that battle," Sam says with a grin. "She might, however, stare you down with her famous death stare, so just try to stay away from her."

I see Mrs. LeBlanc in the distance and can't help but think about how cold and hateful she really is under her sweet southern demeanor... Nothing like Lance's mom's warmth. Mr. LeBlanc is decked out in an LSU jersey and ball cap and drinking a Coke, surrounded by his friends who are all dressed the same. Both of the LeBlancs are way too swept up in talking to their guests to bother with Sam and his friends. I get the impression that this is probably how he spent most of his childhood, and this would clearly explain his cutthroat take-no-prisoners attitude towards life.

The game begins, and I look out at the sea of people cheering and wearing their purple and gold. A huge screen begins to play "Callin' Baton Rouge" with a montage of famous Baton Rouge landmarks and exciting moments from past games; even the head coach is singing along with Garth Brooks. Lance looks down at me and winks, and I think about the first time I met him. My mind drifts to how amazing last night was, minus burning the place down during sex. I see all the beautiful cheerleaders (Lance has probably dated most of them.); I see the mascot running around on the finely manicured field, and it all finally clicks. There is something magnetic in the air. This isn't just about a football game; this is about pride. It's about the spirit of Louisiana. I couldn't be happier to be here and to be a part of it. I finally get it and realize I'm in love with Louisiana, just like so many who have come here before me.

At half time, Mrs. LeBlanc asks Sam to go get some soft drinks because the fridge in their suite is out. Sam and I make our way through the crowd to the concession stands.

"Sunny, I have something to tell you. I have been trying to figure out a way to say this all week, but it's time I let you know. When my parents got home from Europe, they basically sat me down and said if I don't have a job within the next month, my trust fund will be cut off completely. Now you and I both know that can't happen, and I'm sure as hell not going to stay here because there's nothing for me here. I decided to take a job that was offered to me when I first graduated, and they have begging me to come out ever since." I look at him in shock.

"So you're leaving me here and taking off? Where will you be working?"

"It's a public relations firm...in Los Angeles."

"Sam LeBlanc, are you fucking kidding me? You're going to L.A.??"

"Listen, Sunny, don't give me that bullshit. I'm not even going to waste my breath asking you to come with me. You and I both know you're head over heels in love with Lance Arceneaux, and you're not going to leave that boy in Louisiana, even if it is to go to Hollywood and pursue a career in the movies, although that's all you've talked about doing since the day I met you." He looks at me challenging me, and I can see his temper rising.

I can't believe this. I have never been more torn in my life. Should I go with him or stay here? He's right, as much as I want to go, there's no way I can give up what I have right now. Momma always told me when you find love, you hold onto it because it can disappear in the blink of an eye, and you don't know when you'll see it again. She also told me she wanted me to go out to L.A. and pursue everything we worked hard for so many years. This started out to be an amazing night. How quickly it's changed. Sam takes a deep breath, calms down, and takes a seat on a nearby bench.

"Sunny, sit with me for a second." My mind is swirling as I take a seat next to him. "Now listen to me. I can't believe I'm saying this, but...I think Lance is a good influence on you. I've known him a long time and haven't always been sure about how he is with girls, but when I watch you two together, I see something special. There's some kind of weird connection between y'all that I don't even know if either of you see. The other thing is that you listen to him. He's got an effect on you that no one else has. It's kind of easy for you to get off track and into trouble, not with him though. You're calm and happy with him. I've never seen you like this. It's weird, but I think he's able to tame you in a way that I don't think anyone else can. I know you're happy with him, and I want to see you that way. What Eric did was awful, and you deserve what you have right now. Just keep working, save up some money, and then come out to L.A. In a year who knows, he might come with you. You're young, and Hollywood isn't going anywhere...More than anything I feel safe leaving you here with him; he'll protect you while I'm getting shit together out in California... Just don't ever let him find out what you're doing in New Orleans, or all of our heads will roll."

I SPEND THE NIGHT at Lance's apartment, and when I wake, he's already left for his morning classes. There's a note on his pillow that says "coffee's made" with a smiley face. I lie back in bed and smile. I take in a deep breath and can smell his sexy scent on the sheets. I love the way his room smells, and I love falling asleep wrapped up in his arms. He's always warm, I'm guessing because of his Cajun blood.

I LEAVE LANCE'S apartment and head to La Madeleine, a quaint French bistro, to have breakfast and coffee (Lance makes his way too strong, but it's the thought that counts.); then I head to the store to buy stuff to make dinner. I haven't cooked for Lance yet, and I'm praying he enjoys it. I spend all day cooking Momma's famous rosemary chicken, Brussels sprouts, and mashed potatoes that end up being so spicy I had to throw them away. I watched Lance's mom put this stuff called Tony Chachere's on potatoes at the seafood boil, but I clearly put way too much on the mashed potatoes. Around 6 p.m., Lance comes strolling into the kitchen with a surprised look on his face.

"You cook?" He looks at me perplexed.

"Obviously." I look at him grinning, as he stands in place staring at the food. After what seems like an eternity, he finally speaks.

"Hell, yeah…I love Brussels sprouts!!" I can't help but laugh. He's in a chipper mood, and he's decided it's ok that I've taken over his kitchen this time.

A few minutes later I hear Lance answer his phone in the living room.

"Hey…no buddy, I'm not going out with y'all…No, I'm seriously not going…You know better than to ask me that…I don't care what she said, I'm not going…" His voice lowers, and of course I get closer to the door so I can hear. "I don't give a fuck about what Heather said, I'm not going!!!…BECAUSE MY GIRLFRIEND IS COOKING ME DINNER!!!!" I hear him yell into the phone and hang up. Wow...I wonder who that was. And who the hell is Heather? And did he just call me his girlfriend?? That's the first time I've heard him actually say it. This is a lot to take in... I wait a couple of minutes, and then cautiously make my way into the living room. He is sitting on the couch, arms folded, staring out the window. I stand in the doorway of the kitchen awkwardly and finally work up the nerve to speak.

"Is everything ok?" I ask quietly.

"Yeah. All good. Let's eat."

He doesn't speak to me during dinner or for the rest of the night. His demeanor is cold compared to the great mood he was in earlier. I know better than to push him about the phone call, even though I'm dying to know what happened. I climb into his bed by myself while he finishes watching the game. When I wake up the next morning, Lance is gone, and there's no note. Around 2 p.m. I head back to New Orleans, hoping he will calm down and call me later.

A WEEK GOES BY and not one word from Lance. Sam tells me not to call him and just let him brood over whatever he's mad about.

"Sunny, pushing him is the worst thing you can do," he says. I shrug it off and try not to think about it, but in my gut I know something's wrong. *You can only control what YOU can control.* I hear Momma's voice in my head. So it's back to work at the Circus. Brittany, two other girls, and I are performing a new number we've been rehearsing all week. It's the only part of working here that I do like. I imagine myself on a soundstage somewhere in New York City preparing for the Video Music Awards; at least this helps me keep my mind off Lance.

CHAPTER THIRTEEN
Drug Fiends, Drag Queens, and Solo Dreams

TODAY I WAKE up around ten and decide to go to my favorite little cafe and have eggs benedict served over fried green tomatoes, one of the best things I have found in New Orleans. I walk through the streets of the French Quarter looking at the homes. My favorite is a two story chateau that has a balcony on the first and second floors with dozens of iron fleurs-de-lis across the tops of the rails. There are giant gas lanterns that burn all day and night across the front and pots with pink and purple flowers lining the balconies, along with thousands of Mardi Gras beads in every color. For some reason I am very drawn to this particular house. It looks as if New Orleans royalty should live there. I fantasize about Lance and me living in it one day and how amazing that would be. I can't help but smile. Of course the thought of not hearing from him for the past week flashes into my mind. I would have to be a millionaire to buy such an extravagant home. I decide to take the long way home so I can visit another one of my favorite places, Jackson Square. I pass by the eccentric artists painting beautiful portraits of the city, trying to make a buck as they fast-talk tourists. Next I pass the many fortune tellers and palm readers lining the sidewalks. The Quarter is a strange, exciting place. At the end of the square sits the most amazing church I've ever seen, the St. Louis Cathedral, which Brittany tells me was built in the 1700s. It's so cool to see all of the history here that dates so far back. There's definitely something dark and mysterious about New Orleans, though.

When I get to the corner of Dumaine and Bourbon, I hear someone call my name from one of the balconies on the second floor of a bar. I look up and see Jake, one of the dancers from the Circus. He tells me to come up, so I head inside and make my way up the stairs. When I get to the second floor, there sit all of the male dancers from the Circus, several drag queens who look like they are still wearing the same outfits from the night before, Larry and Burt, the twin midgets who work the door, and smack dab in the middle of everyone is Lisa Beaumann looking every bit the grande dame. It's eleven a.m., and she's wearing a beautiful pink ball gown and a pink oversized top hat with the biggest feather sticking out of it I've ever seen.

"Well hello, dear, come sit!!" she says to me. "We're just about to order brunch!!" She pulls out a little toadstool chair and motions for me to sit next to her. "You know, Sunny…should I call you Sunny or Dixie?" she asks curiously.

"Oh, please call me Sunny. I hate that the ringleader named me Dixie."

"Mmm… hmmm, I can imagine; Herman Toulouse does like to have his way, doesn't he?" she purrs at me and flutters her big eyelashes.

"Can I ask you something? Do you call him Herman instead of ringleader because you know how mad it makes him?" I ask her honestly. She grins at me.

"Well, you're catching on quite quickly, aren't you dear? I mean, how absurd, this whole call-me-the-ringleader nonsense!! I've known him since he was a teenager sweeping the floor at Lafitte's when God was a boy!!

And don't ask me how long ago that was because I'm not telling. Anyway, I think it's high time you did an amazing solo. I've been watching you, and you really do have something special about you. You're not like the other girls. Honestly, I don't know why you're even working at the circus, but if you're going to do it, I think you should come out and do a number that shows everyone what you're made of. I mean after all, we get more requests for you in the V.I.P. room for lap dances than any other girl, and I've had several customers ask me why you're not performing solo numbers."

"Really? I didn't know that," I say to her.

"Yes dear, now let's make a deal. I'll scratch your back if you scratch mine. You have a car, correct?" I nod. "I can't ever get anyone to take me to the fabric shop in Metairie. You take me today, and while we're there, we will find some fabric and rhinestones to make you something amazing to wear for a solo performance...Bartender!!! One more round of Bloody Marys for Sunny and me!!!!" Lisa demands.

Later that day during the thirty minute drive to Metairie, Lisa is inquisitive about where I come from and how I ended up at the Circus, so I share all the details of my journey.

"Well, that's quite the story, dear, one of the most interesting ones I've heard yet!!" She laughs at me. "You keep using this word, *shifty*; whatever does it mean?"

"Well...I don't know how to explain it. It can mean several things: people who play both sides of the fence or someone who's very clever. It can also mean someone who is very resourceful or even that you're shifting gears to stay two steps ahead of everyone else."

"Huh... shifty...I love it!!!!!! Just watch how shifty I can be!!! I'm always shifting gears faster than the other queens in this town, and now I have a word to go with the action!!! Watch out, bitches, Sunny and Lisa, the shiftiest girls in Louisiana, coming through!!" We can't stop laughing, and I could never have imagined how much I've enjoyed hanging out with her.

Later in the day, I go home and get ready because Lisa wants me to come out with her and meet her "adoring fans." I still haven't heard from Lance, and I have to find a way to keep my mind busy, so why not go out on the town, I think to myself. At 10 p.m. I make my way through the French Quarter to Lisa's apartment, which is located one street off Bourbon on St. Ann. The outside doesn't look like much, but I've learned that these little hidden places in the Quarter can be very deceiving. I walk inside, and I'm amazed. The walls are draped with pink silk, and a beautiful sparkling chandelier hangs in the center of the living room. There are plush pink furniture and a pink grand piano with a huge arrangement of assorted white flowers setting on top in a crystal vase. It looks like a fantasy out of a storybook, not anything like a normal apartment. Lisa is in her bathroom looking into a huge vanity mirror that has lightbulbs all around it. Connected to it is the biggest closet I have ever seen with hundreds of the most outrageous gowns, costumes, and wigs. She chooses a nude mini dress covered in silver shimmering fringe, silver shoes, and huge sparkly chandelier earrings. I feel extremely underdressed compared to her, considering I'm wearing a simple cream colored dress I found at one of the local shops and flats, and my hair is up in a high ponytail. Then again, I think anyone would look dressed down compared to Lisa Beaumann.

She says our first stop is Oz, which I've only been to once before on the first night I came to New Orleans. I'm not really excited to go there because it sits across the street from the Bourbon Pub. It reminds me of the first time I kissed Lance and what a magical night that was. As we climb the third flight of stairs, I look around at the old French architecture of Oz. I can't help but be fascinated with its strange beauty. I hear faint music flowing through the giant doors, and I am curious as to what awaits on us the other side. A tall, handsome, blonde haired man stands at the door with a solemn look on his face that changes as soon as he recognizes Lisa.

"Well hello Miss Beaumann!" he beams at Lisa.

"Hello, Jake dear. Are the queens gossiping away?" she asks with a chuckle.

"Oh, well of course, Persana Shoulders is holding court," he says with a coy smile.

"Is she now? Well, tell the princess that the queen has arrived."

"My pleasure, Miss Beaumann." He turns and opens the massive doors revealing a giant oval-shaped room filled with dozens of drag queens, New Orleans socialites, and all of the French Quarter VIPs. Tiny crystal chandeliers are dripping from the high ceiling, and all around the room are plush purple couches. Across the room, huge French doors open up to a long balcony, and I can spot the Bourbon Pub's balcony directly across the street. I try my hardest to put Lance out of my mind and let my curiosity about all of these new exciting people set in.

"Come, Sunny, my audience waits," Lisa purrs at me as she swishes her dress back to make her grand entrance.

I follow behind, and I can't help but stare towards the center of the room. A giant round white marble table sits in the middle with a huge arrangement of white orchards perched in the middle. I see a short very glamorous boy sitting on the table wearing an all-white Chanel pantsuit with a giant magnolia pinned to the breast of his jacket and sparkly white Louboutin heels. His wrists and fingers are covered in diamonds, and a long strand adorns his neck. His skin is very white, and his black pixie-cut hair swoops across his face. I watch as he flamboyantly waves his arms in the air regaling a group of people with a story, ending it with a boisterous laugh and obviously enjoying being the center of attention.

"Sunny, pay attention!" Lisa hisses as I look down and realize I'm stepping on her dress.

"Finally, Lisa, we've been waiting on you all night. The party can finally begin!" a very tall queen who reminds me of Carol Burnett says as we approach the corner of the room.

"Sunny, I want you to meet one of my closest friends. This is Electra Kitty and her partner Maude Toulouse."

"Hello, very nice to meet you." I say politely and a little intimidated. Both queens are at least six foot four. Electra gives me a fake smile, and then pulls out a long cigarette and lights it up. Maude Toulouse, who has curly blonde hair and somewhat resembles Kathy Bates, doesn't even acknowledge me. I look around the room nervously. *Look, Sunny just pretend that this is an episode of "Sex and the City." You're Carrie Bradshaw right now, and you've just walked into a room full of glamorous people in New York City*, I tell myself. The thought makes me feel a lot better.

"Here, Sunny, best blow in the south." I turn around, and Electra Kitty has a small white bag open. I watch as she dips a car key into it, scoops up some white powder, and places it close to my nose. "Have a bump, dear; you look like you need it." I awkwardly look at Lisa, who shakes her head *no*.

"No thank you, I'm allergic." *The dumbest thing I could say*, I think to myself as Electra rolls her eyes and does the bump herself.

"Lisa, don't look now, but Persana is shooting daggers through your back with the look she's giving you," Electra whispers to Lisa.

"Well of course she is, darling; she hates it more than anything when I walk into the room and steal her thunder," Lisa says laughingly. "C'mon, Sunny, let's say our hellos to the rest of the queens."

I follow Lisa as she introduces me to several different groups of people around the room, and then we finally make our way to the group surrounding Persana Shoulders herself.

"Well hello, Lisa darlingggg!!!!" Persana says while uncrossing her legs and getting off the table to greet Lisa. She takes a sip from a martini glass, and then reaches out for both of Lisa's hands as they air kiss on both cheeks.

"Hello, Persana," Lisa says in a cheeky tone. I can tell they are both trying to be the bigger person as everyone in the room is now watching.

"I see you brought a real fish with you; is she one of your 'circus girls,' dear?" Persana looks me up and down with a cynical grin.

"Persana, I'd like you to meet Sunny Collins," Lisa says nonchalantly, ignoring Persana's question.

"Hello," I respond shyly.

"Well, I can't even imagine what you're doing with Lisa Beaumann." She laughs. "But the more the merrier!! That's what I always say!!" she says with another overpowering laugh.

"Sunny, this is Tammie Tarmac, Tamia Watson and her drag mother Cabrina Watson, Vivica Devereaux, and last but not least, Tiffany Alexander."

The group is very polite shaking my hand, but all look more interested in the banter between Lisa and Persana.

"So, what are you doing with a real girl?" Tiffany Alexander asks Lisa.

"She might be the real thing, but I'm the sure thing," Lisa says as she turns her nose up rather snobbily, as the rest of the queens break out into laughter. Just then, the doors of the room burst open and in storms the biggest, scariest drag queen I've ever seen. She has caked-on drag makeup that looks like she's been wearing it since the night before, and her dress is too small for her body.

"Miss Simone!!!" Persana shouts nervously. Miss Simone stomps towards Persana fuming mad.

"Persana, just the little bitch I was looking for," Miss Simone says in a low eerie rumble. I look around the silent room and observe the frightened faces watching what's happening. "So, I heard you decided to talk shit about me during your opening monologue last night, something about me cutting my cocaine with carpet freshener," Simone says in a frightening tone.

"Persana hosts the drag shows all over town," Lisa whispers in my ear.

"Oh that was just a joke, dear; you know everyone enjoys your refreshments!" Persana says laughing nervously.

"Oh, it was a joke alright," Lisa chimes in. "One that Bianca Del Rio told onstage three years ago. Get some new material, Persana," Lisa says taunting Persana.

"Carpet freshener! I knew this smelled funny!" Electra Kitty yells out as she dumps out her little white bag on the floor. Miss Simone slowly turns her head back to Persana.

"You're affecting my sales, bitch; you owe me money," Miss Simone growls threateningly.

"I owe you nothing. Beat it, queen," Persana says dismissively, and then turns towards the table, grabs her martini, and gulps down the rest of it.

Just then, everything happens very fast. Simone lunges for Persana, Lisa pushes me backwards onto one of the couches, and I hear a loud crash and screaming all around the room. I look up, and the table in the middle of the room is broken into thousands of pieces, and Miss Simone is dragging Persana across the floor towards the open doors of the balcony. Simone flings Persana over the railing, holding onto Persana's foot with one hand. Persana flails about like a fish out of water while screaming bloody murder. I watch as one of Persana's white Louboutins falls off, and I imagine it hitting the pavement on Bourbon Street three stories down. I'm guessing the tourists down below are as mortified by this sight as everyone in the room.

"Now!! I want everyone in the city of New Orleans to know that you owe Miss Simone money, then, bitch, you better have my money!!" Simone yells out to everyone in the room.

"PLLEASSEEE DARLING, IM TOO FABULOUS TO DIE!!! ILL GET YOU YOUR MONEY, I PROMISEEEE!!!!" Persana begins to sob uncontrollably. Simone pulls Persana up and slams her onto the ground.

"You have one hour, bitch," she says as she turns and stomps out of the room. Lisa walks over and pulls me up off the couch.

"I'm so sorry, Sunny. Simone carries a knife on her sometimes, and I didn't want to risk you getting hurt."

I brush off myself and decide it's time for cocktail. I'm really starting to realize that as glamorous as the French Quarter can be, it can be even more dangerous if you piss off the wrong person.

CHAPTER FOURTEEN
Hookers and Hold-ups

I T'S FRIDAY NIGHT in New Orleans, and I've been sitting on the end of the stage at the Circus for half an hour nursing the same Grey Goose and soda. It's been pouring down rain all day, and only four customers have trickled in since the doors opened for the evening. I look up to see Brittany making her way through the empty tables and chairs in the audience. She is pissed, and the look on her face shows it.

"Sunny, I'm telling you right now, this is bullshit; these Gulf Coast storms are fucking with my money!! I have rent due tomorrow, and there is no way we're making any cash tonight." Brittany yells in outrage, her Scorpio temper boiling over.

"Yeah, I can see that," I say worriedly because I've spent a ton of money and don't have enough to give Brit my part of the rent either.

"Yeah, the worst part is that we still have to give the ringleader his nightly cut whether we make money or not," she says as she plunks down on the stage next to me pouting. It's never a good thing when Brittany is in a bad mood. A couple of minutes go by, and she jumps up and turns towards me excitedly.

"Ok, I have an idea! Weren't there a couple of guys heading into the lap dance room earlier? Or did they already leave?"

"No, I think they're still in there," I say to her perplexed.

"Ok, don't move; I'll be back in a minute. I think I recognized one of them, and he's a baller," she says to me and hurries off towards the V.I.P. area. What on earth is she planning? My curiosity begins to eat away at me. After a couple of minutes, she comes strutting back towards me, a look of triumph on her face.

"Ok, so here's the deal; I was pretty sure I saw this guy who's a regular here when we got to work. He comes over from Mississippi once a month, and he always spends a ton on the girls when he's here. He usually begs them to come back to his room at Hotel Monteleone." I've seen the hotel a couple of times in passing, and it supposedly one of New Orleans' swankiest. "So I always say no, but I know a couple of the girls have gone to his room to do privates, and he pays really well. He travels with a safe that's loaded with cash!!"

"Oh no, Brit, are you serious? Now you wanna go do a private dance in some guy's hotel room?"

"Sunny!! He's already had a lot to drink, we'll be there ten minutes tops, and he'll pass out!! We'll have enough to pay rent for this month!! Have you already forgotten about the little shopping spree we went on at Saks? Neither of us has any money left!!"

"Oh my god fine, let's just go..."

"Good girl." She grins at me. "Trust me, this is the perfect plan." Ten minutes later, we are following a middle-aged, overweight casino owner from Biloxi named Wilbur Smalls through the sprinkling rain down Royal Street and into the decadent hotel.

"Ok ladies... *hiccup*...right this way into the elevator!! *Hiccup*," he says to us swaying from side to side with a jolly smile on his face, his eyes half closed. I honestly can't believe we are doing this, and I have a bad feeling in my stomach. But Brittany's right, we need the money. I mean, what could go wrong? We'll do a quick dance and then get out of here. We exit on the top floor and follow him into one of the beautiful suites. He wobbles over to the bed and takes a seat.

"Wilbur, darling," Brittany coos to him in a baby voice. "I'm going to need you to pay us first before my friend and I can dance for you."

"Oh, well of course, beautiful!!" he says with a big smile on his face. I watch him as he heads over to the dining room table where a large safe sits. He spins the dials for what seems like forever until finally the door of the safe flies open. Brittany and I peer in at the same time, and there are literally stacks and stacks of hundred dollar bills.

"You were not kidding," I whisper to Brit.

"Ok little miss hotcakes, how much do I owe you?" he asks as he begins to count out money. I see Brittany trying her hardest not to lose her temper with him. I've learned over time that she doesn't tolerate idiots very well.

"I told you at the club, Wilbur; it'll be two thousand dollars."

"Two thousand? Are you outta your mind? The other girls charge me five hundred for a private!" His face turns from sweet and jolly to suspicious and disgusted.

"Well, we're not just any girls, Wilbur; we're the best. You want the hottest girls in the club, you're going to have to pay for it," Brittany says to him matter-of-factly with her head cocked sideways.

"I'll tell you what, how 'bout instead both of you get the hell out of my room. I don't even want a dance from you!!" he says with a drunk yet triumphant look on his face.

"Ok that's fine; we can leave, but you know the rules; you still have to pay us for coming to your room even if you change your mind about wanting a dance. We don't leave the club for free." Everything after that moment happens very fast. The look on his face again changes from triumphant to furious, and he apparently has sobered up rather quickly. He spins around to face his safe, reaches in, and pulls out a small handgun and points it towards Brittany.

"Nooooo!!" I scream. "Please, don't shoot her sir, please!! We're leaving, right now!" I plead with him.

"Get the hell out of my…" Just then he stumbles and falls to the floor, and the gun goes flying. To my surprise, instead of running towards the door for dear life like me, Brittany runs towards the safe and grabs two huge stacks of hundreds. I feel terror rush over me as I see Wilbur Smalls stand up quickly and reach towards Brittany. The next thing I know, I'm running towards him. I push him as hard as I can, and he stumbles backwards and onto the bed, and his feet go up into the air.

"RUNNN!!!" Brittany screams at me. We head for the door, swing it open, and run towards the elevator. We get inside, and the door cannot shut fast enough. I feel my heart beating out of my chest; we almost got shot! Brittany hits the lobby button and stares down at me as I sit on the floor of the elevator out of breath. She begins laughing uncontrollably which I feel could not be more inappropriate at this time.

"Did we seriously almost just get shot? Like who knew that old geezer would have a gun, Sunny!!"

"I just can't. I don't even know what to say." I look at her and shake my head.

The door opens, and we step out into the opulent lobby. We begin walking to the exit doors slowly, smiling as we pass the concierge and hotel staff. We make it almost to the exit when I hear another elevator ding, and the sound of the doors sliding open. I turn and see Wilbur Smalls standing several yards behind us pointing a gun. The first blast goes off and shatters the glass in the entryway of the hotel. I hear the staff screaming as I grab Brittany and pull her through the shattered entryway. We take a right and run as fast as our heels can carry us to the next side street that will take us back to Bourbon. We hear another gun shot as we turn the corner and can hear Wilbur running behind us. I can't help but let out a scream because this is literally the most terrifying thing that's ever happened to me. All I can think is how I'll never see Momma again, how I'll never see Lance again, and how this will be my legacy: to be shot to death as a stripper in the French Quarter. We finally make it to Bourbon Street, shots ringing out behind us.

"Take a right!" I shout to Brittany. Luckily, the rain has stopped, and the crowds have picked up. All I can think is to keep running until we find N.O.P.D., but unfortunately there are none in sight.

"Sunny, where is your car? Didn't you park close to the Circus tonight? We need to get out of the Quarter until things calm down." Brittany's right; we need to jump on the freeway and haul ass until we get to Baton Rouge. I turn and look behind me and don't see him anywhere.

"Ok, I don't see him anywhere; maybe we lost him." Still in panic mode, we race to find the alley where my car is parked. We finally see it and run for our lives, but half way there, we here another gunshot ring out. Brittany screams, and we run to the other side of the car and duck. The passenger side window of my car shatters, and the car rocks. I grab Brit's hand, close my eyes, and begin to pray out loud.

"Dear God, please, I'm begging you, let us make it out of this alive. Please, don't let us die like this. It just can't end this way…" I begin to sob uncontrollably. Then, I hear a scuffle and cars pulling into the alleyway, and voices. I turn and peek over the hood and see the New Orleans police. We're saved!! I see the police throw Wilbur Smalls on the ground and handcuff him. I look up at the night sky and thank God. The police make their way over to the car and carefully approach Brittany and me.

"Hi officer, we're ok, just a little shaken," I begin to explain.

"Oh, you are? Ok, good. No injuries? No reason to go to the hospital, right?" one of the officers asks kindly.

"No, we're fine," I say relieved.

"Great!" He looks at us with a grin. "You're under arrest; put your hands behind your back." The officers grab both of us, slam us up against the car, and handcuff us.

"What the hell are you doing? I DEMAND to know why we're being arrested, asshole!!" Brittany screams at the cop.

"Ha! Like you don't know. Your little customer over there ratted out you guys. You're being booked for prostitution."

"PROSTITUTION??" Brittany screams. "We are NOT prostitutes!! We were hanging out with him at a club, went to his hotel, and he went crazy on us!! Started shooting a gun at us!!"

"Really? He says he paid you $2,000 for sex, and you stole his money and ran." I watch in terror as the officer reaches into Brittany's jacket pocket and pulls out the crumpled stacks of one hundred dollar bills.

"$2,100 to be exact. Take 'em to the tank!!!" he says to the other officers cheerfully. "They can rot with the other French Quarter whores."

WHEN WE'RE BOOKED in at the station, Brittany whispers to me and tells me to give them my stage name. They book me in as Dixie Daniels, and luckily I don't have an ID on me with my real name. They take our mugshots, fingerprint us, and then put us in a holding cell.

"I'm really sorry, Sunny. I could have never imagined this would happen."

"I know, Brit. I'm just scared. How long do you think we'll be in here? What happens next?" I ask her.

"Well, my dad's an attorney. I'll tell him we were just walking through the Quarter, and we were in the wrong place at the wrong time. He'll never buy their story about us being prostitutes. Believe me this isn't the first time a couple of girls have been arrested in the Quarter and falsely accused." Just then an officer walks by our cell escorting Wilbur Smalls to the exit. He waves at us with his stupid grin as he passes by.

"Enjoy jail, ladies!!" he sneers.

"He must have posted his own bail," Brittany says with her face in her hands.

Four hours later, an officer comes to the cell and asks Brittany to follow him.

"Your father's here; he posted your bail," he says to her.

"What?" I ask terrified. "Brittany, you can't leave me in here!! I don't know anyone's number; they're all programmed into my cell!"

"Sunny, chill, I will figure out how to make your bail, or I'll call Sam or Lance."

"NO!!" I scream hysterically. "Don't call Lance whatever you do!!"

"Ok, ok, I'll figure something out…I'm sure my dad is already furious for having to put up my bail, but I'll find some way, I promise."

The guard slams the door shut and escorts Brittany away. I begin crying uncontrollably. I'm terrified being in this cell by myself with no idea how long I'm going to be here. Every scary thought imaginable takes over my mind, and I feel my anxiety level go through the roof. This could be it for me. If no one gets me out, I could be here for an eternity. Only one person knows I'm here. I don't know Sam's number; Lance isn't speaking to me and won't wonder where I am. How did I go from getting on a bus heading to Hollywood to being locked up for prostitution in a New Orleans jail cell?

I finally fall asleep on the hard cement bunk and have nightmares for hours. I'm not sure what time it is when I wake up; bright lights of the cell are shining on me, and a female guard tells me she'll be back in twenty minutes to take me to general population. I'm terrified beyond belief. I can only imagine what will happen to me in here. I'm going to be placed in general population with murderers and gang members in one of the most dangerous cities in the country. This is a living nightmare. Just then I hear the door at the end of the hall open. She's coming for me, the female guard. The door swings open, but instead of the guard stands Lisa Beaumann. She's wearing a sweeping midnight blue ball gown, matching satin gloves that go up to her elbows, and a blue feathered head dress that looks like it came straight off a Vegas showgirl. I look at her in absolute shock.

"Well come on, dear, you know I can't stand being in this terrible lighting for long!! We have places to go and people to see!!" I have no words. I follow Lisa and a guard out of the jail and back into the streets of downtown as she hails us a cab.

"Lisa, how did you know I was in jail? How did you get me out?" I ask perplexed.

"Darling, seriously? The entire Quarter is talking about the shooting last night!! You're famous! Your name is on everyone's lips! Dixie Daniels, the runaway stripper they're calling you!! You've officially hit star status on Bourbon. And how did I get you out? Well, of course, it only took one phone call; the chief of police is a close, personal friend. He comes in every week for a hand job in my dressing room!! You think you're the first girl from the Circus to be arrested? Anyway, I can't wait to take you out tonight; everyone wants to hear the story!! Who knew you were such a bad girl underneath that innocent exterior!"

I slink down in the seat of the cab and look out the window as Lisa goes on and on about where she wants to go this evening. Lance stops speaking to me for no reason whatsoever, I've watched a drag queen dangle someone over a balcony and almost plummet to his death, I've been shot at numerous times, and now I'm infamous in the French Quarter for being arrested as a prostitute. Now I'm expected to regale everyone with the exciting details of it all tonight. What a week! Is this really my life?

CHAPTER FIFTEEN
The Caterie

A FTER A LONG night out in the Quarter, I wake up on one of the plush pink couches at Lisa Beaumann's house. I have a splitting headache, and I'm annoyed that she has the doors to her balcony open letting in the morning sun.

"Oh good, you're up, dear!!" Lisa pops out from the kitchen wearing her white satin robe that drags the floor, the neck and ends of the sleeves covered in white feathers. Her hair is still as gorgeous as it was last night, although I can tell she still hasn't taken off her makeup. "I've made beignets and coffee. Come and get your plate, and we'll have our breakfast on the veranda," she says.

I go into the kitchen and make a plate, grab a cup of coffee, then head outside. Lisa's patio is beautiful. There are dozens of petunias in every color imaginable, potted all around the edges of the balcony, and white wrought iron patio furniture right in the middle. She has set up everything as though she's getting ready for a tea party, always the eloquent host.

"Now sit down, dear; we have some things to talk about." I look at her inquisitively, and then take seat at the little table.

"What do we need to talk about?" I ask her, sipping my coffee.

"Last night at Oz we were having a marvelous time, then you became very emotional, and I, of course, had to take care of you. I'll know better next time not to let you drink so much!!" she says in a sassy tone. "Not to throw shade, dear, but getting messy drunk and crying is not something you want people in the French Quarter to witness!! Never let them see you fall, or they will kick you while you're down the first chance they get!!"

"I was crying? Oh great. That's just awesome," I say feeling mad at myself.

"Yes darling, you kept mentioning a boy named Lance; who is he? Where did you meet him? Tell momma everything." She looks at me sweetly then winks. "We will figure it out, Sunny dear; I can't have my shifty little partner in crime crying on the job!!" This makes me laugh. I sit up and take a deep breath and begin to explain how it all started.

"So, anyway, I've been torn between the two this entire time. Part of me knows that I have to go to Hollywood. Everything I've ever wanted is out there in California, but the other part of me has always yearned for love, the kind of love that is timeless. The kind that sends sparks flying through the air. The moment I saw Lance, I knew that he was the one. That day, the pursuit of fame became irrelevant, and all that matters now is my pursuit of love. The problem is that I don't know if he feels the same way about me. Do you think that's possible? That you can love a person with every fiber of your being? That you look at that person and just know that you are meant to be with him? But for that person not to feel the same way about you, that's just..." I can't even say it. "...Anyway, I feel like he's the Mr. Big to my Carrie Bradshaw," I say with a smile. "I just hope I get the same happy ending that she did."

"Well. That's quite a story. I had no idea you had such strong feelings about a man," Lisa says to me lost in thought, looking out to the roof tops of the surrounding buildings. "You know, dear, I have learned over the years that love is a strange thing. It can build the tallest palace and can also tear it down. Empires have risen and fallen due to love. You have to make a decision about this Lance and decide if you're willing to do anything to be with him. He sounds like quite a complex man, and this journey will not be an easy one. I can tell you now; you will have to go the ends of the earth to create this life you're telling me you want. I mean, could you have chosen anything more difficult? You want to be an actress, one of the most extraordinarily hard dreams to make come true, and you have chosen to love a man who is going to be impossible through the years. If I can say one thing about you, Sunny, you sure do go big or go home!!" I feel a smile come over my face.

"I know, Lisa. Sometimes I think maybe I'm crazy. Why couldn't I just settle for a normal life with a normal job and a normal guy?" I say with a sigh.

"Because there is nothing normal about you, dear. I watch you, Sunny. As pretty as you are, you still stand out awkwardly when you're dancing with the other girls in the show. When you're in a crowd, you're always easiest to spot. You just...stand out!! You need to learn to embrace the fact that you are different and figure out what it is you want most and go after it with everything you've got." Lisa sounds more serious than ever, and I hang on her every word. "Now!! Enough of the mushy stuff!! Let's get dressed and head to Lafitte's; I need a Bloody Mary!!" she says, changing her demeanor to light and fun as she stands up and heads inside.

As she's walking away, my phone starts ringing, and I run inside to grab it. It's Sam calling. I'm hesitant to answer because I'm almost sure word has gotten back to him by now that Brittany and I were arrested. On the other hand, I may as well get it over with, so I hit *accept*.

"Hello, Samuel," I say in an annoyed tone.

"Sunny, I have Brittany on three-way; where are you?" Sam says panicked.

"I'm fine, I'm fine, no thanks to either of you by the way, luckily Lisa Beaumann got me out of jail, and I spent the night at her house last night, and I..."

"Sunny, listen, you're going to have to take off work tonight at the Circus; shit is going down in Baton Rouge, and I promise you're going to want to be here."

"Why, what's happening now?" I ask Sam trying not to sound too on edge.

The truth is that it's been two weeks since I've seen or spoken to Lance. I finally broke and started texting and calling and got nothing in return. I have no idea what I've done. Brittany and Sam both tell me they aren't sure what to do because they've never seen him act like this and that we're swimming in unchartered waters.

"Listen Sunny, I'm just going to tell you the truth. Brittany and I didn't want to tell you about Heather Savoy because... well...she's the girl Lance was seeing right before we arrived in Louisiana. I've heard she's been asking everyone on LSU's campus who this new girlfriend of Lance's is because, quite frankly, he doesn't have girlfriends. Heather is a sorority girl, her family owns Acadian Meat Company, and she has quite the reputation for being the biggest bitch on campus. What Heather Savoy wants, she gets. And now she is coming for you. I honestly didn't know this was going to be a problem, but now it is. Everyone seems to be trying to figure out who you are, and it's time we show them. Tonight's the night." I'm pacing back and forth in Lisa's apartment, trying my best to comprehend what Sam's telling me without flipping out on him.

"So what's happening tonight?" I say, barely able to get the words out.

"Well!! Tonight is the Friday night karaoke contest at The Caterie, which everyone is going to be talking about because Heather and Brittany have this huge feud, and they're going up against each other tonight!!" The excitement in Sam's voice tells me tonight is no doubt going to be a drama filled shit show. "The local college kids compete for a cash prize, blah blah blah, no one cares. The exciting part is that Heather and Brittany fought fiercely for head cheerleader last year and for Miss LSU when Brittany was still in school. Everyone in town is going to be there!!! Including Lance..." Sam is literally about to burst with excitement on the other end of the phone. He lives for this.

"Sam, let me talk for a second!!" Brittany yells. "Sunny, look I'm really sorry about what happened with me and you, but I promise we have much bigger fish to fry right now. You need to get over here and get ready, and I'll explain all the details to you on the ride to Baton Rouge, ok?" Brittany says this with desperation in her voice.

"Fine. I'll be at your apartment in ten minutes. I hit the *end* button and feel a tidal wave of anxiety wash over me. How is this my life?

"Damn, y'all got here fast," Sam says to me as I whisk past him into his parents' mansion. "Thanks for hanging up on me, by the way," he says nonchalantly. "Where is Brittany?"

"She's outside on the phone with Drew, the new guy she's dating who she met at the Circus." I head for Sam's room and throw my bags down on his bed. "Do you not realize how upset I am right now?" I look at him exasperated.

"First of all, sit down and take a deep breath. You know I don't like it when you get overdramatic." *Overdramatic?* "Yes, overdramatic, I know what you're thinking, Sunny Collins. Second, have you not learned anything? I have been trying to teach you for quite some time that this whole thing is one big game, and it's all about how well you play it. Just think, all the players will be in the same room tonight, and I mean all of them. So what is the objective? What is it you could hope to gain from tonight?" Sam asks me as he paces back and forth holding his hands behind his back like he's a college professor.

"Well, honestly, all I care about is finding out what I did to make Lance stop talking to me." Sam stops in his tracks and gives me a disgusted look.

"Are you serious right now? I mean, are you an idiot? You didn't DO anything!! This isn't about *you*, it's about *him*!!" Sam yells. "Look I know you look at him like he hung the moon, and you have him up on this pedestal and all that nonsense you keep blabbering about, but at the end of the day he's a small-town guy from the sticks of Louisiana. He has the pressure of everyone at LSU judging his every move, and on top of that, Heather Savoy is making his life miserable, and his feelings for you confuse him!!"

"Oh…well, I didn't really think of any of that."

"Sunny, listen. You have all of the tools to play the game; you just have to learn how to use them."

"Why are you and Brittany just now telling me about Heather and this feud? Why is this just now being sprung on me?" I ask him. He stops pacing and looks at me with as much sincerity as Sam is able to muster.

"We talked about it when you and Lance first started hanging out and agreed we should let things happen organically. You didn't need to be worried about her at the time, and honestly we never thought you and Lance would make it this far. Like I've told you before, he goes through girls pretty quickly. Anyway, now it's become a problem, and we're going to face it head on tonight. So take a shower, get ready, and we'll have something light for dinner. I'm sure your stomach is churning, and the last thing I want to see is you blow chunks in front of everyone tonight."

8888

At 9 p.m., Sam, Brittany, and I pull into the enormous parking lot of The Caterie. I feel another rush of anxiety as we walk past the hundreds of cars, and I realize the whole town has shown up tonight. Then, parked right in front of the venue, I see Lance's truck. My heart drops. I can't do this. I am in way over my head, and I'm terrified.

"Sunny, come on." Sam turns and looks at me, irritated. "Look, you have two choices. Either run away and look like a fool, or step foot in this building looking hot with your held high and show these Louisiana bitches you're a force to be reckoned with. Besides, Brittany has been a good friend to you, and you need to be here to support her."

I decide right then and there. My love for Lance Arceneaux is more powerful than my fear of some crazy LSU bitch and her friends. I take a deep breath, swing open the door to The Caterie, and march into the building... straight into Lance... who spills beer all over me... and himself. He looks down at me like I'm some random stranger, turns, and makes his way into the crowd towards the stage. I'm shell-shocked, frozen in place. I finally turn and look at Sam and Brittany who are equally as shocked and frozen in place.

"Did that really just happen?" I say in disbelief. For the first time in forever, Sam is speechless.

"Well, I definitely didn't see that coming," Brittany says quietly.

"Go to the bathroom and wash up; I'll get cocktails. I have a feeling we're going to need all the alcohol we can get," Sam says to me looking rather unsure about tonight.

I come out of the bathroom, and Sam is talking to a group of very pretty girls; Brittany is nowhere to be seen.

"Ladies, this is Sunny Collins!!" Sam says with a grin on his face, as he hands me a vodka soda. The girls look at each other, look me up and down, and then turn and make their way into the crowd, whispering excitedly.

"Is this night for real?" I ask him.

"See, I told you that you needed to dress hot!! Everyone is judging you!!" He couldn't be more giddy. After an hour of Sam's introducing me to people who all look at me the same way, we have become the center of attention. Everywhere I look in the enormous venue, people are staring at me in disgust.

"Where is Brittany?" I ask.

"She said she was going outside to take a call again; some shit is going down with her and Drew. Ok Sunny, the contest is about to begin, so let's move closer to the stage to get a better view." As we make our way through the crowd, I see Lance in front of us standing with a group of guys including Chad and Danny. The alcohol has kicked in and so has my anger. Sam grabs my arm as I make my way towards Lance. "Not yet, Sunny, this isn't part of the plan!!" I break free from his grasp and march up to Lance. I reach up and hit him on the shoulder as hard as I can, but he just continues to stand there, arms folded, and his face cold with no emotion.

"Just tell me what I did to you!!" I hear myself blurt out. He doesn't even blink much less acknowledge I'm standing next to him.

"Sam!! What's up, old friend! It's been forever! I've been interning in Shreveport, so I'm just in town for the night!" a handsome but much shorter guy standing next to Lance shouts.

"Hey Mikey, how are you? Good to see you as well...," Sam says awkwardly, then turns to face me. "Sunny, this is Mikey Dubois...Lance's best friend who's down from Shreveport." Mikey looks at me blankly for a second, then a wide grin comes over his face.

"Oh ho ho ho!!! So you're the famous Sunny Collins, huh?" He glances up at Lance who shoots him a dirty look. Mikey immediately darts to the other side of Lance. In that same moment, the music begins to blare, and the curtains start to open. Lance yells something at Mikey, and they take off through the crowd towards the bar. I watch as the two of them order shots and down them immediately.

"Sunny, watch the damn show. Remember we're here to support Brittany. Don't let him think this is all about him!" Sam yells over the music. Christina Aguilera's "Dirty" is blasting over the speakers. I glance over at the bar, and Lance is still doing shot after shot. I have never once seen him do shots like that. Sam taps me on the shoulder.

"There she is...," he whispers excitedly, looking at the stage in awe. From stage left, out struts Heather Savoy.

The crowd again goes wild. Heather has long flowing brown hair, a great body, and is extremely pretty. But her expression is somewhat scary. The ultimate bitch. Her reputation precedes her. She is wearing a coral colored halter top that shows off her bully button which is pierced, tattered jeans with holes in the knees, and coral high heels that match her top. Her long brown hair sweeps down her back, and she definitely has no problem sexing it up. I look down at my outfit and feel somewhat plain. *Great! That's just great!* I think to myself. She's not only singing the song but she's dancing along with it and working the crowd.

"She's head cheerleader this year!!" Sam looks at her in awe.

I really wonder about Sam's loyalty sometimes. It's almost as if he enjoys the drama in a sick way. We're here to support Brittany, yet he loves the fact that these girls really hate each other. Heather finishes the song, and her evil grin is triumphant. The crowd is wild, screaming, cheering. They love Heather Savoy. Just then I see Brittany hurriedly making her way through the crowd; her face is flushed, and she is visibly upset.

"Drew found out about me getting arrested, but he won't tell me how; he just said he got a text from an anonymous number. He said because I work at the Circus that it wouldn't surprise him if I was out being a hooker all night." Tears start to run down Brittany's face, and I can't help but feel sorry for her.

"But who would text him anonymously to sabotage you? Heather?" Sam asks curiously. I think I see a hint of a grin on Sam's face, but it quickly disappears.

"How on earth would she know I was arrested or even who Drew is, and how would she be able to get his number? Honestly, I have no idea how this happened, but there's no way I can go up there and sing next," Brit says wiping the tears from her eyes.

"Sunny. You have to do it. This is your chance. You are going to get up there and sing, and you're going to show Heather Savoy who the real star in Lance's life is," Sam states as he points towards the stage. I look at him with bewilderment.

"Have you lost your damn mind?!! I'm not going up there, period!" I say, looking at him like he's crazy.

"Sunny, listen to me. Tonight is a big night. It's one of those moments in life that will define who you are, and alter the course you're on. If you get up there and sing and sing well, the way I know you can, you will get what you've been wanting: the chance to show Lance Arceneaux you're a fighter. Show him you can't be beaten. Get up there and choose a song you know that will speak to his heart, no matter how guarded it may be." Sam puts his hands on my shoulders and looks me in the eye. "Get up there, be brave, and show him who Sunny Collins is or lose him altogether. Those are the two paths in front of you right now." I look into Sam's eyes for what seems like an eternity, and I can see how much he believes in me. I finally turn to look at Brittany. She nods at me.

"Get that bitch. Take her down for me, Sunny," Brittany says still shaken.

"Ok LSU Tigers, up next we have our girl, Brittany Laveau!! Brittany, please make your way to the stage!!" the DJ announces. I look at both of them, and then without saying a word, I make my way to the stage. I walk behind the curtains and up the tiny staircase that leads to the DJ booth. "Hey there. You Brittany?" he asks.

"No, I'm singing in her place. My name's Sunny Collins."

"Ok, great. What are you singing, Sunny? Let me make sure I have it."

I peer out to the audience and see Lance making his way back through the crowd. He stops when he gets to Brittany and Sam, and I see them explaining to him what is going on. Brittany points towards the stage, and he turns and looks in my direction. Chills shoot down my spine. This is real. This is really happening. I know that if I turn and run right now, I will regret this moment for the rest of my life. I take a deep breath and turn to look at the DJ.

"Would it be ok if I just sing a cappella?"

"Are you sure? That's not easy to do..." the DJ says to me looking uneasy.

"I'm sure," I say, and he hands me the microphone.

"Ok guys, up next is Sunny Collins. Let's give her a big round of applause!!" Some of the people in the crowd clap half-heartedly, but mostly I hear loud chatter.

I step out onto the stage and make my way to the center. I keep my eyes on the ground because I'm afraid of what I'll see if I look out. An overhead spotlight blast shines on me, and the crowd goes so silent that you can hear a pin drop. A couple of people start to giggle, and I finally look up and see Heather Savoy in the crowd with her group of friends. They are laughing and snickering. I feel something strange building in the pit of my stomach. I'm not sure if it's fear or anger. Then without even thinking about it, I look out at Sam, Brittany, and Lance. Sam is grinning, Brittany is covering her mouth with her hands, and Lance stands like a statue, arms crossed, his face emotionless. Without another thought, I hold up the mic and begin to sing. I slowly sing the first verse of "Ain't No Way" by Aretha Franklin, the first song Lance and I heard at Tabby's Blues Bar. I downloaded it the next day on iTunes and have listened to it a thousand times. Somehow I know this is the song. It almost feels like someone else has taken over my body. As the fear fades away, it is replaced by courage and strength. I belt out the song the best I can, hitting every note with a different memory of my time with Lance and of my time here in Louisiana. When I'm finished, I open my eyes and stare out into the crowd. A couple of people are clapping, a couple are cheering, but mostly people look back at me with blank looks on their faces. I glance over at Sam and Brittany who both looked shocked. With hesitation I look at Lance, but alas, he is still stone cold showing no emotion, just staring up at me, his green eyes piercing me like daggers.

"Sunny Collins, everyone," the DJ says rather quietly, and I turn to exit the stage. I hand him the mic, walk down the stairs, and head for the exit. I did what I had to do, and now I'm done. I want to get out of here. I want to get in my car and get the hell out of Louisiana. These people hate me, Lance wants nothing to do with me, it's all a game to Sam, and I'm not even sure if he even really cares about me. I'm done.

Just then I hear footsteps behind me, then a hand rests on my right shoulder.

"No, Sam, I don't want to hear it. Just leave me alone, ok?" I say in a hateful tone. I hear nothing, so I turn, and there stands Lance. I look up into his eyes which are still unreadable. It takes me a second to realize he's really standing in front of me.

"Follow me back inside," he says calmly. Do I object? Do I take off running? Is this even real? Screw it. I hesitantly take his hand and walk behind him back into the building. He makes his way over to the DJ booth and starts talking to the DJ. What on earth is he doing? I look over and see Brittany and Sam talking heatedly in the crowd. Then I look over and see Heather Savoy and her fan club enthralled by every word Heather says. Lance walks over, grabs me by the hand, and pulls me to the center of the crowd. We pass by Sam and Brittany who stop midsentence and turn and look at me in disbelief. The music comes on, and Lance wraps his arms around me.

"I'm not great at explaining how I feel... just listen to the words of this song...," I recognize the song because he's played it for me in his truck. It's "Until You" by Dave Barnes.

I need you, now and forever, just stay right here with me, don't ever leave. Love was kept from me like a secret, and I swore that I was through, until you, until you...

He is towering over me, holding me close, as we sway back and forth. I am so confused; it's unreal. Out of nowhere, I feel a piece of ice hit me in the back of the head. Then another. Then another. I look up, and people with shit-eating grins on their faces on the balcony are throwing ice at me.

"Ignore them," Lance whispers.

All of a sudden, an entire drink is dumped down my back. I turn around, and I'm face to face with Heather Savoy.

"Hey, Sunny!! Just wanted to welcome you to Baton Rouge!" she says with an evil grin on her face. Before I can say anything, Lance steps in front of me. I look around, and the entire club is watching. Sam and Brittany are standing there with their mouths agape. All I can think to myself is that this is a freak show. The crowd has a front row seat, cocktails in hand, and they can't wait for the fight to begin. We're all players in a best-selling show.

"Heather. You just made a very poor decision. Have you forgotten I know your little secret?" I hear Lance say to her in a quiet deadly tone. I can't see his eyes, but I would bet my life they are flashing with rage. I peek around him and see her face change from super bitch to terrified little girl.

"You wouldn't." She looks up at him in disbelief.

"Oh, but I would," he whispers. "Now turn around and walk away. I don't want to see you within twenty feet of Sunny again. Got it?" She stares him eye-to-eye for a second, and then turns and pushes her way through the crowd. No one says a word. The song ends, and a new contestant takes the stage to sing. Lance grabs me by the hand and leads me back through the crowd, out into the parking lot, and to my car.

"Just get us out of here. I drank too much to drive," he says in a dark tone. I get in and quickly stuff my bag full of stripper gear onto the back floor board. He's never ridden in my car before, and I'm not sure if he'll even fit. I unlock the door and put the top down. He gets in, and sure enough, he barely can get his legs in; he puts his seat all the way back.

"Drive," he says, as he stares out the window.

"Where are we going?" I ask him quietly.

"I don't know, just drive," he says irritated. I peel out of The Caterie parking lot, and ten minutes later make my way over the Mississippi River Bridge. "She had an abortion," Lance says as he looks out the window.

"What? Who did?" I ask perplexed.

"Heather. That's the secret in case you were wondering... Last year... She doesn't want her family to find out. They would disown her."

"Are you...I mean...was it your baby?" I ask not knowing if I want to know the answer.

"No. The guy she was cheating on me with was the father. I went with her when she had it done because I was the only one she trusted. The guy also happened to be one of the judges in the Miss LSU Pageant. If it ever got out, it would be one of the biggest scandals in Baton Rouge history. I don't think she'll mess with you again."

"Wow...," I say shocked.

I drive for almost half an hour before Lance tells me to turn. We make our way down a long gravel road that dead-ends at a swamp. He tells me to park, and he gets out of the car. I watch him walk to the end of the road and then pace back and forth; the only light is coming from my headlights. I get out and take a seat on the hood of my car, watching him go back and forth until he finally stops and looks at me.

"I love you. You get that, right? I love you." I feel like he just threw a dozen bricks at me. I'm still in shock from what has happened tonight, I don't know how to process this. This is what I've wanted to hear since I first met him. Unfortunately, I can't seem to get any words out. He studies my face intently, and then hits me with it. "Sunny, what do you want from me? Seriously, what is it you want from me? What are your intentions?

Why are you here? Why did you come into my life?"

"I...I don't want anything from you. I love you, too, and I just want to be around you." Thank God I got it out. He thinks about this for a minute.

"Do you get that I don't trust myself with you? Do you get that you scare me? I have feelings for you I've never felt before. I mean, do you fucking understand that? Do you know how hard that is for me? On top of it, I have all these people on my back criticizing my every move!" He begins to pace again.

Wow. He's scared of me? From day one I've been scared of him. I'm mesmerized. He's telling me he's scared of me? This is just crazy. On the other hand, I'm starting to understand why he hasn't spoken to me in two weeks. All I can think is that Sam was right; that he wasn't ever mad at me, he was just trying to figure things out, and that's his way of doing it. I feel like I was the one hurt, but I also can't help but feel sorry for him. I realize at this moment how opposite we are when dealing with love and our feelings. I walk over and grab him by the hand and lead him into the forest away from the bright headlights of my car. Normally he wouldn't let me take charge, but he doesn't hesitate. I push him down onto the ground and straddle him. Unfortunately, I realize I just made him lie down in two inches of water. We're in a swamp. Luckily, he thinks it's funny. He grabs me and flips me over on my back so that my entire backside is covered in swamp water as well. We both burst out laughing. Despite being soaked, the electricity between us begins to sizzle. We start making out, and next thing

I know were tearing each other's clothes off like animals in the Louisiana swamp. Were both soaking wet, but that doesn't stop us. The craziness of tonight's events has made sex even more intense than ever before. Tonight is the first time a guy has ever told me he loved me, and I actually said I love you back. What an incredible feeling! The truth is that I couldn't be any more in love with him.

CHAPTER SIXTEEN
The Cat's Meow

LANCE IS BUSY with baseball, and Brittany spends all her time with Drew, so I don't see either of them but maybe once or twice a week. I wander around the French Quarter and find odd places like Esoterica, the most famous shop for witches, a place that sells spell books and ingredients to make potions. I also find Marie Laveau's House of Voodoo; she is the most famous voodoo priestess in New Orleans' history. I buy a lot of unusual things to make a really cool gift basket to send to Momma, and I know she'll be tickled to get it.

ON HIS NIGHT OFF, Lance wants to have dinner in the Quarter. He parks his truck in his normal spot in the Quarter and knocks on the front door of Brittany's apartment. I let him in, and he's wearing a lime green button-up dress shirt with the sleeves rolled up, jeans, and his normal boots. His signature style. Every time I smell him, I melt inside, and I can't help thinking about how good he is in bed.

"Damn. You look hot!" He looks me up and down and smiles with approval.

"Thanks! I got my dress today at Neiman Marcus," I say to him without thinking.

"How can you afford a dress from there?" He looks at me inquisitively. Shit, think fast.

"Oh Brittany and I were just there browsing, and it was on sale."

"Oh cool," he says and shrugs his shoulders. Whoa, close one. I stand on my tiptoes and put both my arms around his neck to kiss him. I haven't seen him all week, and I've really missed him.

He takes me to Brennan's for dinner and explains to me that it's one of New Orleans' most famous fine dining restaurants. They serve Creole food, which I'm starting to develop a craving for. We are led through the beautiful restaurant and are seated outside in a courtyard that resembles a secret garden. There are flickering gas lanterns everywhere that give the entire garden a romantic glow. Lance orders a lot of different things from the menu and tells me he has a bunch of favorites that he wants me to try. I eat raw oysters for the first time which are surprisingly good. Lance tells me, along with a wink, that they're an aphrodisiac.

"One of my favorite things about you is your fearlessness with food, Sunny." He laughs at me. "You're like me; we both love food, and we both try anything," he says amused. Over dinner he asks me to tell him more about growing up in Texas. "Why is it every time I ask you about your past, you freeze up? I just want to know more about you," he says, his tone serious.

I'm clearly not comfortable talking about this at all, especially after meeting his wonderful family. What am I supposed to say? That my dad severely abused me and my mom, and that I ran away from home? I try to be as honest as I can, but I have to scoot around the truth a couple of times, which I feel really guilty about doing.

Lance gazes at me all through dinner. He holds my hand and really pays attention to what I'm saying. We laugh so hard, we cry. We really enjoy each other's stories and just being together. *So this is love?* I think to myself. I also think back to when I first met him. When I'm with him, I feel like the sun is shining. He's charming, attentive, sexy, and caring, but then there's the other side: cold, dismissive, self-involved. You never know which side of the Gemini you're going to get, so you cherish the good times.

After dinner we make our way into the Quarter, and Lance tells me he wants to grab a beer. As we stroll down Bourbon, I'm caught up in how wonderful life is with him in it. I just can't stop smiling. I'm in this strange beautiful city with this sexy mysterious guy. Then suddenly I'm shaken out of my bliss. I look up and see Big Louie standing outside the Circus. Shit. It's like a slow motion train wreck. I can sense what's about to happen. I jump on the other side of Lance and pull him to the opposite side of the street.

"What the heck are you doing, Sunny?" he asks me perplexed.

"Um, nothing. I just saw a customer I waited on at the bistro who was really rude to me."

"What do you mean rude to you? Which one is he? I'm gonna go say something to him."

"No, don't, he might go back and tell my manager." I look over at the Circus, which we are directly across from, and freeze. Just then Louie turns and heads inside the front door. That was a close one. I convince Lance that everything is fine, and we keep walking.

"I can't believe how warm it is tonight," Lance says, as he begins to take off his button-up. He has a wife beater on, and he's sweaty from the sticky southern heat. It makes his tan biceps glisten. I'm the luckiest girl in the world. Eventually, we arrive at the Cat's Meow and step inside. "I think you'll like this place. It's usually packed, but it's kind of dead since it's a Tuesday," Lance tells me. "You want a beer? Or something else?" he asks.

"Grey Goose and soda would be great," I say.

"Alright, well go look at the song book because we're gonna sing in a little bit."

"What? Who is?" I ask.

"You and I are. Don't pretend you're shy, not after that performance at The Caterie," he says as he makes his way to the bar.

After a couple of drinks and Lance constantly badgering me, I finally work up the nerve to sing. What the hell do I sing this time? I step on the small stage, and I'm more nervous singing in front of Lance and a few random bar flies than I was singing in front of hundreds of people at the carnivals and fairs as a kid. I thought what happened at The Caterie was a one-time thing, and I felt forced into it. The DJ cues me, and I hear the music begin. I've chosen "Fancy" by Reba McEntire. I feel like the song is appropriate. I begin to sing, and I think I'm doing pretty well, but the look on Lance's face is unreadable. He has a great poker face which makes me even more nervous. Once again I feel tested by the Gemini. I make my way through the song, and half way through it, my nervousness goes away and I let the music take over. In my mind, I'm suddenly in front of thousands of people performing in a stadium with the lights, the fire, and the smoke all around me. The crowd is screaming. I belt out the words the best I can, trying hard not to look at Lance. The song is over, and I open my eyes, step down quickly from the stage, and take my seat back at the table. I finally work up the nerve to look at Lance who's staring at me with a bewildered look on his face.

"Sunny...you are amazing." He just sits there staring at me intently for a minute. "You just continue to surprise me...Life with you will never be boring, will it?" He smiles at me, and I have to look away because I feel myself blush.

After a couple of beers, Lance gets up and sings as well. He, on the other hand, loves to sing in front of people and even does cocky little dance moves as he sings "Where You Are" by Marc Broussard, a Louisiana local who people here love. Watching him sing is very entertaining, and I think to myself that there's a little bit of him who loves the spotlight. He winks at me throughout the song, and he has everyone there clapping along. Later, we walk a couple of blocks to the outskirts of the Quarter to sit on the banks of the Mississippi River. We find a spot on the grassy knoll and sit and watch the steamboats go by, and the lights from the city shimmer on the water.

"So, Sunny, I want you to be honest with me. What do you really want to do with your life? I know your dream wasn't to come to Louisiana to be a cocktail waitress. I mean, I'm really glad you did, but what do you want out of life?" he asks sincerely.

"Well..." I look at him nervously. "Ever since I was a little girl, I wanted to be on stage or in the movies. My mom worked at a theater, and all I have ever wanted was to do was sing and dance on stage someday. Eventually I want to go out to Hollywood and see where it takes me." I smile at him; thinking of my dream gives me goosebumps. His expression suddenly grows dark. "What's wrong?" I ask him.

"If that's what you want, then why are you here? Sam is moving out to L.A. next week; why aren't you going with him?"

"Well..." Shit, I have to stall because I know where this is going.

"Sunny, you can't stay here for me. I think we both know you don't belong in Louisiana." He stands up and looks out towards the water. "Tell me right now, am I the only thing that's keeping you here?" *Yes*. But there's no way I'm telling you that.

"No, of course not!!! I'm working and saving up money to go out there, and I'm enjoying my time here!! I've met some great friends, and I've seen some amazing things I never knew existed...and maybe a little bit because of you." He turns to look at me, his expression has softened, and I think I see a hint of a smile. He puts his arm around me.

"I think you're pretty amazing, in case you didn't know that. You're not like any other girl...You're just...different. I don't know what is. You put some kind of spell on me," he says looking at me perplexed. "Listen. I want you to promise me you'll go out to Hollywood. I want you to make me proud. If being an actress is what will make you happy, then that's what I want for you...And if you ever get nominated for an Oscar, I damn well better be your date on the big night," he says with a grin. I breathe in his ridiculously sexy smell. "You know what? You're lucky you're so damn cute," he says demurely.

"Well, what about you? Would you ever consider living there?" I ask, afraid of his answer. I can't imagine him ever wanting that lifestyle.

"Well actually, I've never told anyone this, but I've always kind of wanted to live on the beach in Santa Monica. Maybe take up surfing. Yeah, that would be cool; I'd be a badass surfer!" he says happily. "My family pushed me hard to play baseball; I never really wanted to, but it turns out I'm good, so I used it for a scholarship. Anyway, I don't think I would enjoy the fast paced part of L.A., but I could definitely see myself living on the outskirts enjoying southern California life. Maybe having some kids..." Wow. I can't believe he would be down for it.

This makes the wheels in my head start to turn. I imagine us living in a condo on the beach, Lance waking up early to go surfing with his friends, me on the way to the studio to work on my latest movie... Taking our kids to Disneyland... Maybe even having a second house somewhere in the south so we're both close to our families. The idea is pure bliss.

"Hey...I love you, kid," he says.

"I love you, too, big guy." The statement is simple, but when I hear it, especially from someone I happen to be head over heels for, it's the most amazing moment of my life. Even saying it back to him changes something inside me forever. Eric blinks into my mind for a second. What a difference. Eric told me I was a fool for wanting to try and make it in

L.A., and he never said *I love you*...Not that I thought I would hear Lance say it any time soon because he definitely takes his time in matters of love and romance. He has to be sure of something first. And he's supportive of my crazy dream. He's the best thing about my world. I love him with everything in me right down to my soul. We sit for hours talking about the future and what the life of a movie star is probably like, and he even says he may come out to Hollywood when he's finished LSU. This couldn't make me happier. I eventually fall asleep snuggled up in his arms right there on the banks of the Mississippi, as the gentle breeze blows in. It's been one of the most memorable nights of my life.

CHAPTER SEVENTEEN
The Governor

THE NEXT WEEK, which arrived quickly, Sam has his furniture packed in a U-Haul in front of the LeBlanc mansion and is ready to make the long drive out to California. Brittany and I go to his house to say goodbye, both of us crying and hugging him, and he of course is rolling his eyes at the two of us. Sam and I are very different when situations are emotional. I cry my eyes out because he's leaving and going far away.

"You're so dramatic, Sunny; suck it up and stop with the waterworks," he says in true Sam LeBlanc fashion. "Listen you two, I know we've pulled off some crazy shit. Getting Sunny a job at the Circus and no one finding out is quite the feat in itself, but just keep a low profile and keep making that money. If anyone finds out what y'all are doing, all of our heads are going to roll. The last thing we need is Lance finding out that all three of us have been lying to him this entire time." He winks, jumps in the U-Haul truck, and makes a speedy exit down the street towards the interstate.

"He has never been good at goodbyes," Brittany says to me. As I watch him drive away, I can't help but wish I were going with him. Someday I'll make it to Hollywood, but for the first time in my life I'm truly in love, and there's no way I'm giving that up.

THE NEXT WEEKEND back in NOLA, Brittany and I wake up early and decide to have breakfast at Dauphine's on St. Ann. It's been a week since Sam left, and I miss him. I also have a sinking feeling about his going to L.A. without me; after all, that is what I had set out to do so long ago, and I pray I haven't missed my chance. It's a little strange being here without him because I feel like I've been left to fend for myself.

"Snap out of it!" Brittany says causing me to jump. "I know you're missing Sam, but you still have me and Lance, and nothing's going to happen to you, Sunny." She has a sympathetic smile on her face.

"I know...He's just been around so long and always walked me through sticky situations that I tend to get into. We've been together since...well since I left Texas." I think back at how long ago that was.

"Ok, well let's get your mind off of it. You still haven't told me what happened with Lance after y'all left The Caterie!! I have been dying to hear this story since it happened!"

"Well, Brit, every time I try to tell you, you are on your way out of the house with Drew."

"I know, I know! I'm sorry! It's just that ever since I met him I've been a little preoccupied. Seriously, Sunny, I think he might be the one. Like, we are inseparable. I can't even begin to tell you how good he is in bed, and he treats me so well; it's insane." Brittany's face lights up as she talks about him, which is rare. Being a Scorpio, she's good at masking her feelings and has a pretty tough exterior. She's told me many times she's had a lot of trouble letting guys get close to her in the past. It's nice to see her trust again.

"Ok, so you have my full attention now, tell me everything that happened from start to finish." I tell her all of the details about our endless drive to the middle of nowhere, Lance yelling at me and using the *L* word, and I end with the juicy details of us rolling around in the swamp. Brittany just stares blankly at me for a minute.

"So he said *I love you*, huh..." I watch as she processes it. "Honestly I'm in shock right now. I mean, Sam and I both literally could not believe he grabbed you and stood there holding you in front of everyone, especially in front of half the school. I know for a fact he's never told any girl he loves her before you; this is just blowing my mind."

"Why do you think it's so crazy? And why do you think he didn't speak to me for two weeks before all of that? I am so baffled by the whole thing that I don't know which way is up or down anymore." I start to feel frazzled talking about it and remembering how crazy the past two weeks have been.

"Well, I'm just gonna be honest with you, Sunny. I've known the guy for a long time, I probably know him better than anyone. Hell, he is one of my best friends. I'm telling you, Lance and I are the same person. He just happens to be a guy, and I'm a girl. We've sat up so many nights talking, and we both have the same problem in relationships. When things get too intense, we run. We will hurt others before they can hurt us. That's just how we do things. I think he knew he was really starting to have feelings for you, so he turned a cold shoulder towards you. You were able to get over his walls, and it freaked him out. A lot of people don't realize how deep his emotions run. You've been swimming in uncharted waters with him for a while now. It's really hard for him to trust anybody, and I feel like you've gotten further with him than anyone else has... Which is actually awful since we both have been lying to him for a while now. I'm just waiting for the day that this all blows up in our faces. Anyway, regardless, I just hope you figure out a way to tell him soon because I'm getting worried that he's going to catch on. I mean if you think I'm joking, I'm not; I'm sure you've caught a glimpse of his temper by now, and it will be Hurricane Lance, category five if he finds out," she says with a laugh, and I sink down in my chair dreading the thought.

Just then, I look up and see Lisa Beaumann strutting down St. Ann. She's wearing her hair up today and closely resembles Elizabeth Taylor. She dons long chandelier earrings, giant black Chanel sunglasses, and a black and white polka dot dress, and she looks like a 1950s housewife.

"Sunny!! I have been looking for you everywhere, damn it!! I've been calling your cell non-stop, and I walked all the way over to your house!" she says exasperated.

"I'm sorry, Lisa. I left my cell on the charger at Brittany's apartment. We just walked over to have some breakfast. What's going on?" I ask inquisitively.

"Well, dear, only the most important event of the day, of course, and I need you!! The governor is in town, and he is taking me and a few other well respected members of the French Quarter out on his newly renovated club car on the railroad. There's going to be a buffet and open bar, and he wants me to invite some pretty girls. It's at two p.m., so you need to go home and freshen up right now!!" she says, as she stomps her heel on the ground dramatically. I can't help but giggle. It's very entertaining when Lisa gets mad. "Don't laugh at me. Oh and Brittany, you come as well. Don't invite anyone else though, this is an invitation only affair." She turns up her nose arrogantly and prances off.

"Lisa sure has taken a liking to you," Brittany says sipping her coffee.

"Yeah she has. I love being around her. She's one of the most fascinating people I've ever met," I say lost in thought.

"Fascinating? I wouldn't go that far. At the end of the day she's kind of a freak, I mean she used to be a guy, Sunny, not someone to admire." I shoot Brittany a don't-cross-the-line look.

"I don't see her like that. I think she's absolutely fabulous," I say in a dismissive tone.

"Oh my god, Sunny, don't get defensive. I'm not trying to be a bitch, I just don't get being transgender or whatever she is," Brittany says to me trying to avoid an argument. I get lost in thought for a moment, pondering the life of Lisa Beaumann: the glittering gowns, her plush pink apartment, nightly performances, and how her presence captivates the audience. I couldn't feel more blessed that she's taken a liking to me.

"Ok, well I guess we'll have to finish this conversation later, Brit. Today will be fun; I've never been on a private train car before. And we get to meet the governor!" I say excitedly.

"Oh sure, let me just run through the Quarter with excitement," Brittany says with yawn.

At ten minutes to two, we arrive at platform 6 inside New Orleans Union Station. There sits a beautiful red steam engine with two train cars connected to it. It looks brand new, but I can tell it's been restored. There's a club car in the middle and a caboose on the end. We see Lisa deep in conversation with a group of men and make our way over.

"Sunny, Brittany, I'd like to introduce you to Governor Bobby Boudreaux," Lisa says very formally.

"Hi, it's a pleasure to meet you," I say shaking his hand.

"Well aren't you a beauty, young lady," he says smiling, with a twinkle in his eye. I must say, he's very charming. I glance at Brittany who is pretending to vomit behind him. A man steps out from the waiting train car and addresses the governor.

"Governor Boudreaux, lunch is served, and we're ready to go."

"Well, everyone, I don't know about you, but I'm hungry. Let's eat!" the governor says with a jolly laugh, and everyone begins to walk towards the awaiting club car.

We enter, and the train slowly begins to move. It's more posh than I could have imagined. Plush gold velvet booths line one side of the club car, topped with dozens of decorative pillows. On the other side is a beautiful array of berries, po-boys, smoked salmon, crab cakes Benedict, and beignets, all set up as a buffet.

"These are all of the governor's favorites," Lisa whispers in my ear as we make our way through the buffet line. Brittany whisks past me and makes a beeline for the very elegant bar at the front of the club car where a handsome bartender is making cocktails.

"Sunny, be sure to have a Bloody Mary; Cory my bartender makes the best one this side of Alabama," the governor says as he piles food on his plate.

"I sure will, Governor Boudreaux," I say with a polite laugh.

"Oh Sunny, we're all friends here, please. Call me Bobby." I smile, grab a beignet and some raspberries, and then head over to the bar.

"Well, it sounds like he's pretty impressed by you," Brittany says condescendingly.

"Brittany, he's the governor of Louisiana; are you not even the least bit impressed?" I ask to her, not understanding her attitude.

"He's sleazy, Sunny. I just came so I wouldn't piss off Lisa Beaumann... and because I can't resist a good Bloody Mary."

We spend several hours making our way through the swamp lands, over huge bridges, and finally we turn a bend and circle back towards New Orleans. I'm definitely feeling buzzed and enjoying myself as the governor and Lisa swap stories with the group of men who are all somewhat tipsy at this point. Some of them have rolled up their sleeves, drinking brandy, and puffing away on cigars. I decide I should use the restroom before we get back to the Quarter, so I make my way to the back of the club car, through the sliding doors, and into the caboose where the tiny restroom is. I sit forever waiting to pee and have to hold onto the railing inside the bathroom as we make our way over a rickety bridge just outside New Orleans. When I'm finally done, I stand up and realize how buzzed I am.

I need some water and fast. Just then, I hear a knock at the door. I open it expecting to see Brittany who is probably wondering what's taking me so long. To my surprise, it's the governor.

"Well, hi there. I was just making sure you're okay, darlin'. I wouldn't want anything to happen to such a sweet little southern girl." He has a strange grin on his face, and his eyes flash wildly.

"I'm fine, thank you, just had one too many Bloody Marys." I giggle nervously and try to duck past him. His arms shoot up, trapping me in the tiny bathroom, and I feel my heart drop. This is not happening. He then pushes me back into the bathroom and shuts the door behind him. He reaches for my skirt and pulls it up, and then reaches for my panties. I'm terrified, and my heart is beating out of my chest. Then Lance pops into my head. *I love you, Sunny. Don't let this guy violate you like this*, I imagine Lance saying. *You're mine, not his.* My fear turns into anger, and with everything I've got, I slap the fire out of the governor. He looks at me stunned, and his grin turns into "You little bitch! How dare you slap me! I'm the most powerful man in the state of Louisiana!" he hisses through gritted teeth.

"Get off me, you bastard!" I scream back. "HELP, SOMEONE PLEASE HELP!!" I scream as loud as I can. The governor cups his hand over my mouth, reaches down and rips off my panties, and unzips his pants. I feel the train begin to slow and realize we must be close to the station.

"Stop trying to resist me," he whispers into my ear. "I know you Circus girls are all whores and prostitutes. You want a big dick so bad, you can't stand it." *Think quickly, Sunny.* I nod *yes* slowly, and he removes his hand from my mouth.

"You're right. I just like a good struggle," I whisper to him seductively. The grin spreads across his face again.

"Is that so?" he asks surprised. "Well don't worry, I can tame a little mare like you," he says, slowly running his hand down my leg. I pull my arm back and with all my strength sock him in the groin as hard as I can.

"Ahhhhhh!" he yells out in pain. I shove him as hard as I can to the left, and then kick the door of the bathroom which goes flying open. I climb past the governor, out of the bathroom, and haul ass to the back of the caboose. I hear the governor wrestle his way out of the bathroom, and then he starts making his way towards me. The train is still rolling to a stop, but I swing open the back door and jump off the train. I hit the gravel between the tracks hard. *Run, Sunny*, I think to myself. I get up, brush myself off, and take off running towards the station platform and finally into the crowds of people waiting to board their trains.

I wander through the French Quarter wearily, trying to wrap my head around what just happened. Am I going to end up in jail? Will the governor have me arrested for assault? I'm sure I would end up in prison if he did. There's no way he would want that kind of publicity, being accused of rape. Should I go to the police station right away? God, please tell me what to do. It begins to rain, so I run inside the Bourbon Pub and order a Grey Goose and soda. I feel hot tears begin to roll down my face. *I know you Circus girls are all prostitutes and whores.* The sound of his voice plays over and over in my head. I have never felt so ashamed in my life. I've never been treated with such disgust. What have I done? How did I get here? I set out with big dreams, and now I'm nothing more than a New Orleans prostitute, sitting in a bar, drinking by myself. How pathetic.

I OPEN MY EYES, and everything is still spinning. I realize I'm in my car, but I can't make out where I am because of the rain. I'm guessing I'm somewhere in the Quarter. I search everywhere for my phone and finally find it stuck in between the seats. Thirty two missed calls and text from Brittany...and eighteen calls from Lance along with one text.

LANCE: I'm in New Orleans looking for you. WHERE THE HELL ARE YOU!

Shit...oh shit. That was two hours ago. I bet he is madder than a damn rattle snake by now. All of a sudden there's pounding on my window, and I jump up terrified. I can barely see through the window because the rain is coming down so hard.

"Sunny, open the goddamned door!!!"

Oh no, it's Lance. This is gonna be bad, and my head is still spinning from the alcohol. I unlock the door, and he swings it open. He's soaking wet, rain is dripping down his face, and anger flashes in his eyes, so much so that I don't want to get out of the car. He reaches in, grabs my keys, pulls me out, and throws me over his shoulder. All I can see are the heels of his boots as he walks through the flooded street. His body feels warm, even though his clothes are completely soaked. After what seems like a very long time, we get to his truck, and now I'm drenched as well. He opens the passenger door, pitches me in rather roughly, and puts my seat belt on me, which he jerks tight, and slams the door. Shit. I know what's about to happen. He's about to light into me like I've never seen before. He is genuinely pissed. I know he would never hit me, but he wouldn't have to. Just being around him when he's this mad is terrifying enough. I slink down in my seat and put my knees up on the dash. He opens his door and gets in, fires up his truck, and we're off. It's dead silence for the first couple of minutes, and then sure enough, I was right. His temper boils over and explodes.

"I cannot fucking believe you would do something so stupid!!! You're sleeping in your car, no passed out drunk in your car, all day and half the night while Brittany's hysterical and looking for you everywhere and calling me at work!! Have you lost your goddamned mind??Are you ever going to fucking understand how dangerous New Orleans is!! These people will murder you and not think twice about it!! But I guess you don't care right? Don't care that you mean something to me and I would be devastated if someone murdered or kidnapped you?? No you're too goddamned selfish to care how what you do affects anyone else!! This is unbelievable!! I tell you I love you, and this is how you repay me? I had to leave work and drive an hour to get here, and then walk the streets for another two hours in the rain until I found your goddamned car!! But does any of that matter to you?? Somehow I doubt it!!" His anger has hit fever pitch.

"You know what, just shut up, Lance. Where the hell were you for two weeks when I was calling and texting you?? Were you worried about me then?? Was I not supposed to be worried about you?? But that doesn't matter right? Because Lance does whatever he wants and everybody else just has to tiptoe around him!!!" I yell at him for the first time ever.

"Ohhhhh no, I already apologized to you and told you why I did what I did, so don't try and pull that shifty shit on me," he yells back, making a valid point.

I have to think for a minute about what to say next because I don't have a comeback. I also am still frazzled by the events of the day. Do I tell Lance about the governor? No, I can't. If I tell him part of the story, I'll have to tell him everything, and that means telling him I work at the Circus.

A couple of minutes go by, and Lance starts to speak.

"Why are you still here, Sunny? Go out there to L.A. and live your dreams, make me proud. I don't want you to stay here for me," he says in a solemn tone. He can't be serious. Is he trying to push me away from him?

"I want to be wherever you are," I say, and then suddenly burst into tears. "I'm supposed to be right here, beside you. That's where I belong. I've known that since the moment I saw you. Now you want to push me away again? Well good luck. No matter what you do, I will always end up wherever you are." I wish the words wouldn't have come out, but it's too late. There's no more playing games; I've put it all out on the table. Lance stares out the window as the rain pounds against the windshield of his truck. After a couple of minutes of silence, he finally speaks.

"I want you beside me, too...," he says and reaches for my hand.

Neither of us says anything. As we make our way over the spillway of Lake Pontchartrain, I am sobered up, and my mind races thinking about what I just told him and his response. Holy shit. I unbuckle my seat belt, scoot over, and lay my head down on Lance's lap. I can tell he wants to object, but he doesn't. After a minute or two, he rests his free hand on my head. I look up at his handsome face as he stares out at the road in front of him. I still see a hint of worry on his face, and it finally hits me. He was really worried about me. Baton Rouge's number one playboy was worried about me. Underneath all his confusing layers, it's clear as day. I smile and close my eyes, and he begins to run his fingers through my hair.

"I really was scared something was going to happen to you...," he mumbles under his breath. I smile and drift off to sleep.

When we get back to his apartment, the sun is beginning to rise. He gets me a bottle of water, and then brushes past me still brooding. He changes into basketball shorts and hands me a big t-shirt. He climbs into bed and turns onto his side so he's not facing me. I change, climb in next to him, and slowly slide my hands around him.

"Stop. I'm still mad," he says as he pushes my hands off him and turns back on his side.

I can't help but be turned on being next to him, not to mention the fact he left work and drove all that way to come save me. I try again, and this time he doesn't push me off. He just lies there pretending he's already asleep. I rub his back, which I know he loves, then his shoulders and his smooth chest. I slowly make my way down to his shorts and am just barely able to slide them off his long muscular legs. I touch him as sensually as I can, and finally he turns over towards me, still pretending to be asleep. Really? Ok, so we're playing that game. I giggle as I watch him try to keep his eyes shut. He suddenly grabs me and pulls me close to his warm chest. We fit together perfectly. I love being curled up next to him with his bulging arms wrapped around me.

"What the hell am I gonna do with you?" he whispers to me. "Should I buy you a leash?" The thought turns me on.

"That actually sounds kind of hot.' I answer him playfully. His eyes spring open.

"Come here, you little freak!" He grins at me and begins to kiss me uncontrollably. The Gemini seduction is underway, and my body feels like it's on fire every time he caresses me. He flips me on my stomach and grabs my hips with his massive hands. "You've been pretty bad tonight, haven't you? Are you ready for your punishment? Say it. Let me hear you say you want it."

"I want it," I whisper. He's driving me crazy making me beg like this. Slowly, he slides into me, then deeper and faster.

"Yeah, you like to be punished don't you? Tell me how you want it," he says in a low rumble.

"I want it bad," I whisper. He pulls out of me, and then picks me up and slams me up against the wall above the headboard.

"C'mon baby, let's burn this motherfucker down," he jokes. He's back inside me, and it feels amazing. We move around the room, getting rougher and rougher until I can't take it anymore. "Come on, I'm not gonna stop until I see you explode," he says. I feel the electricity between us shooting sparks everywhere. I tilt my head back and hear the beautiful cinematic music that plays in my head whenever we have sex. I feel him inside me pulsating, creating so much heat, and then I burst at the seams. Fire engulfs my body, and I explode. I watch him do the same, his face dark and staring right into my eyes; it's ecstasy. Pure ecstasy. Better than any drug, any cocktail, anything else in the world.

CHAPTER EIGHTEEN
The Gulf Coast Storm

A WEEK HAS GONE by, and Friday finally rolls around. Lance's mom called me last night and told me that Maw Maw has requested my presence, and that she's ready for me to come and help her redecorate her house. She also requested I come alone, so I don't tell Lance I am going. I'm curious what this means but also excited to have some one-on-one time with his grandmother. He's so complex and hard for me to understand, and I'm hoping I will come away from this with some answers. The long drive from New Orleans to Black Bayou and back will totally be worth it if I leave Black Bayou understanding him even just a little bit more. I make my way down I-10 through rural Louisiana and turn south when I hit Lake Charles. My convertible top is down, the wind is blowing in my hair, and there are thousands of pine trees as far as the eye can see. The smell of the fresh pine is intoxicating. Dave Barnes, Marc Brossard, and Michael Buble blast through my speakers thanks to the CD Lance burned for me. Not the kind of music I would have ever listened to before living in Louisiana, but it's growing on me.

When I finally get to the address Lance's mom gave me, all I see is a mailbox and a little dirt road that leads around a bend. I follow it and eventually pull up to a quaint little house painted eggshell with baby blue shutters. A staircase leads to an enormous porch that wraps around the house with a swing on one side and table and chairs on the other. Huge pecan trees grow on both sides of the house, shading it from the bright Louisiana sun. I make my way through the wrought iron gate in the front yard and up the steps. I peer through the screen door and wonder if I should knock or just head in. What sounds like 1920s French music is playing on an old record player inside.

"Miss Dot?" I yell through the screen door. "It's Sunny!! Lance's… um…girlfriend." I feel weird saying that since I've only heard him say it once. I don't hear anything, and there's no sign of her, so I make my way around the porch to the backyard. I peer over the fence and see a chicken coup full of chickens, goats galloping around the yard, and horses in the distance nibbling on grass. I take in a deep breath, and the smell reminds me of home. Just then I spot Maw Maw in the middle of a huge vegetable garden. She is so tiny compared to the tall stalks of corn growing in rows all around her. She is wearing spectacles, a paisley top with tiny flowers all over it, and an enormous straw hat. *A true southern woman*, I think, and I giggle to myself.

"Maw Maw!!" I yell. "I'm here!!"

"Well there she is!!" She looks up at me startled. "I was beginning to wonder where you were!" I make my way through the gate to the garden and bend down to hug her.

"Sorry I didn't mean to scare you!" I say to her.

"Yeah, what are you trying to do, give me a heart attack? You better be careful about sneaking up on me, especially when I've got these in my hand. I might be old, but I can still whip some ass!!" she says warning me, as she shakes her garden shears at me. I can't help but laugh. "Well come on in, darlin'. I'm done out here, so let's go sit down for a minute and have something to drink." I follow her through the back door and into the kitchen. "You want Coke or sweet tea?" she asks looking up at me suspiciously.

"Coke, of course!" I say grinning.

"Good answer," she says with a smug look on her face. "I knew you were a Coke kinda girl." She pops open two cans, and we make our way to the front porch. We sit at the table, and she lights up a cigarette, and then leans back and relaxes. She studies me like it's her first time seeing me.

"So what all do you have planned for me to do today?" I ask, trying to sound like I believe that's why I'm here. She looks over her spectacles at me with the same disapproving look Lance has given me so many times.

"Now darlin', I thought you were smarter than that. We both know you aren't here to decorate anything. God only knows what you would have my house looking like if I put you in charge," she says with an eye roll as she takes a puff of her cigarette. A wide smile slowly spreads across my face. I can't help it. "Uh huh!! Just as I thought!! You know exactly what you're doing here," she says matter-of-factly. "So let's get down to business. What are your intentions with my grandson?" This catches me off guard and my smile fades to a worried expression.

"What do you mean *intentions*?" I ask her honestly.

"You know what I mean," she says as she takes another puff of her cigarette. "If you want my help, you have to be honest with me. What are your intentions?" Her help? Now I'm confused. How does she know I need help with him?

"Well...I don't really have intentions. I love Lance, more than anyone else in the world. Those are my intentions," I say honestly, and I watch as her eyes widen listening to my statement.

"And have you told him that?" she asks wide-eyed.

"Yes ma'am."

"And has he told you he loves you?" she asks suspiciously, disbelief in the tone of her voice.

"Yes ma'am," I say, thinking back to that night. Even I was in shock hearing him say it.

"Oh lordy...," she says with a sigh, shaking her head. "Well before we go any further, I need you to promise me something," she says with a stern look.

"Of course, anything," I say, feeling as though I have no other choice.

"Promise you won't do anything to hurt him."

"Ok, that's easy. I promise."

"No darlin', I don't think you understand. There's a reason Lance is the way he is. His temper, his way of shutting you out if you've upset him... Things happened when he was a child, indescribable things. It took me and his momma years to get that boy sorted out. The fact that he's such a stable young man, getting good grades, playing ball at Louisiana State...It's a miracle," she says with a shudder, looking out at the surrounding fields. A look of sorrow caused from awful memories of the past washes over her face.

"I'm sorry, I...I didn't know...What sort of things, if you don't mind me asking?" She comes out of deep thought and looks me in the eye, searching for a sign to let her know whether she can trust me or not.

"All in good time, darlin'," she says sweetly. "Today's not the day. I will say one thing, though; you two do look good together. You fit well, like two peas in a pod." I feel my face turn red, and I smile. "It's more than that though, there's some kind of connection between you and my grandson."

"Really? You can see it, too?" I ask looking at her curiously.

"Trust me, young lady; I've been on this earth a long time. It's rare, but I've seen it before. If I didn't think there was something special about you and him, we wouldn't be having this conversation. And trust me when I tell you, if you break his trust, it's over, and it'll take a lifetime to get it back... Now for the fun part!!" she says with a mischievous grin. "What good dirt do you wanna know? Should I tell you his nickname as a kid? Or all of the embarrassing things that happened to him in high school?"

I curl up in my chair with excitement as Maw Maw trails off into stories of the past. Unfortunately, a part of me is burning to know the dark secrets of Lance Arceneaux. What happened that damaged him so badly? Would he still be the same guy today had it not happened? Would I have fallen in love with him if he were normal like any other guy? Lance's grandmother has opened a whole new can of worms, and I pray my curiosity doesn't get the best of me. A couple of hours later, I hug Maw Maw goodbye.

"You be safe driving back now. They said on the news this morning that we have a huge storm blowing in from the coast, and it's gonna hit New Orleans first," she says as she walks me to my car.

"I will; I'm gonna get back as fast as I can so I don't get stuck in the rain." She reaches out and grabs my hand, putting it in hers.

"Listen to me," she says looking up into my eyes, a kind expression on her face. "Just remember to follow your heart, Sunny. I know he can be difficult at times, but he's worth it. True love is hard to find. It can make you soar above the clouds one day and make you wanna kill somebody the next. Just stay true to who you are and follow your heart." She winks at me and kisses my hand. I feel my eyes welling up with tears. She's right. Sometimes I feel like I'm on top of the world, and sometimes I feel like I'm in hell. I put my arms around her and give her one last hug.

I MAKE MY WAY down I-10, and all I can think about is telling Lance the truth about working at the Circus. After what I've learned today, I have to tell him. I also have to face the fact that he may never speak to me again, but I know if he finds out any other way, it'll be the beginning of the end anyway. I see the turn off for New Orleans coming up. Do I go to Baton

Rouge and tell him right now? Shit, I'm already going to be cutting it close, and there's a storm rolling in. Tonight is my first solo, and Lisa Beaumann has been working tirelessly for weeks on my costume for my first solo performance. I swerve right and head to the New Orleans exit. Ok. I'll tell him after this weekend. I just need a couple of days to think about how I'm going to say it. God, how am I supposed to know what's right?

As I WALK DOWN Bourbon Street, I see posters on the side of the building with my picture on them. *Dixie Daniels, Texas Cowgirl* is sprawled across them. I can't help but roll my eyes; I hate the name. I make my way inside, and I'm shocked to see that the entire place is already packed. The storm rolling in hasn't affected business tonight, that's for sure. I walk backstage and see Lisa. I begin to apologize to her about the train, but she interrupts me.

"Sunny don't apologize. I overheard the governor frantically telling his security staff what happened. I think he is afraid that you will accuse him of rape, and he's scared of the consequences. I promise you, I will never put you in danger again, and I hope you forgive me." I nod my head *yes*, and hug Lisa tightly. "Ok, I need to finish putting the final touches on your outfit!"

Lisa has spent weeks sewing, cutting and gluing Swarovski crystals to my costume, that consists of a hot pink halter top with a matching pink thong, pink chaps that have no back, pink fingerless gloves, and pink lace-up boots. I barely move, and the entire outfit sparkles like nothing I've ever seen before. It ties in with the cowboy theme to match the ridiculous name Dixie Daniels.

The best part about tonight is that Lisa, the DJ, and I worked out a remixed version of "Baby One More Time" by Britney Spears and "Pour

Some Sugar on Me" by Def Leppard, and Lisa convinced the DJ to let me sing live even though it will infuriate the ringleader. She says he'll just have to get over it, and he just may let me sing in all my solo numbers when he hears how good I am. Well, here's hoping I don't lose my job. I've been rehearsing with Brittany all week, coming up with the sexiest dance moves we can imagine, some I'm not even sure I have the guts to walk out there and do. I wish more than anything that Brittany were here tonight, but she's in bed at the apartment with a terrible case of the flu; however, the show must go on.

It's finally show time, and Lisa wishes me luck, and then takes the stairs high up into the rafters where her swing awaits. Tonight she and the boys perform "There's No Business Like Show Business." I run to the dressing room and down three shots of vodka and spray my cotton candy perfume all over me. The DJ brings down a small mic'd headset for me to wear on my ear, and it's almost invisible. I thank him as he runs back to the DJ booth.

"Well, gentlemen, since you've all been so good tonight and obeyed me so well, I have a very special treat for you!! Yes, you!!! You've been requesting a solo performance by her for quite some time, and I've decided that since you've been so obedient, you deserve a present!! Here she is... our very own little cowgirl from Texas, Dixie Daniels!!!!"

I hear the crowd roar with excitement, and I feel my heart beating out of my chest. The lights go out, and I walk down the runway to the center of the stage while Lisa and the dancers run past me and through the curtains. The fog begins to pour from the edges of the stage, the music begins, and one single spotlight pours light over me from above. This is it.

Oh baby baby........Love is like a bomb............Oh baby baby............ Love is like a bomb........Oh baby baby, how was I supposed to know............C'mon, take a bottle.....Shake it up... Pour some sugar on me!!........ Pour some sugar on me!! You got the peaches I got the cream, sweet to taste saccharin, cuz I'm hot, say what sticky sweet, from my head, my head, to my feet...

I do the wildest moves ever. I'm up, do a full circle around the stage, and then drop back down to the floor into a sexy crawl to the front of the stage. I head back to the ramp, turn and look at the audience, and it's time for my big finale. I walk down the ramp just like Demi Moore in *Striptease*. I rip off my halter top, and the audience goes wild.

I must confess that my loneliness is killin' me nowwwwww... Don't ya know I still believe, that you will be here and give me a signnnnnnnn.....Hit me baby one more time!

The main pole drops to the stage floor from above, and I run, jump, and twirl, whipping my hair back and forth, while a shower of sparks come down behind me, and the stage lights up in a circle of flames all around me. It's one hell of a finale.

I smile out at the audience who is standing and screaming for more and throwing money onto the floor of the stage. I look up to the DJ booth, and the DJ gives me a thumbs-up; I look to the side, and there's Lisa Beaumann beaming at me, waving away, her wrists covered in jewels. Then I look out into the audience, the spotlights are in my eyes, the crowd is screaming for more, and suddenly it hits me like a ton of bricks. Sheer horror. There, leaning on one of golden pillars at the back of the theater, is Lance. Hell hath no fury. The look on his face is pure, unadulterated rage. My skin goes clammy, and my heart drops. I can feel the complete disgust and hatred from him even though he's several yards away. He shakes his head slowly, turns, slams into a customer, and storms out of the club.

Minutes later I'm running down Bourbon Street through crowds of loud drunk people, wearing only a bathrobe and heels. My running is frantic, and I feel like I'm about to throw up. I know that even if I find him, I'm chasing a lost cause. Lance is the best man I could ever ask for, everything I always dreamed about in a guy, the first man to truly love me, and I've lost him forever. It takes a long time for a guy like him to trust a girl, and when that trust is lost, it's lost forever. A million thoughts are going through my head.

I keep running in the direction where he normally parks his truck, and I see it parked on the side of Bourbon. There he is. Tall, brooding, breathing heavily, with that look of fury still on his face. I run up and grab his arm, and he shoves me off, and then turns to look at me.

"Lance, I'm sorry... just please let me explain!" I cry out, as hot tears begin streaming down my face, and words are coming out of me robotically. I'm saying what I know I'm supposed to say in this situation, even though I know it won't make a damn bit of difference. We are standing in the middle of Bourbon Street. It's sprinkling rain, and there are thunder and lightning in the night sky. The raging storm is blowing in from the coast. Hundreds of people are passing us, bumping into us, and going on their merry ways, while I've just lost the love of my life. Lance looks down at me, his eyes wild with rage.

"Now, you listen to me very clearly because I'm only gonna say this once. Yeah, I'm fucking pissed at you for lying to me the entire time you've been in Louisiana and for showing your body to all these fucking strangers and that I had to find out from some letter, but more than anything, I'm disappointed in you." He takes a breath and looks away. "Sunny... You are smart, you are talented, and you are beautiful..." He looks me up and down, studying me like it's the first time he's ever seen me, like I'm a stranger. "You could do anything in the world with your life." I wish he would just keep yelling in rage because that would be easier than hearing he's disappointed. "Instead, this is what you've chosen to do. I trusted you. I told you I love you. Hell, I brought you home to meet my parents!!" He tilts his head back and laughs at the sky as it flashes with lightning. "God,

I'm such a fucking idiot!!"

"Lance, I…"

"I don't want to hear a fucking word out of you, Sunny." His face grows dangerous and dark again. "I don't ever want to see you again. I hope that's crystal fucking clear." He gets in his truck, slams the door, fires it up, and peels out through the French Quarter. It's over. Everything I worked for all this time, and it's over in the blink of an eye. I've never felt so ashamed. I decide right here and now that I will never step foot in the Circus again. I'll go to Hollywood and find Sam. There's nothing left for me in Louisiana.

Suddenly I feel a hand grab hold of me tightly. I turn and see the ringleader.

"That was quite a performance you gave just now, my dear, inside the Circus *and* out here in the middle of Bourbon. Tsk, tsk, love can be such a sad, sad thing. I've seen it happen time and time again with my girls. They fall in love, and they want to leave me and the Circus behind. It makes me so sad." He has an eerie grin on his face, and then he fakes a pout. "But it never works out well for either of us. I lose a girl from my show, and she ends up at the bottom of Lake Pontchartrain!!" He laughs a wild, evil laugh. Tears well up in my eyes. I was forewarned about this. Sam told me I wasn't ready for what this lifestyle would bring. "We don't want that now, do we? After all, you will make me more money than any other girl can!! They're dying to see you, dear! Forget the boy and come back to your adoring fans!! Shall we?" He's gleaming at me. I have to think fast. Lisa. I need Lisa, and I need Brittany, but she's sick. Ok, I'll just walk back with him. I look at the ringleader, nod, and head back towards the club with him escorting me. When we get there, he brings me into the dressing room.

"You have fifteen minutes to get to the lap dance room; the line to get a dance from you is a mile long so make it quick!!" he says cheerfully.

I'm horrified. The last thing I want to do right now is have men touching me. I'm even more terrified of what he will do to me if I leave, but it doesn't matter because I'm out of here. Just then, Lisa rushes into the dressing room.

"I've already talked to him, so I know what happened. Get dressed fast." She starts grabbing clothes frantically out of my bag and handing them to me.

"What? What are we doing?" She stops and looks at me.

"Listen to me. He has this group of thugs who do his dirty work for him; they come over from the Ninth Ward. If he needs someone roughed up like a customer who won't pay his tab or a dancer who tries to flee, he calls them. I walked in the office, and he was on the phone; they're already on their way, and they'll be following you for weeks to see if you try to leave New Orleans. You understand if you don't leave right now, you will be his prisoner here?? He makes thousands of dollars each night off you girls, and he's not going to let you leave unless it's to go to a watery grave. Sunny, it's happened many times before to good girls just like you; this is why I don't get attached." I see a tear roll down her face.

"So what do I do? How do I get out of Louisiana?"

"Get dressed and follow me, dear, but we have to move fast," she says to me with a look of fear on her face.

We head down an old creepy passageway I didn't know existed that leads out to a back alley.

"Hurry, we have a very small time frame to do this," Lisa says to me.

We race to Brittany's apartment on foot because I normally leave my car parked in the alley behind her house. As we walk in the house, Brittany is sitting on the couch visibly upset.

"Sunny, Lance was here. I tried to call you at the club. He was pounding on the front door and screaming at me asking me if it was true that you've been working at the club this whole time, and he kept asking me how I could lie to him after knowing him for so long, and he was pissed that he had to find out from someone sending him a letter telling him you were working at the Circus. I seriously think someone is out to get us!! First Drew gets an anonymous text about me getting arrested, and now Lance gets a letter telling him about you. What the hell? It was awful, and I didn't know what to do so I called the club when he left, but you were already on stage."

"Who would send a letter to him?" I ask, as tears start to well up in my eyes again.

"Sunny, we don't have time. Throw what you can in a suitcase; you'll have to leave everything else behind," Lisa says to me. I start grabbing everything I can, stuffing my suitcase and backpack full of clothes, and I empty the drawer of money I have saved up. Then there's a pounding on the front door.

"Go!! Now!! Out the back door!!" Brittany starts crying, hugs me quickly, and Lisa and I head out into the alley. We throw my stuff in the trunk and jump in the car. I hear the front door crash open, and I look up in the rearview mirror and see two men running down the alley towards my car.

"GOOO!!!" Lisa starts screaming. I put my Mustang in reverse and peel out backwards, almost running over both of the men. I can't make out their faces in the dark alley, but I can see that they both have guns. I hear two shots fired behind us.

"They are trying to shoot us!!!" I scream to Lisa. All of a sudden my back windshield shatters. I throw the car in drive and speed out of the alley as fast as I can.

"Take I-10 to the airport!!" Lisa screams. Twenty minutes later, we arrive in front of the terminal at the Louis Armstrong New Orleans International Airport.

I know that they will track my car if I try to drive to California, so Lisa was right to advise me to head to the airport.

"Listen, I want to thank you for taking me under your wing and helping me so much, Lisa. You're one of the most fascinating people I have ever met," I say as I fight back another round of tears.

"Oh, stop, dear, you're going to make me start crying, too!" She smiles at me, looking fabulous even in the awful lighting of the airline terminal. "Sunny, listen to me; you can't ever come back to Louisiana. Herman Toulouse won't stop looking for you, and if there's even a hint or whisper that you're here, you know what he will do. You're a very special girl. I think this was just a stop on the road to finding something much bigger and better for you, whatever that is. I'll miss you terribly," she says smiling and holding back tears.

"Lisa, I want you to have my car; it's all paid for, just park it for a while till things calm down." She sniffles and nods.

"Thank you, dear. You know, Sunny, you've been like a daughter… I mean, younger sister to me. Go out there and make me proud. You have star quality young lady, and I know you can make it. And if they ever make a movie about your life, I'm playing myself, got it?" I hug her tightly as hot tears run down my face.

I feel like I'll never see Lance, Brittany, Lisa, or Louisiana again. Everything I've known for the past year is ending all in one night. I hurry inside to the airline counter and buy a one-way ticket on the next flight to Los Angeles, California.

A true love story never ends…

45411279R00154

Made in the USA
Lexington, KY
26 September 2015